THE BOXER

Also by Jurek Becker

Sleepless Days
Bronstein's Children
Jacob the Liar

THE BOXER

A NOVEL

Jurek Becker

Translated from the German by Alessandra Bastagli

Arcade Publishing • New York

FIRST ENGLISH-LANGUAGE EDITION

The characters and events in this book are fictitious. Any similarity to real persons, living or dead, is coincidental and not intended by the author.

Library of Congress Cataloging-in-Publication Data
    Becker, Jurek, 1937–1997
      [Boxer. English]
      The boxer: a novel / Jurek Becker ; translated from the German by Alessandra Bastagli.
        p. cm.
    ISBN 1-55970-615-5
    I. Bastagli, Alessandra. II. Title.
    PT2662.E294 B6813 2002
    833'.914—dc21   2002019147

Published in the United States by Arcade Publishing, Inc., New York
Distributed by AOL Time Warner Book Group

Visit our Web site at www.arcadepub.com

10 9 8 7 6 5 4 3 2 1   ·

Designed by API

EB

PRINTED IN THE UNITED STATES OF AMERICA

Translator's Note

This story is related by a man, presumably a writer, interviewing a Holocaust survivor, Aron Blank, several years after the war. In the original German, Jurek Becker uses italics only when the interviewer is quoting Aron's exact words rather than to indicate spoken emphasis. I have maintained this usage throughout the translation.

In two instances I chose to keep the original German terms because they seemed more effective. The translation of these terms can be found in the footnotes.

I wish to thank Christina Kiel, who continued to offer me her time and insight in spite of my pestering her with late-night phone calls. Warmest thanks also to my editor, Richard Seaver, a patient and inspiring teacher.

THE BOXER

AFTER GIVING HIM ENOUGH TIME to suggest it on his own, I ask Aron if he wouldn't at least like to take a quick look at it.

"No, thank you," he says.

To my following, surprised question for his reasons, he answers, he's simply not interested. I don't understand. After all, the story is about him. It's his story. Although I know it's a waste of time, I bring this fact to his attention. He smiles. He looks at the five green notebooks that lie between us on the table, eyes me skeptically, or with disapproval, or contempt — I am not good at interpreting facial expressions — in any case with no curiosity whatsoever, and says quietly, "I shouldn't have told you so much."

I think, How strange. Or isn't it strange that he should suddenly pretend to have doubts? Now, after two years during which we spoke of nothing else, or virtually nothing else, but him? The sole purpose of our meetings was to identify Aron Blank, or at least a significant part

of him. They were like open interviews, even though I
wasn't working with a tape recorder or a notepad. Nothing happened that wasn't perfectly clear to Aron, he
wasn't tricked or pressured. On the contrary, he knew the
extent to which I depended on him and his readiness to
communicate, and he never gave me a particularly hard
time.

It also occurs to me that he might be afraid that,
since the work, as it were, is done, my sympathy will turn
into indifference. There lie the five notebooks; there
won't be a sixth. Perhaps he thinks that my interest in
him will fade. No further acts of kindness, because all the
previous ones implied an ulterior motive, which no
longer exists. And therefore it doesn't seem altogether
impossible that our separation will guide him back to the
road he was on when we first began working together.
Not to spare me an embarrassing retreat, in other words,
not out of generosity. Rather, I suspect, to prevent any
possible distress an emotional farewell might involve.
Perhaps he wants to erect a barrier before I declare all
trust that has grown between us to be nothing more than
part of the deal, a lubricant for his memory.

However, I won't base my attitude on hypotheses.
In the end, none of my conjectures is appropriate. In the
end, Aron is simply in a bad mood — among his symptoms is an overwhelming susceptibility to mood swings.
I'd sooner ask why he's not interested.

"Think about it," he says.

I had done that, I say, and, "I still don't understand."

Aron shakes his head, apparently amused, as if he
can't see how someone who professes to be intelligent

can overlook such obvious motives. I've grown used to that attitude. He is often satisfied with hints that, combined with other gestures or with a certain way of looking at me, he thinks are informative enough. I soon learned that he found my occasional pleas for greater detail aggravating, unworthy, and foolish. So in order not to inhibit his flow of words, I would withhold my questions as often as possible, preferring to accept temporary — or for a longer stretch of time — lack of clarity, and try to fill in the ensuing gaps by deduction. But today things are different. I don't mind insisting on explanations, we are no longer working. Today my inability to understand is, so to speak, purely personal. Nevertheless, I take pains to proceed cautiously; he mustn't sense that anything is different than it was. I use his weapons. I tilt my head a little to one side, look at him for a long time, my questioning eyebrows raised, and my hand, which till now has been lying unnoticed on the table, is turned palm up.

This is a language Aron understands. He says reluctantly, "Why don't you leave me alone? I'm not interested. Isn't that enough?"

"No," I reply. "How can that be enough? You can't convince me that you aren't interested in your own story."

Another couple of strokes to his outline: as soon as Aron decides to explain something, he suddenly finds it difficult to begin. He likes to use introductory phrases, tentative approaches to the subject, he often says, "Listen" or "All right, let's see." He always wants his listener to understand that the explanation implies a great effort on his part, an effort he considers unnecessary, and that he nonetheless gives in only because his listener is so stubbornly insistent. Sometimes he hints that the sentences that are to follow will require complete concentration from his listener. He might say, "Pay attention."

This time, Aron says, "Listen. You claim that you wrote my story, and I claim that you're mistaken, that it's not my story. At best, it's something you think is my story."

"What do you mean — at best?" I ask.

He says, "Don't look so hurt. I'm not blaming you. I knew it from the very first."

This said, he is now someone who has performed an uncomfortable duty. He stands up, his hands in his pockets. He walks to the window and looks at the chestnut tree that has grown so thick it blocks the view and darkens the room. A few seconds later he adds, "There's no other way."

"What did you know from the very first?" I ask.

"That what I tell you is one thing," he says, "and what you write is something else. Again, I'm not accusing you of anything. I understand there's a mechanism from which you can't defend yourself."

"So, you do understand that."

"Or had you meant to be perfectly satisfied only with what you heard from me?"

A brainteaser that requires no answer, one of his rhetorical questions. My comprehensible no would only annoy him. As a reward for my self-restraint he goes into greater detail: of course I hadn't meant that, I had meant something completely different. I had wanted to improve him, to make him publishable, to use him as raw material. From the beginning I had had my own ideas about a story, and then I had made choices. I had taken what I found useful and listened politely to the rest. And even what I had chosen had become different, nothing remained as it was. Why? Because we had always been interpreting — incoherently he uses the plural, confusing me. Because we had felt that damned urge to seek a hidden meaning behind everything. Because we had been suspicious of every harmless thing, as if in reality it served as a disguise for God knows what. Yes sir, says Aron, sitting down again and answering the further questions in my eyes, he had known that very well and had participated nonetheless, out of pure egoism. I mustn't believe that it was only about me. Or did I think he was a Samaritan, who sits down and does a two-year-long favor? Of course, our conversations had been useful for him, too; of course, he had been happy that someone had finally come to listen to everything he had to say. Aron claims that those who only brood and never talk about it will eventually suffocate. He has told me so much about himself, he was amazed he had played a role in so many different situations. Often the question came to mind: Had that really been he? Then, painstakingly, he'd have to explain to himself: Yes, it had been he — who else? — no one else was there. And over time, as the essential was gradually revealed, things became a little easier for him, knowing this should reassure me. In reality, he hadn't done me a favor, I'd done him one — he had fewer headaches, he hoped I wouldn't be getting them now.

"That's a pretty strong statement," I say when he stops to catch his breath, "almost outrageous."

"What?"

I knock on the notebooks and say, "You talk about them as if you had read every word. Maybe you're right about some things, but isn't it rash to attack me with a thousand hypotheses and act as if they were facts? Don't you want to make the slight effort, and read?"

Aron leans back in his chair and repeatedly breaks out into smiles that are not his usual sad or thoughtful ones, but rather cunning and unconditional. One could say that Aron's whole face lights up. He even twinkles, and I will soon know why. It's as if he's worked out a painless method that will finally shut me up.

Very well, he says, for the fun of it let's assume what he had said was total nonsense, from start to finish, as I would have it. Let us assume that in writing everything down I had kept to his exact words; my notebooks could just as well be his notebooks. If so, and therein lies his own story, why should he read it? He knows it inside out, and a purely literary interest, as I well know, does not exist.

I find nothing convincing to refute this, not right now anyway, but for Aron I have not been humbled enough. In these cases he is merciless. He takes the last card he has up his sleeve, and his eyes reveal that he considers it his ace of spades. Or do I want him to read the story so that he can later say how satisfied he is with me? That wouldn't work for different reasons. First, he isn't an expert on the written word, more a layman who tends to pass coarse judgments; and, second, he isn't a controller. Therefore I should think long and hard about exactly what it is I want from him. Evidently I had subconsciously wanted him to authorize my writing, but he warned me away from that — if we should start we would never finish. And that couldn't possibly be what I wanted.

1

IT WAS NOT LONG BEFORE an identity card was required. Aron wanted to have one quickly, preferably right away, he says. But that was easier said than done, all sorts of formalities stood in the way. He listened quietly to all the things that had to be provided — the questionnaire with many categories, passport photographs, a birth certificate — and the man at the counter wondered why the applicant left without saying good-bye. After all, he had been friendly enough in explaining things. So, a photograph. Aron didn't want to ask anyone; he thought that in a city this size it must be child's play. He started off at random and looked closely at the surrounding houses. All he found were traces of photographers — relics in the form of company plaques that still hung on the façades, testifying that long ago, in that location, there had been a shop like the one he was looking for. The buildings no longer stood behind them, as if, of all shops, the photographers had pointedly been done away with. This had happened to Aron three times when he finally decided not to trust chance any longer and to ask for directions from a local after all. But the street was spitefully empty. He didn't like the few people he met; they had *provocative* faces, or at least there was something evocative about their manner. Aron was looking for a photographer, not a fight.

He went into a bar. To his amazement, or rather to his frustration, he says, the room was full of people who were drinking, though there was nothing to drink, and the air was full of smoke, though there was nothing to smoke. They had stopped talking when he came in, at first only a few, who had noticed him right away, then more and more. Silence rolled over the tables like a wave. At the same time, he knew that before he had come in they had not been speaking of things that an outsider isn't supposed to hear, *because they only talk about unimportant things, from which evil develops as a side effect.* The sight of him rendered them speechless. It would take a long time for them to get used to the fact that someone with his looks, someone so unmistakably similar to the pictures on the National Socialist posters, could be walking around freely and look them straight in the eye, and that he hadn't escaped from a camp but that he had been freed. Aron pulled himself together, went up to the bar, and asked the scrawny barmaid if she knew a photographer in the area.

It took her a couple of seconds to *cope* with his appearance, the typical nose for example, but then she called out, "Does anyone here know a photographer?"

Aron waited, without turning around. Behind him, he heard people start talking again, more quietly than before. In spite of his resolve, when someone touched him, he turned around instantly. A small boy stood in front of him. Ten years old at most — though to be able to estimate a child's age takes practice, he says. "Come with me," the boy said and, without hesitating, Aron followed him. But at the door the boy's courage dissolved. He stopped and, frightened, looked back into the room. A woman nodded encouragingly and said, "Go on."

They went a fairly long way. At a certain point, after they had turned left twice, Aron thought, If he goes left again, he'll be taking me in circles. He could think of nothing to say to him, or of any reason to ask him his name, and he could expect nothing at all from the boy. So they walked along in silence, the boy always a couple of steps ahead of him. In a courtyard they came to a halt. The boy pointed at the building across from them and said, "There. On the third floor."

Aron reached into his bag to look for a reward, but the boy had run away as soon as his assignment was over. There was, in fact, a sign next to a door on the third floor and, after repeated knocking, the photographer opened. Many people wear white coats, but by the way in which the light obviously bothered this man, the time it took him to stop squinting — though it wasn't bright outside — one could immediately guess what his profession was. "Are you a photographer?" Aron asked.

"What else?"

"I need four passport photos."

The young man moved aside so Aron could step into the narrow corridor. Aron had to allow for a brief but aggravating visual inspection to brush over him.

"You shouldn't evaluate me, you should take pictures of me," he said.

"Of course. Do you know how many people need photographs these days?"

"Where's the stool?" Aron asked.

"Easy, easy, first we have to talk about the price."

"Why? Don't you know how much four passport photos cost? I'm sure I have enough money."

The young man laughed and said, "You're funny. What would I do with money, the house is as good as new. Do you have any cigarettes? Coffee?"

"How much would the pictures normally cost?" Aron asked.

Something must have impressed the young man, perhaps the seriousness of the question, or the emphasis with which it was posed. Either way, he felt he owed an explanation. "There are no normal prices. I could tell you what the pictures used to cost before the war, four photos for two marks. But what difference does that make today?"

"Just take my picture," Aron said. "Somehow or other we'll work out the price."

The photographer hesitated but finally decided to run the risk. When they had finished, Aron said, "Listen, I agree we can't base ourselves on prewar prices. Let's assume that in the meantime prices have increased five hundred percent. So I'll pay ten marks for the photos. When will they be ready?"

The photographer ground his teeth and felt betrayed — he had exposed his precious film under false premises — but he wasted no more words over the payment. He took out a thick notebook, leafed through the pages, and said, "Six weeks. At the earliest."

"That's unacceptable," said Aron. "You mustn't get back at me this way, I haven't done anything to you. On the contrary, I'm willing to pay an unlawfully high price. I'll come by to pick up the photographs tomorrow, all right?"

And the next day they were ready?" I ask.

"Naturally."

"Naturally is good," I say. "You threatened him."

"Threatened? Are you crazy? What would I have threatened him with? All I said was what you just heard. Where was the threat?"

"It must've been in your voice. Or in your eyes, how should I know?"

"Young man," Aron says, "you're letting your imagination run away with you. But if you mean that he was afraid, that's something else again. A fear that had nothing to do with me. At the time, almost everyone was afraid."

"And you really gave him the measly ten marks?"

"And a pack of cigarettes to boot," says Aron. "But why should I have told him beforehand?"

The questionnaire was a bigger problem, which began with the very first question. Only after a long hesitation did Aron decide to put down his real last name. It appeared, after extensive consideration, neutral, harmless — anyone could be called Blank. Blank didn't tell them anything.

His first name was a different story. It was revealing, gos-
sipy. The name Aron had to go if Aron's ultimate effort
was to rid himself of his past. He knew that not everyone
could draw a conclusion from such a name, only those who
had been inculcated. But they were the whole issue; *only
one would have been one too many.* He knew from experience that those who were inculcated could not keep their
mouths shut. So they were exactly the ones he needed to
throw off track. Then there was the problem of his appearance. He would deal with that later, if there was anything that could be changed. Yet it was clear to him that
he could use this appearance, should it be necessary, in
a deceitful, misleading way. Besides, if a man can look
like a horse, he said to himself, and everyone will believe
him when he claims he isn't a horse, then in his case, too,
an attempt to put matters straight would not be utterly
hopeless. However, this could work only if he had a different first name. With this Aron, people would just smile
knowingly and not believe him.

Aron proceeded in a most unusual manner. He
swapped two letters. In the appropriate column he wrote
his new name, Arno. In case of a formal inquiry, it could
be explained as a spelling mistake that had been ignored
out of laziness.

But why did he falsify his date of birth?

Why did you make yourself six years younger?"

"Can't you figure it out for yourself?"

I try, and say, "Because you wanted your son to have
a younger father?"

"That too, perhaps," says Aron. "But why precisely six years?"

This is his only clue. For several days, I think of what meaning the number six could have. At first a biological reason occurs to me. Six years could lie near a medically significant border — one can't make oneself randomly younger but only within certain thresholds. Aron would satisfy these conditions with his six years. But he would have told me that.

Only several days later do I find an illuminating explanation, and the number six appears in a new light. The war lasted for six years. Aron was a prisoner in concentration camps for six years. Is he referring to those six years? If so, he could have canceled out a bad time and tried, with the only means at his disposal, to reattach the stolen piece of his life. But he makes no comment.

Aron provided the remaining details truthfully, except for trivial issues, like the question of his place of birth. He wavered only one other time, when he had to name his job. For a moment he was tempted by the idea of changing all things past. This had less to do with the plan of erasing tracks, he said, than with decade-old dreams and his appearance. Yet he soon gave up the idea of raising himself to the status of professor or doctor, or some other profession. It was immediately clear to him that such a declaration would require verifiable knowledge. So he wrote: Employee.

Aron was given the number of a room in which sat a man who wasn't really a policeman, for his armband didn't

indicate any sort of rank, it showed only that the occupying forces did not consider him particularly suspicious.
Aron handed over the documents. The man verified them
and said, "The birth certificate is missing."

"I don't have one."

"What do you mean you don't have one?"

"It's gone, burned. Like everything else. Is that so
unusual?"

"Please," said the man, "there must be some sort of
proof of who you are. I don't want to insinuate anything,
but I'm sure you'll understand that these days there are a
lot of people who want to cover up their past. We have to
be very careful."

Aron had expected some such complication, even
though he was basically pleased that *someone with his face*
could be taken for a man who wanted to hide his past. He
took the certificate of discharge from his last concentration camp out of his bag and simply held it up to the
man's face, very calmly, and ready to take it back — as if
its worth could be diminished by excessive looking.

B ut I mustn't believe, Aron says, that he was particularly
restless. On the contrary, he had been overcome by an astonishing coolness. He knew exactly what he was letting
himself in for, he says, and his nerves had, fortunately,
held up very well. The man, even if one presumes that he
was one of the well-meaning ones, could easily have noticed the discrepancies between Aron's declarations and
the entries on the discharge certificate. After all, in these
situations, it should not be entirely insignificant if some-

one is called Aron Blank and was born in Riga in 1900 or
Arno Blank, born in Leipzig in 1906.

"Why did you think of Leipzig, of all places?"

"My late brother was born in Leipzig."

Aron had been fully prepared, he says, to distract the
man somehow — with a heart attack or an emotional out-
burst — if he had suddenly become interested in the details on the discharge certificate. But, to his relief, that
turned out to be unnecessary.

The man just glanced at it and said, "All right, all right,
thank you."

Thus it was clear that people who possessed such an
ID had, in his eyes, an inexhaustible source of credibility.
In an instant he had forgotten his suspicions. Yet this *penetrating* compassion in his eyes, a sort of participation —
Aron found it revolting from the very beginning, but he
now bore it for practical reasons. He quickly stuffed the
certificate back into his bag, and a couple of hours later
he had his papers.

For the first few days, the apartment that was assigned to
Aron felt far too luxurious, considering the widespread
poverty of the time. It consisted of two spacious rooms
with parquet flooring, a kitchen, a bathroom with green
tiles, and a long corridor, at the end of which was a large
storage space, almost a third room. There was plenty of
furniture, carpets, linens, and kitchenware. When Aron

first stepped into the bathroom, he found perfumed soap
in a container and eleven bottles of bath oils. The whole
inventory became his as soon as he moved in, without a
receipt or any kind of formal transaction; not a word was
said about it.

The decor wasn't to Aron's taste but, at first glance,
he says, he had been completely satisfied. Yet it was hard
for him to get used to the fact that all these objects belonged to him, that he could sell them, use them, or
throw them away as he saw fit. At first he reduced his con-
tacts with the apartment to an absolute minimum. There
was a luxurious king-size bed in the bedroom, painted
white, with soft blankets. When he went to bed the first
night, he sighed with pleasure — at last, a decent bed.
But the anticipated pleasure proved to be fleeting; *a bed
does not necessarily mean sleep.* Aron lay awake and found no
protection from the past. His thoughts rummaged in it, in
death and suffering, his two starving children lay beside
him, his wife was repeatedly dragged from the room crying. The nauseating smell that his bedmates in the concentration camp exhaled — to which he must also have
contributed — would not leave him. He took the oils from
the bath and sprayed them around the room. Hours later,
he figured that the bed was too wide. He took a blanket,
searched the apartment for another place to sleep, and
settled in the storage room, which was separated from the
corridor only by a curtain. He lay down on the floor, immediately felt the improvement, but nonetheless had to
wait until he collapsed from exhaustion.

Now and then, through the curtain and the door to
the apartment, he heard steps on the stairs. Time and

again he would get up and sneak over to the peephole. Thus he got to know his neighbors, who were still up and about at night. Then that wasn't enough, and he observed them during the daytime as well. He pushed a table up against the door and put several pillows on it, so that he could sit comfortably while he watched. He noticed six different men, sixteen women, and seven children; then he kept seeing the same people over and over again. His apartment was on the third floor, so Aron never saw the people on the first and second floors unless they were visiting someone upstairs. That was definitely a disadvantage. Then one day Aron saw himself sitting like that, on the table, on three pillows, his legs crossed like a tailor, hiding behind his door, in the dark corridor, in the middle of the day. He was shocked, he says, he thought, My God, who in his right mind ever behaves like this? A madman behaves like this, a cretin. How lucky you are that no one sees you like this. But the restlessness didn't last long. He simply left his observation post and resorted to the window. Many people look out the window.

He was terribly startled when the doorbell rang for the first time. Through the peephole he recognized the short man with an amputated leg who had given him the key to the apartment — the superintendent. Before he opened the door, Aron let him ring again.

"Thank God," said the superintendent.

Aron couldn't understand the man's initial concern, or his subsequent relief. He led the super into the kitchen and asked him what he wanted. "Nothing specific, I just wanted to make sure everything was all right," said the super.

"Why shouldn't it be?"

"Let's be frank," said the super. "No one has seen you leave the house for at least two days."

Aron thanked him for his concern, which was totally superfluous in this case — he simply led a withdrawn life. As he spoke, he had to suppress a smile. That someone who had been persecuted for years, who had succeeded in eluding numerous traps only thanks to a thousand tricks and ruses, that this person should now hang himself, or turn on the gas — he found such a thought highly amusing.

Since the man was already in the kitchen, Aron thought he might as well offer him a cigarette. The superintendent thanked him effusively and volunteered his services for any necessary repairs. Aron asked who had owned the apartment.

"You weren't told?"

At this point the superintendent embarked on an overly long story. Until three weeks before, exactly until two days after the end of the war, a man called Leutwein, who owned the house, lived in this apartment with his wife. A man in his mid-fifties, he had been a party member since the very beginning; his membership booklet had a very low number. Everyone knew that; Leutwein never lost an opportunity to brag about his low membership number. During the war he worked for the government — not in a very important post, he didn't have sufficient expertise, but he must've had influential friends because he was spared service on the battlefield. In return, he was impudent, made great speeches, threw around words such as *Wehrkraftzersetzung* and *durchhalten*, he would not toler-ate any *Elemente* in his house.* So he terrified people and was considered an informer. Whether he really was, the superintendent couldn't say; personally, Leutwein never did him any harm. At the end of the war, everyone wondered why he didn't clear out immediately. Where to? At least to an area that wasn't occupied by the Rus-sians. But just then his wife had come down with typhus. Leutwein loved her — these people have feelings too, said the super — he took care of her until the Russians came to get him. They even took his wife, picked her up in an ambulance; that was as much as the super knew.

With this information, Aron felt less awkward about taking possession of the apartment and its contents. It suddenly appeared legitimate. He couldn't imagine a more just property exchange than the one that had taken place between Leutwein and himself.

Imagine another case," he says. "Imagine that the apart-ment had belonged to someone who was more similar to me than this Leutwein. There also must've been apart-ments like that."

However, he now made a critical selection. With careful eyes, he went over the rooms and tried to look at the

---

Wehrkraftzersetzung: undermining of military morale; *durchhalten*: perseverance, *Elemente*: elements.

objects in the light of their history. Whatever he thought could have contributed to the specific well-being of a National Socialist he put aside. Mainly ornamental objects fell victim to Aron's censorship. Hardly any furniture, which was for the most part considerably older than the lowest membership number, and was therefore above suspicion. Vases had to be trashed, paperweights, couch pillows and blankets, also the cuckoo clock, and all the pictures. Not just the family photographs, oil paintings as well. He describes one of them to me: a farmer follows a plowshare, which is pulled by a strong horse and digs a rut in the dark soil. He had observed this painting often, even before the superintendent had come. It hung in the corridor, and until that moment had been carefully painted and had pleasant colors. Yet now it disturbed Aron, though he could not logically explain why. He could only convey, in passing, random concepts: return to nature, love of the land, the innocent word *Arbeit*.*

(At this early stage, it seems worthwhile for me to provide some details of Aron's biography. These should serve simply to intimate that he grew up and lived not in a particularly exotic environment but rather in one where concepts of value and taste were those of the common man. He was born in Riga, into a family to which piety was a curious phenomenon to be smiled at. While he was still a child, his parents moved with him to Germany, where he lived in Leipzig for a while and later, until the year 1934, in Berlin. Then a woman called Lydia, whose only relationship to Judaism consisted of the fact that she loved Aron, convinced him to leave the country. Aron chose

---

*Work.

Bohemia, because the textile factory where he was employed had a branch there. Lydia pleaded for an exile even
farther away, but he declined; he didn't have any savings
and was entirely dependent on his salary. In Bohemia
they married and had three children. After the German
invasion they were sent into a ghetto — Lydia too — and
then one day she was taken away. Presumably for inflam-
matory speech. Aron never saw her again; he was left alone
with the children, two of whom died before his eyes.)

Aron cleaned out the apartment, throwing things
away, tearing them up, and burning them. He also rearranged everything, because he realized that a certain way
of thinking can find expression even in the way objects
are organized. Sometimes he would hesitate, uncertain
whether what he held in his hands or observed deserved
his disapproval. Yet the hesitation seemed to be a sort of
proof, and so, in case of doubt, he made decisions to the
disadvantage of the object. He threw a stack of handker-
chiefs into the fire because they were embroidered with a
monogram, E.L.

Aron wondered how he would react if one day Mrs.
Leutwein would come back and demand her property.
Or, worse still, if she would beg for it. A likely possibility;
there have been cases of people who recovered from typhus. Aron waited hourly for her to knock. He felt fully
prepared for demands or the invoking of so-called rights;
he wouldn't mind calling the police or resorting to some
form of violence, even without anyone else's help. But he
was terrified at the thought of entreaties. He imagined
the woman sitting in front of him, pale and emaciated
from her recent illness, with tears in her eyes or sobbing unrestrainedly, begging him to leave her the bare

necessities. She would say that she was on the street, destitute, her husband was in jail and, besides, she was somehow attached to the things they had lived with for so long. Wouldn't he let her take at least this object or that? And he heard himself say, after she had begged long enough, "Take whatever you want." But then, when the expression intended to arouse his sympathy would vanish from her features and she would start amassing things, he would throw her out. In case of emergency, he resolved to think of Lydia.

But Mrs. Leutwein did not come — pride, or death, kept her away. Instead two men visited Aron. They showed their staff ID issued by the occupying forces and said they had instructions to search the apartment for documents that may have been left behind.

"What types of documents?" Aron asked warily.

He learned that in Erich Leutwein's trial, certain murky points had arisen that might possibly be cleared up with the help of correspondence or certificates of a certain kind. The men also said that they had already been to the apartment once but had perhaps overlooked something at the time.

"You won't find anything," Aron said. "I turned everything inside out, there's nothing. There was only a folder with a couple of letters, and I burned it without reading them."

"It's a pity," the men said, and made as if to leave. Aron's words had made the search seem unnecessary; they could think of no good reason why he of all people should want to cover for Leutwein. Aron held them back and asked what the unclear points in the trial were. The men looked at each other hesitantly until one nodded to

the other. Aron learned that Leutwein had tried to portray his party membership as something he was forced
into, his behavior during the war as disapprovingly passive and, as for the undeniable fact that he had not been
called to arms — he had always found it incomprehensible. Naturally no one believed him, the men said, yet
without proof the outlook was in doubt, and witnesses
were nowhere to be found.

"Go to the superintendent," Aron said, "he knows
Leutwein really well."

They had already been to him, they responded, and
to most of the other tenants of the house, yet everyone
claimed they knew nothing either good or bad about
Leutwein.

Once the men had left, Aron sat for a long time and
was annoyed about the absurd care with which these investigations were being carried out. Documents, witnesses,
proof, were nothing more than obstacles in the way of
a crystal clear deduction. As if there weren't millions of
obvious proofs, as if Lydia wasn't proof. As if they didn't
know that they were dealing with a sworn gang from which
they couldn't single out witnesses by using tact and by
following some rule from an aged law book. Aron simply
hoped that what he had just seen was an extremely unusual case, that in other cases procedures were more reasonable and less shortsighted. But already this one case
felt like an immoderate dissipation; it was impossible for
him to let it rest. He rushed down the stairs and rang at
the door of the ground-floor apartment. The little super
opened and smiled at his acquaintance. "Oh, it's you."
Aron grabbed him by the collar and shook him; the superintendent gasped for air and could not free himself.

"Listen to me," Aron said. "If you don't go immedi-ately and confess everything you know about Leutwein, I'll turn you in. Mark my words, I'll send you to jail."

The superintendent didn't answer, either because he was scared or because his shirt was pulled so tightly around his throat. He simply stared with bulging eyes and had stopped struggling. Aron repeated, "Right now. Is that clear?"

The superintendent nodded. Aron let him go and watched while he pulled on his jacket and his single shoe and left the house.

So you were your own police?"

"Why do your questions always sound as if you were against me?"

I deny this vehemently. I say that constantly agree-ing with him would help neither of us. "I'm just trying to understand an event I didn't participate in. What else do you hear in my questions?" I ask.

"I hear that you have decided to be objective, and I don't like that. If you insist on being objective, then go and write about a soccer game. That doesn't work with me, I'll be exposed in a distorted light."

Aron maintained confident hope in one child. To this day, it remains uncertain whether or not this hope was fulfilled, but you can't talk to him about it.

The transport that led from the Bohemian ghetto to the camp was meant exclusively for the men who were fit to work. Aron's youngest son had to stay behind. This Mark Blank, barely two years old at the time, was left in the care of a neighbor, a certain Mrs. Fisch. She didn't make a particularly good impression on Aron, but at the time the circle of people who could have been trusted to carry out such a delicate task had become remarkably small. Aron brought everything he still owned into her room and in addition promised her mountains of gold for her self-sacrificing care — yet he didn't really believe things would work out.

Immediately after his release, he had found the address of an American organization that, among other things, dealt with the search for missing Jewish relatives.

You wonder why I didn't go to Bohemia myself?"

"Yes."

"It was terribly far. My feet hurt."

The organization was called Rescue. Aron was sent to a room that looked like someone lived in it. He was given a cup of coffee and told his whole story. The woman who listened to him was, he found, remarkably young, seventeen, nineteen at most, he says; she had long, black hair and tear-swollen eyes. She took notes during his report and interrupted him only once with the request to spell

the name of the little Bohemian town. He presumed that
she heard similar stories daily and wasn't as yet used to
them, hence the tear-swollen eyes.

"As soon as we know something, you'll be informed,"
she said as they parted.

Aron assumed there would be a long wait — in those
days a lost child was like a needle in a haystack — yet only
a week had passed when Rescue knocked on his door. A
man, who wasn't a postman, handed him a package that
didn't in fact contain the missive he was hoping for but
held powdered milk, cigarettes, chocolate, and other food-
stuffs from overseas. Aron ate his fill, smoked, and waited.
Everything he did at that time, he says, just served the purpose of getting through the waiting period. For example,
the gradual occupancy of the apartment. For example, he
went to the barbershop and had his hair, which had become gray over the past years, dyed black. (Since the effect, after a short period of adjustment, pleased him, the
dyeing became an established habit. He repeated it every
four weeks until the matter became too time-consuming
and troublesome. From the start of the sixties, his hair was
allowed to grow the color it wanted to — yellowish white.)

Two weeks later, a postcard arrived, bearing the Rescue stamp. Aron read the exciting news — "I think we
have something for you" — signed by a certain Paula
Seltzer, presumably the girl with tear-swollen eyes. Not
an hour had passed and he was there, again the cup of coffee, again the girl. This time, Paula seemed more relaxed.
"I like you much more with dark hair," she said.

She looked so pretty, Aron's task should've been to pay
compliments, but he just asked, "What did you find out?"

Paula started with the most important issue, she said that the child was alive. Traces of the woman, this neighbor — Fisch — were nowhere to be found, but for Aron it should be more important to know that all the children of the ghetto were transferred to a children's camp at the beginning of '43. The chances of survival were desperately small, but when the Allied troops had conquered Bavaria, where the camp was, Mark was still alive.

"There is, however, something curious," Paula said. "In the lists of the camp, your son was entered under not the name Mark Blank but Mark Berger. But he is the only Mark. One explanation could be that the lists were compiled carelessly; precision was not apparently their prime concern. It's lucky these lists exist in the first place."

"Did you look through the lists of the dead children?" Aron asked.

"Of course. There was no Mark Blank among the dead. And no other Mark either. Mark is an uncommon first name; we can be pretty sure of our case. Even the age is more or less right."

"What do you mean, more or less?"

"There are no dates of birth in the lists," Paula explained, "only the years. We have a Mark Berger, born in 1939."

Doubts arose only later; at the time Aron was convinced that every other suspicion was superfluous. He had swum into a cloud of happiness, he says; the years had taught him that in every kind of undertaking the most unhappy outcome was also the most probable. Now delight somersaulted in his head. For minutes he looked at Paula as she spoke, without understanding a word. At a certain point he interrupted her and asked, "You are Paula, right?"

Surprised, she said, "Of course my name is Paula."

Perhaps she took what happened in the next few seconds as an attempt to seduce her. But I swear it wasn't, it was nothing at all. I must have concentrated and reflected for a long time, I must have then stood up and given her a kiss. She was Rescue, you understand? Where else should I have kissed Rescue? It had nothing in the least to do with the question about her name."

It's a pity," Aron said, "that we can't drink a schnapps now."

Again Paula was surprised, but now she also smiled. She dialed a number, asked someone if it was already open, hung up, and told Aron, "Come with me."

They stepped out into the street; Aron followed her blindly. After a short distance, Paula pointed to a house. An American soldier stood at the entrance; Paula showed him her permit and made as if to go in. Looking at Aron, the soldier asked her a question in English. Paula answered him, whereupon the soldier nodded and let them pass. Not only that, says Aron, he even winked and, oddly, the wink was directed not at the pretty Paula but at him, Aron.

There was a restaurant on the first floor. They had barely sat down when a waiter with a white smock came to their table. Paula ordered, this too in English. "This is an officer's club," she said.

"Are you an American officer?" Aron asked.

"God forbid, I'm very civil."

The waiter brought a cognac for Aron; Paula had a glass of whiskey in which ice cubes clinked. Aron was curious about his first glass of liquor in years. "Let's drink to you and your plans," Paula said.

"All right," he said, "no one has drunk to that in a very long time."

But then there were still some details that Aron absolutely had to know. He found out that the camp where Mark was when the war ended had been turned into a sort of hospital right after liberation. The sick children — and almost all of the survivors were sick — could therefore be treated from the start by trained personnel, Paula intoned. Mark was still there, Paula said, no need to worry, he wasn't suffering from one of the many well-known illnesses. The letter in reply to Rescue's inquiry read: Malnutrition with all the usual collateral symptoms. It would take a couple of months, Paula said they had written, before Mark would be completely recovered, but there could be no talk of serious danger.

"Let's have another drink," Aron said.

"As many as you want."

Paula said he should take some time to think of how to proceed with Mark. For the next few weeks it would probably be best to leave him where he was. "Do you have a decent apartment?"

"A luxurious one in fact," Aron said.

"Naturally, once he is released, you can take him with you. But I think it would be more reasonable if he went to a convalescent home first. I mean, only until he is all better. Children who are just skin and bones do not turn into healthy people from one day to the next."

"I'll take care of it."

She had already taken care of it, she said. Rescue had a number of convalescent homes at its disposal, some for children. In Berlin there was only a small one, in which all the places were spoken for in the long term, but if Aron wanted she could probably see to it that Mark was taken to another place in the American Zone, or in Switzerland.

"That's very nice of you," Aron said. "I'd prefer it if he was transferred near me."

They drank a third glass; Aron felt the unfamiliar schnapps comfortably rise to his head. His limbs, he says, became noticeably heavier and his thoughts more light. I will buy myself some schnapps and drink a glass more often, it does one good, he thought. He observed that Paula emptied her glasses of whiskey with a certain nonchalance. In any case, she drank with no visible effort, unusual for a girl who was no more than nineteen, he says appreciatively. "How old are you?" he asked.

"Twenty-six," Paula replied. "Why?"

"Because you look really young and you like to drink."

"I used to like drinking," she said. "Now I only drink with company, like today."

Aron found this a little brash, almost as if she were an adolescent wanting to impress an adult. They were silent for a while. Aron looked around; he remembers an amazing number of details — even the pattern of the tablecloths. He mentions that a young soldier, who sat a couple of tables away, was trying to attract Paula's attention by giving her penetrating looks. "Would you like to go to Bavaria for a couple of days?" Paula asked.

This suggestion baffled Aron, not because Paula had guessed his most secret wish, but because until then that idea hadn't arisen. Now he knew that he wanted to go see Mark, it just hadn't occurred to him before. Paula could arouse desires, he says, that would only have awakened much later and, what was more, she delivered the key to their realization. He was a little afraid, he says, because he doesn't like having debts.

"What's the matter?" she asked.

"Of course I'd like to go."

"You're so passive," Paula said. She would take care of the ticket and the authorization, Aron should report to her in three days. She then called the waiter and signed the bill.

Back home, Aron lay fully clothed on the bed, closed his eyes, and tried to imagine Mark. Not the way Mark might look today, not an image conjured by suppositions, but his two-year-old child whom he had had to leave behind with his neighbor Fisch. Yet despite all his efforts, he could not. Everything possible was reflected behind his closed eyelids. Two dead children, the trip to Prague with Lydia while she was pregnant. Lydia's deportation, incidents from the camp, roll calls, hard work, blows, over and over the face of a particularly hated prison guard — the child Mark never surfaced.

*   *   *

Can you understand that?" Aron said. "It was enough to drive me crazy. It was as if you had lost a picture and, to make things worse, you forgot what the image was. I only knew that it was a son of mine, and that his name was Mark. Nothing else."

I'm a little amazed at the degree to which his forgetfulness still angers him after all these years. "You had simply forgotten what he used to look like, why was that so important? You saw him again soon after that anyway?" I ask.

"But I couldn't recognize him, you idiot!" Aron says impatiently. "Do you think it didn't give me a headache that in the papers it said Berger? Why did it say Berger and not Blank? Paula could repeat a hundred times that Mark was an uncommon name — naturally it bothered me. Don't you understand that it was particularly important for me not only to see him but to recognize him?"

"Sure, I understand."

"It would have been far easier if he suddenly had three eyes or eleven fingers. Then I could've said, No, that's not my child, I remember clearly, mine had ten fingers. Do you think that in the ghetto my mind was free to make note of moles? Lydia would have definitely recognized him."

"Something else, Aron," I say. "How did you make your living?"

"In due course."

He looks at me disapprovingly, as if it were presumptuous to change the topic or to interrupt the flow of his story. He also says, "I decide what the order will be."

Perhaps, I think, he doesn't want to tell me. Perhaps
there are some things he doesn't want to talk about.

After a while, Aron recognized the uselessness of his
search. He opened his eyes, stood up, and somehow got
through the day. In the late afternoon, somebody knocked.
Aron didn't feel like opening the door. By now knocking had ceased to frighten him. Usually when someone
knocked, it was the super who, since the day Aron had
shaken him and forced him to testify in court, never lost
the opportunity to demonstrate his good behavior and sub-
missiveness. The pushy fellow kept knocking until Aron
sullenly went to the door. There stood Paula. She held a
bouquet and a package; she smiled and said, "I'm not disturbing you, am I?"

"No, no," Aron replied.

Don't forget, I was still fairly young back then, only
forty-five. And since I had lied to this Rescue lady, just as
I had to the police when I needed my papers, in Paula's
eyes I was six years younger."

He put the flowers in a vase, then they sat across from
each other at the table in the living room. Paula looked
embarrassed; Aron found her less self-assured than that

morning in the office or in the club, where she had been his host. Aron was embarrassed, too. He guessed that she hadn't come for business. The fact that this was both a determined and a shy attack on his affection was suffi- ciently evident from the flowers and her face, he says. Yet the reason for his embarrassment was not this knowledge. Paula's sudden materialization had made him happy, he had liked her from the start. Neither was Lydia the cause, for at that moment she played a negligible role. Rather, the reason was to be found in Aron's reaction to women in general, which, according to his account, I would describe as tense, uncomfortable from the very first.

(First experience: a visit to the brothel at the age of seventeen in the presence of friends. *Embarrassing result.* Then, to prove himself, an affair with a secretary that was conducted with greater seriousness on his part than on hers. She dumped him in favor of an acquaintance of the same age whom he couldn't stand anyway. Then a long pause, accompanied by sexual desires that he found ex- cessive and of which he was consequently ashamed. Fol- lowing the advice of a book he had bought secretly, he tried to reduce these urges by practicing physical activities, primarily swimming and tennis. At the age of twenty-two he fell in love with Agathe. Like him, she was reserved. Months had to pass before one could speak of marriage, of a sunny future, but before the plans were carried out, Agathe had drowned in a swimming accident. Thoughts of suicide. Only at the age of twenty-seven did the next story *worth mentioning* take place. The driving forces were his father and the owner of the aforementioned textile fac- tory in which Aron had been working in the interim. This owner, a practicing Jew by the name of London, not only had placed Aron in his heart but also had a daughter for whom he wanted an honest man. According to ancient custom, the fathers sat down together and worked out the details. The engagement went through unopposed. The girl, Linda, did not object; the wedding took place a year later. A marriage of convenience rather than conviction. Aron could never get rid of the thought that this was a bond dictated primarily by social goals. They had no children. Toward the end of 1931, Linda announced she'd like to move to America, and Aron answered, "Fine. Go ahead." A short while later she left, as did London senior, who took tearful leave of Aron and hoped that his son-in-law would have second thoughts and follow them. Aron thought about it and stayed. A few months later he and Linda were divorced, but this did not alter London's behavior toward Aron in any way. London delegated all sorts of powers to him; perhaps he was actually happy to have such a reliable man in Europe. A relatively comfortable time followed in which Aron concentrated on his job; the business was doing better than ever. Then, finally, Lydia.)

With this as his past experience, Aron now sat in front of Paula at the living room table, with flowers on it. They smiled at each other and hardly knew what to say.

(I want to add that Lydia was the last woman Aron held in his arms. Unlike most of his fellow prisoners, he hadn't used the few occasions that had presented themselves, first in the ghetto and later in the camp. They often talked about it, incomprehensibly often, he says. For him, this had been the most bearable side effect of his imprisonment.)

"You still don't know why I'm here," Paula said.

Aron found this strange. He thought he knew very well why she was there. In fact, he could have bet his life on it. But Paula said, "One of our cars is going to Munich tomorrow morning. The route takes it close to Mark's home, it would be just a tiny detour. Or is this all too sudden?"

"It is sudden," Aron said, "but it's good."

"Tomorrow morning at eight, at our office."

At that moment, the prospect of seeing Mark so soon excited Aron more than anything else. He stood up, paced the room, and smoked. He thought of his futile attempts to imagine Mark, and he tried again. Paula didn't disturb him, whether out of courtesy or because of renewed embarrassment is not clear. She sat still and watched him. After a while, she stood up and left the room. In the middle of his wandering Aron stopped. He was troubled because Paula was no longer sitting in her chair. It was definitely not very exciting to watch a middle-aged man as he paced to and fro. From that moment on, he was determined to be more attentive if only she hadn't already left, or he would be the next time he saw her. Luckily, he says, he found her in the kitchen.

"I'm looking for glasses."

"There should be some in the living room."

In the living room she finally unwrapped the package, a bottle of cognac. Aron remembered his wish in the club to buy some liquor for himself; he didn't remember now if he had just thought about it or had said it out loud. He put the glasses on the table and poured the drinks. Then Paula said this *puzzling* sentence, "If we wanted to forget everything else first, then we would never get around to living."

Again, Aron had something to think about. He wanted, he says, to take her words as a familiar noise, as a kind of music, but they had to be decoded — what could Paula have meant? One of the meanings, the somewhat philosophical aspect of her sentence, was obvious.

Or should I explain it to you?"

"No, keep talking," I say and ask myself why in the world he so often suspects, at precisely the wrong time, that I'm unable to follow his reckoning.

But Aron racked his brains over the other meaning, the second. Did she want him to understand that it was time to put an end to his past life and start a new one, perhaps with her? Or were her words directed less at him than at herself? Presumably it had also happened to me, says Aron, sometimes one says things that are not intended for other ears but only as a validation. Had Paula wanted to bolster Paula? Had she wanted to gather up some favorable wind, like soldiers do when they storm over a field shouting, "Charge!"? If we wanted to forget everything else first. She was twenty-six. Sure, he says, she wouldn't have been spared experiences that are best forgotten, *from the point of view of continuing to live.* Then we would never get around to living. Aron couldn't figure out exactly what that meant, and he didn't like to ask — he drank.

Suddenly she took his face in her hands and kissed

it. Aron's surprise quickly receded into confused delight
and intoxication that the taste of a woman caused him.
The bottle fell to the floor, cognac soaked the carpet.
Days later, when Aron came back from Bavaria, it still
smelled. But Paula didn't let go. And then she said again
a word that must have been jarring to his ears: "Arno . . ."

It was the first time that someone called me by that
name, especially in a situation like that! At first I thought,
She means someone else. No, it wasn't so tragic, I soon
got used to it. Everyone calls me that today, except you,
but never again did that name feel so hateful and inappropriate."

Why are you doing this?" Aron asked.
    Paula looked at him as if she hadn't understood his
question, then she closed her eyes and kissed him again.
He asked no more questions. His renouncing all resistance was made easier by her embrace, which, as he emphasizes several times, was in no way uncomfortable. (A
difficulty arises that I will often have to fight against.
Aron becomes very hesitant in naming important details;
he temporarily changes his method. Instead of describing
an event, he finds it sufficient to list the attendant circumstances.) He was no longer just letting it happen to
him, he also kissed her. He was intrigued by how things
would proceed. He felt her breasts, she smelled like pep-

permint. It became dark outside, early for that time of year. Paula stood up and opened the window. She lay down on the couch and said, "Come over here."

Aron had never sat or lain on that couch before. He lay down beside her. They embraced and kissed again. According to Aron, when one kisses while lying down it is always with a clearer intention than in any other position. He let himself be captured by the moment, though love had no role, he says, at least not on his side. Rather lust, also vanity and, as he says, control.

Control?"

He rolls his eyes and explains reluctantly that he finally had to test if he had, at least in relation to this, survived the camp unscathed. Or would that have been a matter of indifference to me in his position?

He was soon uncomfortable on the couch. In case of necessity, two adults could easily lie on it, assuming they each lay in an ideal position, but such was not the case. He thought, *Well, if it's going to happen*, then why not go to the other room with the big, wide bed? Yet he had scruples about making such a suggestion, and Paula didn't know the apartment, though in a certain way she was playing the host. So they lay and caressed each other on the couch, which was far too small, and only later, when the time had come to sleep, did she follow him into the bedroom.

Seeing the bed, she stared at him with a mixture of amused amazement and annoyance. Embarrassed, Aron shrugged. They took off their remaining clothes and lay down. He immediately fell asleep.

To Bavaria.

The next morning it took a couple of seconds before Aron understood that it was Paula who had woken him up. He was happy about it, and he also found no sign that she regretted anything. Obediently, she let herself be kissed. All she said was, "You're going to be late."

"For what?"

"The car. It leaves from the office at eight on the dot."

He jumped out of bed; the office was half an hour away and it was already past seven. Paula wasn't in a rush. While he washed and dressed, she went into the kitchen and prepared something to eat. There was no time left to shave. "You're not coming with me to the office?" Aron asked.

"Can't I stay here a little longer?"

"As long as you like," Aron said. "Here's the duplicate key."

He was afraid he'd miss the car, so he decided to eat his breakfast on the way. He took leave of Paula and was sorry they had to part so soon.

"Do you know how long I'll be gone?"

"No."

Something quite childish — Aron lifted Paula from the chair and carried her to the bedroom. At the end of the corridor — he almost collapsed on the way, but now he had already committed himself — he laid her down in the bed. He then forgot his breakfast in the kitchen and left.

Rescue's office was still closed. Wherever he looked, he couldn't see a car worth considering. Aron waited in front of the house and was afraid there could have been an accident or, worse still, a misunderstanding. Yet at around half past eight a foreign car pulled up across the street. Aron timidly raised his hand to attract attention. Someone called out the window, "Mister Blank?"

Aron got into the back next to a bald man who shook his hand, smiling, and introduced himself as Clifford; the driver sat alone up front. Even before they had gone around the first corner, Clifford started talking. Paula must have forgotten to tell him that Aron didn't understand English. Aron made up for this oversight. Clifford nodded and was silent, even morose, or so it seemed to Aron. Apparently he didn't care for long, silent journeys. Aron hoped they would find an interpreter at their destination; he had to come to an understanding with Clifford about their return trip. He kept looking out of the window; he preferred the open highway with fields and woods on both sides to towns and cities, which reminded him more of the war that had just ended. The driver hummed merry songs.

When Aron had seen enough, he started preparing himself for the encounter with Mark. That means he reconfirmed for the hundredth time that he loved him boundlessly and that he couldn't imagine a greater joy than that of being reunited with him at last. Besides, it was firmly established that he would not be shaken in his love by a wretched sight — for he knew very well what terrible physical changes hunger and illness are capable of causing. He didn't expect to meet a rosy advertisement kid. And, finally, he was still angry with himself because, even now, he was unable to project Mark onto his closed eyelids. He couldn't do any more; the road ahead was still long, and a permanent repetition of the aforementioned three lessons wasn't a very entertaining prospect. Clifford offered him a pack of cigarettes.

Aron smoked and started to think of the second person who had become important for him in the meantime, of Paula. Of the last question she asked, whether she could stay a little longer, here's the key, did Paula have the intention of moving in with him? If so, then surely not out of homelessness — Rescue cared for its people, why did she want to live with him? But that was not yet clear; it could just as well be that he would come home to find the second key under the mail slot, with a couple of embarrassed lines — Thank you for the nice evening, I don't know what possessed me, all the best, Paula. This or something similar was more likely than anything else, and Aron admitted to himself that if such were the case he would be disappointed.

A possible return home — Aron wants to open the door but does not succeed because the second key is in the other side of the lock, he must knock. Paula opens the door smiling, seductively attired or not dressed at all; Aron is wrapped in her arms. The best meal that may lie on the table will detain them only briefly, then the bedroom. The embraces achieve greater enjoyment than the first time, when everything was overshadowed by embarrassment and discomfort. Days like this, only in a longer, more reliable series.

Aron asked himself if such a plot would suit him, and he came to the conclusion: yes.

I was still a man in the prime of life."

I ask him if it was a blurred attraction, like a fever, that comes fast and leaves fast. Caused, for example, by the understandable need for a woman. Or had Paula suddenly appeared in a new light in the car, clearer, and more lovable?

"That's hard to say. The truth is that I thought about her for the first time during this journey. And how nice she had seemed since the very first day; you can already tell that it never occurred to me to mistrust her. Otherwise why do you think I left her the key?"

The contemplation of Paula lasted to the border. (From Aron's account one can conclude that, when picturing his life with Paula, he had only her in mind, never himself. By this I mean that he imagined, according to his desires, how she would behave in a certain situation and never thought of how he would act.) Then the car stopped for the first time; there were Russian soldiers outside and a barrier. Clifford had fallen asleep. A soldier walked up to the car, the driver rolled down the window and showed him a green paper. Careful looks around the interior of the car, which made Aron uneasy — he had no papers that gave him the right to cross the border, only Paula's promise to take care of it. Yet the soldier gave a satisfied sign to move forward, the barrier rose, and the journey continued. Not a word was spoken.

Aron knew this much, that he was now in a different zone, which one, however, he didn't know. After a bumpy bend, Clifford woke up, rubbed his eyes, and started talking, but he immediately interrupted himself because it occurred to him that Aron didn't understand. Aron didn't want to sink any further into his thoughts and wouldn't be blessed by a nap — he wasn't tired, merely hungry. All that was left was the landscape. At this stage, he would not have been averse to a little conversation. A chat about God and the world — it would make time pass faster — yet how to communicate with Clifford? German aside, Aron spoke Yiddish and a passable Russian because his mother was born in Petersburg and had taught him the language while he was still an obedient child. It occurred to him that Clifford could be Jewish, a possibility not to be excluded in the case of a Rescue man — perhaps Paula was Jewish? He made an attempt, without success. Clifford smiled at him and didn't understand, yet now he also appeared to be thinking of a way to establish communication. After a couple of strained seconds he said in Russian, "Do you speak Russian perhaps?"

At Aron's amazed expression, Clifford almost died laughing. Aron asked, "Where did you learn Russian?"

"What do you mean, where? I learned it. And you?"

They exchanged facts about themselves. Aron discovered that Clifford hadn't mastered this language by chance; it was because Rescue needed a man who knew Russian. It was inevitable, now and then, to have negotiations and correspondence with Soviet departments. "It can't hurt at the border either," Clifford said.

"We've passed it already."

Clifford looked out the window, exchanged a couple of words with the driver; they had actually passed the border. After the initial surprise about their knowledge of the language, it turned out that they didn't really know what to do with it. A flowing conversation did not develop, only single observations thrown in — the scenery, the extent of destruction, the Germans, Clifford complained about his illnesses. The only appreciable advantage for Aron in this new situation was that he was given a box of cookies when he told Clifford that he had skipped his breakfast that morning.

In the afternoon they left the highway and turned into a forest road. Aron asked if they had arrived. Not yet, Clifford said. On their way to Munich they always had to stop for gas at this place; it was an American garrison. Driving past, Aron saw soldiers sitting in a field, in a circle, with some young women among them. He wouldn't have noticed the group if the driver hadn't stuck his head out the window and emitted a loud whistle. Aron asked Clifford, "Are you Jewish?"

"No, I'm Protestant."

"And Paula?"

"Who's Paula?"

"Paula Seltzer."

"I don't know anyone called Paula Seltzer."

After a brief inspection, they drove through a gate and halted next to a brightly painted fuel truck. The driver got out and left.

"Come, let's stretch our legs," Clifford said. "It always takes a while."

They walked through the camp, stone barracks on sand. The flow of pedestrians was remarkable. Aron was surprised to see so many black soldiers. He started talking about the return trip; Clifford said he would pick Aron up from the children's home two days later. "So you'll have the whole day free for your son. We'll come around ten, but don't be impatient if we're a little late."

Aron found the garrison miserable; he even thought that most of the soldiers looked depressed. His shoes were full of sand, and with every gust of wind dust clouds whirled through the air. They sat on a bench and waited until Clifford looked at his watch and said that it was time.

When they arrived at the home at sunset, Clifford wished him good luck. He said, "Day after tomorrow, in the morning."

Aron climbed out and watched the car until the rear lights disappeared in a bend in the road. A former concentration camp, now arranged to take care of the children, Paula had said. And somewhere in there, Mark. Aron worried that some sort of authorization might be required from him; he hoped Paula had announced his visit. He shuddered at the idea of having to explain to an official why a Mr. Blank wanted to visit young Mark Berger.

The iron gate had no inscription and was closed; there was no bell and no guard. Aron called out "hello" several times, but nothing happened. He stood there puzzled, hungry, and tired, he says, alone in Bavaria. After a while he decided to climb over the gate; he figured he could manage it. As he let himself down on the other side, he heard a dog barking. Aron picked up a stone. Still today he has a phobia of dogs; he closes the window every time a dog starts barking. Yet his precaution proved to be exaggerated; the dog who immediately came running up was, as he says, a ridiculously small dachshund. Still, he had to stop himself from kicking it. He refrained only in view of the reasons for his visit; he didn't want any unnecessary trouble, and kicking a dog almost always led to a fight. He threw away the stone, at which point the dachshund appeared momentarily unsure whether to fetch it or not but then resolved to keep on barking. Suddenly a small, breathless man stood next to Aron in an undershirt and slippers. He reminded Aron immediately of his wooden-legged superintendent. The man grabbed Aron by the sleeve; his eyes revealed that this was a rare catch. He asked excitedly, "What are you doing here?"

"Let me go," Aron said.

The man wanted to let go, but he was nervous, Aron saw, and was waiting for an explanation.

"There is no bell on the door," Aron said. "I called for an hour. Take me to the director."

"So, you called for an hour? And then you simply broke in?"

"Listen," Aron said, "I came from Berlin and I'm tired. Where's the director?"

"There's no director here now. Only tomorrow morning."

Aron had an ugly thought. "This is the children's home?" he asked.

The man scrutinized the intruder and didn't reply, at which point the hostility vanished from his face. With a sigh he invited Aron to come with him. "And you be quiet."

They went into a barrack; the man knocked on a door, a woman in a nurse's uniform sat in the room. The man said that Aron wanted to speak with her, without however mentioning the break-in. She introduced herself as the night nurse, and Aron explained his request. She listened attentively, occasionally nodded understandingly; he didn't get the impression that his story particularly interested her. When he was finished, she said, "I'm sorry but you'll have to come back tomorrow."

"Why can't I see him now?"

"First of all, I am not authorized to let just anybody in and, second, the children are already asleep."

"Couldn't you wake Mark?" Aron asked. "This is something that doesn't happen every day."

"I don't know who Mark is," said the night nurse. "We have two hundred children here. Besides, he doesn't sleep alone. There are at least twenty children in each room, do you want to disturb them all?"

Disappointed, Aron left, accompanied by the man and the dachshund, which in the meantime had calmed down. On the way, the man laid his hand on Aron's shoulder and said, "Don't be angry, that's just the way it is here. You'll see him tomorrow."

When they reached the gate, he clapped his hands angrily; he had forgotten the key and wanted to fetch it.

"Never mind," Aron said, "I know the way."

He climbed back over the gate. The man made himself useful by giving directions, at least for the first half of the way.

"Thanks and good-bye."

"See you tomorrow," the man said.

Aron went along the asphalt road without knowing where it led. It was half past ten and dark; after a bend he saw the lights of a village set hard against a small mountainside. He walked toward it. Yet the closer he got to the lights, the more he questioned the sense of going to the village. He did have some money with him, even in the form of the alternative currency — which presumably was valid here too — cigarettes. It would certainly be enough for a bed, dinner, and breakfast. But his scruples were of a different kind, he told himself, a village that lies so close to a former concentration camp must be swarming with *unbearable* people. He came to the conclusion that the annoyance they could cause him would have been greater than the comforts of civilization that, in the best case, such a village could offer. He left the road and stepped into the woods.

At least it wasn't raining. Aron looked for a soft place, not too far from the road, and lay down. He was so tired that dampness and cold could not prevent him from falling asleep. With his last thoughts he damned the circumstances. He woke up very early and felt unexpectedly well. It was, he says, as if someone had cleaned out his lungs; only his clothes were moist. The clock read four, the sun was shining, he saw several rabbits and a deer. A lake would be ideal, to wash and drink, but he didn't find one. Birds, he says, so many birds, and yet he didn't know the name of a single one. Aron considered how soon he

could go back to the home without having to stand in front
of a closed gate again. He passed his hand over his face
and felt the stubble of his two-day beard. He didn't want
to appear like this to Mark and the doctors, not to mention his crumpled clothes. He ambled around the woods
till seven thirty. Then he did go to the village after all. It
turned out to be small, so small that he soon stood in the
marketplace. He found a barber.

Aron was the only client; he sat in front of the mirror
that confirmed the necessity of his detour and said, "Hair-
cut and a shave."

The barber, while he was preparing Aron, mentioned
that he had never seen him before, did he have something to do with the home? Nowadays one couldn't buy
anything reasonable with money, except for a shave. Aron
answered only with a yes or a no. When it was over, Aron
paid and inquired where he could get something to eat.

"You must be joking," said the barber.

Aron wanted to leave, but when his hand was on the
door handle, he was asked if he had anything besides
money to pay with.

"Only cigarettes."

For five cigarettes he was given bread and a piece of
cheese; he ate while he walked. By the time he had left
the village behind, his hunger was stilled, at least for the
moment. The road was longer than he had expected.
Aron didn't reach the gate, which was now open, until
around ten. He saw something he hadn't noticed in the
dusk yesterday, that barbed wire lay on the ground all
along the high walls that surrounded the home. Not too
long ago it would have been fixed on top. It must have
been since dismantled but not yet removed.

Several children played in a large free space, *definitely the mustering grounds.* Aron stood in their vicinity and observed them; he wasn't interested in how or what they were playing, only in their condition. The children were mostly pale and very scrawny; their eyes, Aron says, were disproportionately large. He bent down to a boy and asked, "Do you know a Mark here?"

The boy shook his head and went on playing. Aron heard someone calling him. He looked around; his acquaintance from the previous night was waving. The man hurried closer and shook his hand. "I've been waiting for you," he said. "We'll work things out now."

He guided Aron to a different barrack from yesterday's and said that he had already been to the director of the home and had announced Aron's visit. By the way, his name was Weber, Alois.

The director of the home was a middle-aged doctor. From the very first moment, Aron found her disagreeable. His request was known to her and not just because of the mediation of Alois Weber. She said, "I have received a phone call from Berlin. Can you explain why your son was registered here as Mark Berger?"

"No," Aron said, "it must've been a mistake."

W hy did you find her disagreeable?"

"Is that important?"

"Perhaps. And if not, explain it to me all the same."

"She had lipstick and painted fingernails," says Aron.

"Oh, my God," I say, "millions of women go around like that. That's not a good reason to dislike someone."

"Normally not," Aron says, "but it simply didn't fit in there. You didn't see the children. At the very best it was tasteless."

How is he doing?" Aron asked.

"Well, considering the circumstances," said the director. "He is weak and emaciated and must stay in bed for another few weeks. Did you know that he had pneumonia?"

"No."

"But it's over. Luckily we received some medicines in the nick of time, otherwise things might have been different."

She walked out with Aron, crossed the square; the children took no notice of them. Aron says he thought she could have pointed to any boy at all, anyone approximately the right age, and tell him he was his, he would've had to believe her. *She could decide who my son is.*

2

THE DIRECTOR SPOKE TO A NURSE who took a stool and placed it by one of the beds in the hall. "That's him. If you need me, send for me. And please don't be too loud," said the director.

Aron stood by the bed and savored the longed-for sight. Tears welled in his eyes, not just at the joy of reunion but also in shock. The face he saw, he says, looked like that of a small skull. It evaded all possible similarities with a previous appearance; the eyes were the only proof of life — alert and black. Aron immediately remembered that this was the color of his Mark's eyes. Not to think what would have happened, he says, if they had shown him a green-eyed child. He pulled himself together and didn't kiss Mark, he didn't touch him, he wanted to proceed carefully and *not frighten him.*

He wiped his tears away and noticed that the black eyes followed his every move, yet the head didn't stir. He moved the chair closer, so that Mark wouldn't lose sight of him, and sat down. He smiled for a long time while he considered what his first words should be — if it were better to start with questions or with statements — far too long, evidently, because Mark closed his eyes. Aron said, "What's your name?"

The eyes opened immediately; he heard the answer, "Mark Berger."

Happily, Aron found that Mark's answer sounded normal, not excessively weak or frail. Rather, it sounded strikingly obedient, almost military, as if Mark had been beaten into giving quick and exact answers.

"Does something hurt?"

"No," in the same manner.

"Are you scared of me?"

"No."

"Were you told who I am?"

"No."

"I'm your father."

At last not a question. At last a fact. Mark took note of this with composure. His face betrayed neither joy nor emotion.

"Do you know your father's name?"

"No."

"If I'm your father, then you're my . . . ?"

For the first time, Mark disobeyed the rules of the interrogation. He didn't answer but shrugged. Under the little white shirt, Aron says, which until then had appeared to be lying empty on the bed, shoulders moved up and down.

"Then you're my son," Aron said. "Do you understand?"

"No."

For a couple of minutes it was a mystery to Aron

what Mark didn't understand about it; the director hadn't mentioned that he was also *meshugge*. He said, "What don't you understand?"

"That word."

"Which word?"

"The one you just said."

"Son?"

"Yes."

"It's really easy," Aron said. "I'm your father and you're my son. Those are simply the words for it. Do you understand now?"

"Yes."

"Then say it again."

"You are my father, sir," Mark said, "and I am your son."

"Right. But you mustn't say sir to me. Say it again, You are my father."

"You are my father."

"I am your son."

"You are my son."

"No, that's wrong," Aron said.

Suddenly Mark started to cry. He wasn't sobbing, and tears didn't stream from his eyes, rather he was whining like a spoiled child, one who thinks nothing else will get him out of an uncomfortable situation. Aron was frightened and didn't know what he should do to soothe Mark. The nurse stood behind him and said it was enough now, Mark had to sleep.

"Leave the chair here," Aron said. "I'll come back later."

He went to the large square, sat on a bench in the sun, and looked at the children playing. Although a lot of

time had passed since he had last observed children playing on a playground, and although he wasn't in a frame of
mind for comparisons, he soon thought he perceived a
striking difference between the children here and the
ones before. No one fought and, amazingly, the game
proceeded noiselessly, almost as if it were repressed. He
also noticed that most of the children played by themselves. They painted in the sand, shoveled little buckets
full of sand, and kicked balls around, all in a subdued
manner, without children's habitual rush and excitement.

Aron started making calculations about Mark. A
great part of Mark's life lay in the dark of suppositions. It
was quite probable that witnesses would not be found,
and Mark himself wasn't a reliable informer — this much
was clear. Only conscientious calculating remained. Assuming that Mark Berger and Mark Blank were one and
the same, and Aron didn't want to think of any other possibility, then it was certain that at age one and a half he
had lost his mother, months later his father, was de-
posited with his neighbor, and then ended up in a camp.
There he lived until the end of the war, but how? Certainly among children and women who, Aron says, had
worries other than his well-being. Among people who,
forced by the circumstances, stole his food and in doing
so taught him to do the same — with success, as his survival proved.

Or he lay for years in a dark corner. Sick and apathetic, provided continuously with the necessary nutrition by a well-wishing destiny. Perhaps by destiny in the
form of a commiserating woman who shared her meals
with him because, who knows, her own son had died, for
example, or because Mark's face reminded her of some-

one, Aron says, or simply because she was a great lover of children. But how could this hypothetical woman find the time to teach him everything that was known to a child his age, to explain who's the father and who's the son, and to whom one says sir or, simply, you? A further stroke of luck in his thought process, which was almost adventurous in Aron's view, was that Mark could speak German in the first place. He was brought to the camp with almost no knowledge of language; all possibilities were open, his surroundings may just as well have been Hungarian or French or Polish.

Alois Weber sat next to Aron on the bench and asked him, "How is he?"

"He must sleep now."

"I'm the maid-of-all-work here," Weber said. "When there is something to buy, or repair, or carry — the women can't do everything on their own."

Aron thought that they should have hired a bigger man. "What did you do before?" He asked.

"When before?"

"Before you came here."

"I was in Dachau, not far from here."

"In Dachau? Wasn't that also a camp?"

"'Also' is good," Weber said.

"As a prisoner?"

"You think as a prison guard?"

"Then you're a Jew?"

"Do I look like one?" Weber asked. "Political."

A conversation followed, in the course of which Aron learned a thing or two about Weber's past, and Weber learned this much, that Aron would be picked up in the morning and that he didn't know where to spend the night. "If you like, you can come to my place later. There's plenty of room and food, too. I live right over there," Weber said.

"Thank you."

"Where did you sleep last night?"

"In the woods."

"Oh, my God!"

Aron went back to Mark. The chair was still there; he sat down without asking the nurse. Mark looked like he was asleep, but Aron had barely sat down when he opened his eyes and *even* turned his head a little in his direction. Aron felt that Mark was smiling at him in a barely perceptible way.

"You are my father," Mark said, "and I am your son."

Aron's tears immediately began to flow again. Mark hadn't slept for one second, but, like his father outside, he had made calculations. He had arrived at the right result and had understood the lesson. Aron was filled with pride. From Mark's behavior he deduced an uncommon intelligence — in spite of all the neglect — and a gift for analysis, and the rare ambition of not being satisfied with approximations. The tears were collected in a handkerchief; then Aron risked his first kiss, which Mark registered with astonishment.

Mark's performance increased Aron's desire for conversation wherein, he says, the content was less important than the pure joy of hearing Mark's voice. "What can you remember?"

"I don't know."

"Do you know that you were in a camp?"

"Yes, in a concentration camp."

"Did you run around there?"

"Yes."

"Who gave you food?"

"The woman."

"Which woman? What was her name?"

"I don't know."

"Was her name Mrs. Fisch?"

"I don't know."

"Did she live in the same barrack as you?"

"Yes. We slept in the same bed."

"Was she old?"

"No, she was beautiful."

Aron thought it was strange that Mark knew abstract words such as "old" and "beautiful" while he didn't know such an easy one as "son." At the same time he felt pleased with himself because he had succeeded, armed with nothing but a little experience, in deducing that this woman, Mark's savior, existed. Like an astronomer who works out the existence of a distant celestial body, he says, without seeing it, only on the basis of its effects.

Aron resolved to change the subject. Furthermore, he decided on the spot that the exchange should be final; he didn't want to speak about the camp with Mark ever again. He said, "Now I'd like to introduce myself. Because it's rather funny that you don't even know your father's name. My name is Arno Blank."

I interrupt Aron to ask why he had never wanted to speak to Mark about the camp again. Not because I consider his resolution absurd, I say, rather because I can think of several reasons. Aron looks at me for a long time without answering; then he declares that it is enough for today, he's tired now.

However, the expression on his face betrays what he thinks: He who asks such questions can't do much with answers.

It is as hard for me now as it was the first day to come to terms with the fact that time and again I will have to rely on suppositions. Unless I discover a cleverer method, or find something that, to Aron's ears, sounds less crass than a question. Half a day is lost, but we're not in a hurry, no one is pressuring us.

Mark was encouraged to repeat the name several times so that he would get used to its strange melody. He didn't notice the difference between their last names, it didn't mean anything to him. Aron began a series of bewildering explanations — father, marriage, registry office — yet he stopped as soon as he noticed that Mark could keep his eyes open only with great effort. The last piece of information he gave Mark was that the name Berger had been a mistake, caused by a hearing defect or carelessness of the person who wrote it.

"So what's your name?"

"My name is Mark Blank."

"Very good."

Then the director appeared and said that Mark had to be treated, medicine, food, and sleep. Aron walked out with her. He had intended to talk with Mark a couple of hours later but she said, "That's enough for today. You can't imagine how much such a conversation strains him in his condition."

"Perhaps you think," Aron said, "that it's better for him to see nothing but the ceiling all day? He has almost forgotten how to speak."

"Dear Mr. Blank," the director said, "I'm afraid you are confused. We have taken over the task of making your son better, not of entertaining him. Or should we assign someone to do nothing but converse with the children all day?"

"Of course you should!" Aron shouted. He went away angrily, without a specific direction. When he turned around he saw her, puzzled, looking after him. He went back, no longer in a rush and not to excuse himself for his lapse.

She even smiled. "Did you forget something?" she asked.

"Yes. I want you to change the name in the papers. His name isn't Berger."

"I've already seen to that," she said.

Aron had barely stepped into Alois Weber's barrack when he wanted to go out again, he was so shocked. But this would have offended his host. He felt as if he were back, he says; except for a living room, nothing had changed. The well-known smell, thirty or more three-storied bunk beds with rotting straw, and Weber, as if he were joking, said, "Make yourself at home."

"For God's sake," Aron said, "how can you live here?"

"What do you mean 'can,'" Weber said. "I have to. Maybe I'm not as sensitive as you are. You had trouble?"

Aron told of his troubles. "But the nursing is really good," Weber said, "as far as I can judge. The nurses are patient and friendly, the medicine comes from America, and the food is plentiful. What more do you want?"

The barrack made Aron restless; Mark and the woman may have slept in one of the beds. He sat on one of two chairs. Weber had achieved a certain degree of luxury, a cupboard, a table, a radio, a standard lamp, an alarm clock, and a palm tree in a bucket. The invitation to spend the night could only mean that Aron should use one of the many empty bunk beds; he asked himself if the woods weren't preferable.

"I'm thinking," Aron said, "whether I should simply try again later or not."

"Try what?"

"Go to him, without asking."

"I wouldn't do that."

"And why not?"

"It's simple," Weber said. "You're leaving tomorrow but he stays here. Or are you planning to take him with you right away?"

"I can't."

"So you see."

"Where's your dog?" Aron asked.

It wasn't his dog, Weber said. He suggested they go for a little walk, the weather was so pleasant, the surroundings were delightful, and they could eat something on the way. Aron was surprised — it was unlikely that somewhere along the way there would be an inn that was still intact — yet since Weber suggested it he agreed. He also agreed because any way of passing time was preferable to staying in the barrack and, as for Mark, Weber was probably right.

They went in the direction of the small town, only a short way, then Weber turned off the road and led Aron across a wide field. From the very first step, Weber produced an endless flow of words; at first he made a number of general comments about the region, Bayern, the correlation between war and crime, or the fight against crop pests, yet he *skillfully* approached his actual topic, Alois Weber's past. Weber portrayed the thorny career of a Social Democrat, even his grandfather had been a Social Democrat, the field wasn't wide enough for the whole story. Weber interrupted himself only now and then to point out a fleeing animal or a rare bird, which interested Aron as little as his life history. Weber wasn't disagreeable, that's why Aron let him talk; he stopped listening only when Weber got to his twenties. He thought of other things, and Weber didn't suspect that he was talking to himself. For example, Aron says, he had thought that he wanted to bring Mark to Berlin as soon as possible, but how? Once Weber tugged on his sleeve and asked, "What do you think of that?"

And Aron risked the answer "Unbelievable."

That seemed to be appropriate. Luckily Weber didn't challenge Aron a second time by asking him to declare his view of the circumstances, so they both went about their business undisturbed. Later, when they were surrounded by the woods and Weber, after listening briefly, had reached the point of his unavoidable arrest by the

Gestapo, he said, "I'll tell you later how it turned out, perhaps this evening. Now let's enjoy the air."

"You're not just going for a walk with me?" Aron said. "You're taking me somewhere?"

Weber grinned and said, "You notice everything."

"Where are we going?"

"We're going to a ranger widow."

"A what?"

Aron found that Weber's grin took on a suggestive twist while he explained: in the woods there was a ranger's lodge, what kind of a German wood would this be if there wasn't one? The ranger had been killed in the war, yet his widow, pretty and lonely, was still alive; these two facts too were not uncommon in our time. In his heart, Weber thanked destiny for having let him, quite by chance, find the little house during a solitary walk hardly two weeks before. "And we will eat there."

"She sells food?"

"Nonsense. I haul everything I can find over there. She also has a child."

"Why do you do this?" Aron asked.

In spite of the grinning, he says, he expected a philanthropic answer, but Weber teased the obtuse Aron. He said, "You have three guesses," and he supported this with an *offensive gesture.* "That's why I do it. Or should I wait till the ten-year mourning period is up?"

"You're right," Aron said, "life must go on."

"That's exactly what I mean."

When they arrived, Aron concluded that he and Weber held completely divergent views on female beauty. The plumpish woman was introduced to him as Margarete; she was considerably younger than Weber, and

this had probably had a positive influence on his assessment of her charms. A child was nowhere to be seen; only
the dog Aron had already met came toward him. Thus
Aron could infer where Alois Weber had spent the previous night. Yes, he told himself, like this the barrack is easier to bear.

The food was good; it consisted of, Aron remembers,
potatoes, mushrooms, and canned meat, with red wine on
the side. Weber helped with the preparations while Aron
sat on a deck chair in front of the house and enjoyed the
peace and quiet. He decided to invite Weber for a return
visit the following morning when they took leave of each
other.

In the meantime supper was on the table, and the
way back was overshadowed by the rest of the Weberian
story.

Don't you want to tell me his story? At least the gist
of it?"

"I already told you, I don't know it."

When they got back to the home, it was pitch black.
Only a few feet away from the lodge, Aron had offered to
Weber to go back alone; he would definitely find the way,
and an empty bed too. Yet Weber had declined and explained, "At my age one can't always do as one wants."

"Which bed do you want?" Weber asked.

"I don't care."

Aron lay down on the one closest to Weber's living corner. He was so tired that the barrack, contrary to all fears, hardly kept him from falling asleep.

The next morning time for conversation with Mark turned out to be brief because Weber, who was already dressed, woke Aron with the news that the car was already waiting outside.

"What's the time?"

"Six thirty."

"Are the children awake?"

"No."

Aron stole into the dormitory, didn't come across any personnel on the way, and woke Mark up. He put a finger on his lips and whispered, "I have to leave now."

He waited for an expression of disappointment, Mark's "Already?" or if and when he'd come back. Yet nothing of the kind happened, so Aron said, "I will come back soon and take you with me to Berlin."

"What is that, Berlin?"

"Berlin is a big city. But don't be impatient."

"Yes."

"I'll come for you soon. Good-bye."

"Good-bye."

Aron kissed Mark and said, "And now go back to sleep, you must sleep a great deal."

The parting from Weber was heartfelt; it even came, Aron says, to an embrace — initiated by Weber. Weber pressed a package with a sandwich into his hand; Aron assured himself that Weber had noted his address correctly.

Then the greeting with Clifford; Clifford said, "We're early."

They both sat in the car exactly where they had

been two days earlier. Aron breakfasted and drove toward Paula; he already thought, *Yesterday was a day without Paula.* Clifford asked him about his meeting with his son, and Aron gave him some information without going into details.

Normally," he says, "one wouldn't need to waste one word on the return trip. But I already told you several things over which one normally needn't waste one word, and I will do it again often. Listen to what happened on the way home. We sit and drive and talk, I forget about what, only our driver is silent the whole time. I can't talk to him because of the language barrier, you know, but I notice that Clifford isn't talking to him either. Not even when he's not talking to me. Perhaps, I think, they can't stand each other or they drive together so often that they have already talked themselves out. At a certain point the car turns into the wood again and stops next to the fuel truck; Clifford climbs out and beckons to me. I don't really want to get out, everything is full of sand, but he waves and I don't want to be impolite. So I get out of the car. In the meantime it's boiling hot, we walk to the shade, sit on a bench, and smoke. Suddenly there's such a blast that I feel like the world is falling to pieces. A pressure wave as hard as iron tears me from the bench. I fly a couple of yards and fall in the sand, but I'm not unconscious. My ears hurt. I see Clifford lying not far from me. You must imagine, the pressure was so strong that even the heavy stone bench has fallen over. Clifford isn't hurt either; he asks what happened and I tell him to turn around. There's a pillar of smoke. It must be the truck, I immediately think, where our car was parked. Clifford dashes away; I stay sitting on the ground and check if my limbs are intact. In brief, the truck has exploded. Why, nobody knows. Our driver is dead, another soldier is dead, and there are a couple of wounded, too. I think, I only got out of the car because I wanted to be polite and that saved my life. Clifford had to go to Berlin urgently. They found a jeep and a new driver; nothing was left of our car. So we sit again and drive, I'm quiet — what can one say about such a story? — Clifford also says nothing. But suddenly he starts crying, crying like a child. A delayed shock, I think, but he doesn't stop. I see that he wants to stop but he can't. I told you, I had the impression he treated the driver as if he didn't exist, which is why I'm so surprised that this story hurts him so. Until he tells me that the driver was his son. Your son? I ask. His son-in-law. And he cries all the way to Berlin. I imagine how he will tell his daughter, and I remember Weber's asking whether I wanted to take Mark with me right away."

Aron's last thoughts during the drive, when it was already dark, with Clifford moaning softly in the background, circled around Paula. If she would still be there, and if not, if she would come back, if perhaps the feared farewell letter would be lying there. He even started thinking if he could do something to *keep Paula*, but he did not know what.

Paula was there. She was lying on the bed reading a

book in English when Aron walked into the room. (The book, one of only a few keepsakes, is still in Aron's possession. It is entitled *Erewhon, or Over the Range* and is written by Samuel Butler.) She said, "Is it all right that I'm still here?"

From then on she lived with Aron. Little by little she brought everything she needed from her own apartment, which she didn't give up and which Aron never saw. Primarily she brought clothes, but also tableware, some vases because it was summertime, a number of canned goods, a night table, so that soon there was no reason for her to go home anymore. Aron didn't think about their living together, he explains, he virtually avoided the subject. The knowledge of being in love was enough, and he had no further thoughts about Paula's motives. She must, like him, have been in love, what else? He excluded pity; he strongly believes that he would have known if it was pity. Yet days later, coming back to Paula's reasons, he actually can't imagine that a woman like her could have been in love with him. Therefore, he absolutely could not think of any reason why Paula had lived with him, even though, naturally, there must have been one; it's logical, nothing happens without a reason.

Soon their relationship became marriagelike. They respected each other's habits and posed no demands they assumed might be arduous or tiresome. Aron reports that his main occupation during those first days was finding out Paula's habits. He wanted to avoid any accidents that might arise from not knowing these habits, and Paula, *judging from their success,* must have made a similar effort.

As for her past, Paula was discreet. Unlike with Alois

Weber, Aron would have liked to hear a long history from her, but she wouldn't talk about it. Only when he posed concrete questions, never on her own initiative, did she offer information about herself. In these instances, her tone wasn't unfriendly, but her replies were always brief and never went beyond the specifics of the question. From this he concluded that she answered unwillingly, that she said things only so as not to appear curt, which is why he soon stopped questioning her. Once he asked her if she had spent the war in a camp, whereupon she answered, "No, in England." Nothing else, not even later, even though she must have realized from his question that he was interested in more detailed information. So he knew almost nothing about her past.

Aron's knowledge of contemporary Paula was extensive, even if one must take into consideration that ignoring her past inevitably led to a certain superficiality. But the attainment of this knowledge, Aron emphasizes, was delightful. He soon found out, he says, that Paula was primarily a theoretical person. She preferred to talk about problems concerning humanity, the century, or *science*, and talked about the basics of living together only when it was unavoidable. If Aron asked her what she wanted for dinner, he could be certain that she would name the first dish that came into her mind, and that was that. But if he brought the conversation around to the closing of vacant lots, he had to be careful or she would be late for work.

He thought she suffered from an illness. He came to this conclusion because, as long as she lived with him, she took a pill every morning and every night, but she said nothing about this either. She didn't keep it a secret; sometimes she would already be in bed while Aron was still up and she would call out, "Will you bring me a glass of water for the pill?" She simply didn't talk about it. The name that Aron read on the bottle revealed nothing; he wrote it on a piece of paper and intended, if the opportunity presented itself, to ask a doctor what the pills were for or against, but he forgot about it.

He found that Paula exaggerated hygiene. After the smallest household task she would wash her hands, she spent hours in the bathroom daily, the best discovery for her were the bottles of bath oils. Twice a week she would change the sheets, the towels daily, and it often happened that when Aron would have liked to have her with him she'd be standing in the bathroom doing the washing. The corridor was always full of laundry hung up to dry. This obsession of hers, as Aron calls it, wasn't an issue, however; even when it bothered him he stuck with his intention of accepting Paula with all her characteristics.

I don't just mean in this specific case," I say, "but don't you think it's false tolerance when one resolves not to criticize someone under any circumstance?"

"Our relationship," Aron says, "had nothing to do with tolerance. I didn't want to disturb her, just like I didn't want to be disturbed by her."

"But she did disturb you?"

"Do you think I didn't disturb her? Trust me, the person who never disturbs anyone hasn't been born yet. Not disturbing means to disturb as little as possible."

I hadn't asked my question randomly; for a long time I had been looking for a pretext to involve him in a

discussion about tolerance. Since we first met, I have suspected more and more that Aron's solitude lies essentially
in the fact that, in his world, tolerance and lack of criti-
cism are considered one and the same. But the privilege
to be left alone, not to be bothered, in the long run, is a
horrible disadvantage, because it means nothing more
than exclusion from the community. The most honest intentions can be behind it, but that doesn't change the result. Yet suddenly I doubt if it makes sense to discuss this
in detail with someone who is the victim of such a delu-
sion.

In erotic matters, a field that is not irrelevant when considering the prospect of living together for an extended
period of time, Aron says, Paula had been a great experience for him, a revelation. Not because she was particularly refined, nor because of the extent of her demands.
She had never made any, thus there had been no cause
for his fear that their age difference, the real extent of
which only he knew, could lead to complications. He was
much more amazed, and at the same time delighted, at
how much she attracted him, not only during the first
days. And this meant far more to him than any other comfort in that otherwise bleak time. It also helped him enormously in getting over the difficult loss of his wife, Lydia,
about which and of whom he never said a word to Paula.
    An even greater quirk than the excessive hygiene
was, in his eyes, Paula's passion for astrology. She owned
several books on astrology, among them a thick one with
the horoscopes of famous people. She didn't read it from

start to finish, simply because she already knew all their horoscopes; rather she would dip into it now and then. The possibility that constellations could influence people's destinies fascinated her, or at least it preoccupied her constantly, and it wasn't easy for him, Aron, always to keep a straight face when she talked about it. Still, he doesn't think she went so far as to come to any conclusions about her own behavior based on the position of celestial bodies. She never said, "Today Jupiter and Uranus are so-and-so aligned, therefore today I'll do this and that or I won't do this and that." And she didn't think that way either. Her preoccupation with astrology was predominantly theoretical; her pleasure in it was Greek to him. Once he asked her, "Do you believe it or not?" She replied, "It's so mysterious."

A finishing touch to her personality: Aron relates that Paula was — he can't find a more appropriate word — a fanatic flower lover. To my question if he isn't exaggerating the details now, he says no, that characteristic trait absolutely belongs to Paula and I shouldn't always think exclusively of *getting on* with the story. The number of vases she had brought from her apartment had been, in his opinion, incredible. Thirteen pieces in all, and he couldn't remember that a vase ever stood empty in the room, not from the first day of his return.

Usually she would leave the apartment at half past eight in the morning and come back in the evening, around half past six. Aron was alone the whole day, except for Sundays.

One afternoon, when he was getting his monthly aid from the department in the center of the city (the first clue regarding his income), he met an acquaintance who had survived the same camp he had, a certain Abraham Kenik. Kenik came up to him in the waiting room and said, "Is it really you, Aron?" They had last seen each other the day the camp was liberated. "What brings you to Berlin?" Kenik asked.

"Where else should I be?"

"How should I know? Home?"

"You'll laugh," Aron said. "This is my home."

"Right, you are at home here. By the way, Aron, why do I never see you?"

"Where should you see me?"

"Didn't anybody tell you where we meet?"

"Who's we?"

"Our people. Those of us who survived. At least a few of us."

"No, where do you meet?"

"We have a bar. That is, it's not ours, I don't even know who it belongs to, definitely a goy. Do you have pen and paper?"

Kenik jotted down the address on a piece of paper; the bar was called Hessischen Weinstuben. Aron stuck the paper in his pocket and asked, "What do you do there?"

"What do we do? We drink, eat, play billiards, play cards, talk about business, what else?"

"About what business?"

"Come join us," Kenik said, trying to sound enticing. He was called, picked up his aid money, and on his way out said, "Do come, I'm there almost every day."

For several days Aron disregarded the paper in his pocket, did not actually throw it away, yet he didn't think he'd ever need the address. No sensible reason occurred to him why he should go to the Hessischen Weinstuben and meet Kenik there. Besides, he didn't feel like it. The other survivors, *what kind of a relationship is that?* What should he talk to them about? At best about the old times, but he didn't care about that, he couldn't care less. Aron imagined that they had erected a sort of new ghetto, without external obligation, and he didn't want to take part in it. The only attraction was that, as Kenik had mentioned, there was something to drink. Probably there was liquor in sufficient quantity, yet even that prospect didn't compare with the disadvantages that had risen so clearly in his mind.

Then at breakfast Paula said, "Arno, I have to tell you something."

"Yes?"

"I don't like you."

"Already?"

"I'm serious, Arno," she said. "I don't like the way you squander your time. You live like an old woman, like our housekeeper. You go shopping, stand patiently in line, you cook — what kind of a life is that? Are you waiting for something? I mean, you should get some kind of job."

"You think so?"

"Yes, I do. I'm not talking about money, you know that. I just think that it can't go on like this. As if you were an old man."

"And what do you suggest?"

"If you want," Paula said, "I can look around for a job for you. These days there's more than enough work to go around. All we have to do is discuss what would be a proper job for you. Should we do that?"

"No."

Aron felt that Paula was right. He refused her offer mainly because it was exclusively his problem. Before long, though, he was thankful that she had drawn his attention so clearly to an unsatisfactory state before he got used to it and took it for granted. Paula realized how uncomfortable the topic was for him, so she let it lie, remaining silent. He had thought, Aron says, Lydia wouldn't have let off so easily.

The following day he went to the Hessischen Weinstuben. The bar was in a noticeably unscathed quarter; the name was on a large sign across the entrance and window, in letters that looked like they were shaped out of green tendrils of vine. In the middle of the room was a billiard table, surrounded by players. Aron checked to see if among them there was a face that he remembered. One of the players asked him, "Are you looking for someone?"

"A certain Kenik."

"If he's here then he's over in that room," the player said.

Aron was unhappy with this beginning; he had come halfheartedly as it was, definitely not because of Kenik. Now it was as if he were there only because he wanted to see Kenik. He saw no face he recognized. The player said, "What's the matter, don't you want to go and see if he's there?"

Aron stepped into the room. It said "Private" on the

door, and he immediately saw that this was actually the bar that Kenik had told him about — full of smoke, protected from hostile looks, and reserved for the initiated. The survivors were sitting at perhaps fifteen tables. Still looking for a face he knew, Aron heard his name being called loudly. Kenik came toward him with outstretched arms. "There you are at last!" Kenik cried.

He pulled Aron to a table, where three men he didn't know were seated, pushed him onto a chair, and introduced him, effusively. While Kenik had gone to fetch drinks, the three men asked Aron about his background. They named the camp where they had spent the war and wanted to know the name of his, as if all the important details about the past were given in this manner. Kenik put drinks on the table and said, "Don't be angry with me, I'm really happy."

"Why should I be angry?"

"He saved my life once," Kenik said to the others and started telling them the story.

"Don't exaggerate."

The truth is that during their fourth month together at the camp, while working in the quarry, Kenik had collapsed and didn't move. Aron, who accidentally had been working near him, dragged him behind a pile of stones. Not because of the shade, rather to get him out of sight of the *supervisory staff,* who were always on edge and who often used their right of immediate execution of prisoners in cases of feigned inability to work. They first got to know each other, Aron says, behind that pile of rocks. He spoke encouragingly to Kenik. He didn't impute Kenik's collapse to physical exhaustion, but interpreted it as the manifestation of widespread demoralization — Kenik had

had enough. Aron let him lie there; he had to go on working, he didn't want to take on any unnecessary risks.
Miraculously, at the end of the workday Kenik still hadn't
been discovered. Aron went back to him, stood him on
his feet, and helped him back to the barracks. That's all
it was, he says, a glorious rescue. By the next morning
Kenik was his normal self again.

Later the two sat alone at the table. Kenik smiled
and said, "The idea with the hair is good."

"With what hair?"

"Didn't you dye it?"

Aron grimaced and felt uneasy, especially since he
admitted to himself only now that he had come to look
for work, even though he would never ask for it. He was
sitting in front of Kenik like a supplicant in disguise and
waited for an offer. Kenik didn't let him wait long; he
said, "Now, between you and me, Aron, how's it going?"

"How should it go? It's going fine. As you can see, I
didn't die, I wear a clean shirt, what more does one
need?"

"One needs much more," Kenik said. "What do you
live off?"

"You were there when I picked up my money."

"I picked up money, too. But that's not what I live
off."

"I do."

"That's wrong, Aron," Kenik sighed, "that's absolutely wrong. We were the lowest dirt for long enough."

"What exactly do you mean?" Aron asked.

"Don't you think we deserve a better life? Haven't
we served our time? Don't you think we have the right to

a job with enough money to lead a decent existence? That others live miserably today, can that be an argument for us? Isn't it our turn now?"

Apparently Kenik felt like philosophizing, but Aron wanted to hear concrete suggestions, a concrete offer, after which it would be easier to chat about claims and rights and human dignity. "And where should I get such a job?" he asked.

"That's why we're here."

Kenik fetched more schnapps and then revealed the possibilities available. "We are dealers," he said. "Our principle is, buy cheap and sell expensive."

"An original method," Aron said. "But what do you buy, and what do you sell?"

"Whatever people need. Nails, coffee, medicine, wood, cloth, shoes, everything."

"Where do you get it?"

"We get it," Kenik said. "That's not your problem."

"And what should I do?"

"You should help to sell."

"To whom?"

"Anyone who wants to buy."

"I should stand on the street and call out?"

"If you don't have any better ideas, yes," Kenik said. "I can only tell you, you will be surprised how easy it is to sell these days. People tear everything out of your hands."

Aron turned his glass and was disappointed; he knew that this wasn't the right job for him. A pity, he would certainly make a lot of money, but it sounded like the kind of job you must be born to do or be trained for since youth, and he thought he fulfilled neither condition. To spend his days in the black market or in the back rooms of shops, then talk to Paula in the evening and lie with her at night, he didn't feel up to such a double life. *Wherever you are, there is the black market.* "You mustn't answer right away. Tomorrow I'll introduce you to Tennenbaum; he's not here now," Kenik said.

"Who's Tennenbaum?"

"An important man for us, but don't ask so many questions."

Then they talked about the old times. The following afternoon Aron appeared for the announced audience with Tennenbaum. He thought he could just as easily have stayed home; there was hardly any hope that this Tennenbaum would make him a different offer than Kenik had, but then again he might. He went with the firm intention to refuse any and all suggestions that sounded like the initial offer. Kenik was waiting in front of the bar and said, "Come on, he doesn't like to be kept waiting."

I succeeded in luring Aron out of his apartment; the weather helped. I didn't name a destination, just suggested a few steps out the door. To my amazement he stood up and put on his shoes. Had I foreseen his willingness, I would have thought of a destination, some small distraction for him. So we walk, as if it were obvious, to the neighboring park. He takes off his summer coat and hangs it over his arm; he hadn't believed me that it's warm. Swans maneuver on a pond; Aron sits on a bench without saying a word. I think he's in pain. "Do you know what I think of all the time?" I ask.

He doesn't reply, "What?"

I continue, "If anyone but you had told me about the Hessischen Weinstuben, I would have considered him an anti-Semite."

"Why?"

"It can't possibly be true that all the black marketers were Jews."

"Did I say that?"

"Not in so many words. But in the Weinstuben there were only —"

Aron interrupted me. "Is it so hard to understand that I went to the Weinstuben only because Kenik invited me and that Kenik went there only because only Jews went there? There were definitely thousands of other Weinstuben, without Jews. But Kenik didn't go there. And therefore neither did I."

"Yes."

"And something else," Aron says. "I'm not telling you the history of the postwar years, I'm telling you what happened to me. There are bound to be differences. I understand that you have a certain vision and that you worry about contradictions. But that is your problem, my friend, not mine."

He rolls up his coat, pushes it under his head, and stretches his legs. Within five minutes he's asleep. I have never seen him sleep. I observe him and wait for flies to chase away.

Aron had thought that he would meet Tennenbaum in the Hessischen Weinstuben, but Kenik steered him away

from the bar, a couple of streets down to Tennenbaum's
apartment. On the way he drew a portrait of the chief:
very clever mind, erudite, before the war a lawyer or
something like that, in any case a jurist, outstanding rela-
tions with the Allies, not a friend of many words, strict
but just. "The first time he might seem a little gruff, but
that's his personality."

"Did you already talk to him about me?"

"Last night."

"And?"

"I just announced that we would visit him today,
nothing more. Only so he knows who's before him."

An elderly woman opened the door. Kenik said, "We
have an appointment with Mr. Tennenbaum."

The woman led them into a *rich* room, bookshelves
all the way to the ceiling, Oriental carpets, draped cur-
tains. Kenik let himself sink into a leather chair and made
an inviting hand motion, as if all this were his property.
Aron made an effort to appear relaxed; he felt that Kenik's
announcement and the peculiar room were having an effect on him. He was also starting to think of Tennenbaum
as an important man, even though, until then, nothing
spoke for or against that idea.

"Look here," Kenik whispered. He stood near the
door and pressed the light switch. A stunningly large crystal chandelier with perhaps thirty lightbulbs blinded Aron.
Kenik immediately turned it off and sat down, so that he
wouldn't get caught by the owner of the house, a *big baby*.
Aron thought, This Tennenbaum cannot have gotten this
house any differently than I got mine; some Leutwein or
other must have lived here once. With his good relation-

ship to the Allies, the apartment was no proof of his true wealth.

"I don't like to be kept waiting either," he said.

"He's probably very busy," Kenik said. "Please don't be impatient."

"I also have things to do."

Finally Tennenbaum came, inconspicuousness personified, Aron found, average size, thin. The only notable thing about him was a certain gold tiepin with a red stone. "Don't get up," he said.

He sat down; the elderly woman stuck her head around the door and asked if she should bring something, tea perhaps.

"No," said Tennenbaum, and then, "It would be better if we speak in private first."

Kenik stood up immediately, said, "Naturally," and then good-bye. As he left he winked, unnoticed by Tennenbaum; then they were alone.

"So, you want to start working with us?"

"That's not exactly right."

"What do you mean?"

"Kenik has made me an offer. He told me it's better if you inform me of the possibilities. For now I can't speak of wanting."

"So you don't want to work with us?"

"Let's put it like this: First I must hear what kind of job we're talking about, only then can I make up my mind."

"Didn't Kenik tell you?"

"A little. It didn't sound very interesting."

"What did he say?"

Aron repeated the contents of the previous day's conversation and didn't fail to tell him that he wasn't suitable for such an occupation in any way, for buying and selling at a high price. That he didn't think much of a training period. Because of his unsuitability, he also had no inclination. He intentionally chose self-confident words and an appropriate tone. Tennenbaum should know that he didn't have an odd-job man in front of him; *the first impression is everything.*

"What's your profession?" Tennenbaum asked.

"Before the camp I worked as a company secretary in a textile factory."

"Did it belong to a Jew?"

"Yes."

"What was his name?"

"You wouldn't know him," Aron said. He disliked the questions and answers game, he felt like he was under interrogation.

Tennenbaum said, "Don't be rash, and above all, don't be so sensitive. If we're going to work together, I have to know certain things about you. So, what was his name?"

"London."

Tennenbaum snorted. Of course he knew London, though only in passing. He knew who London was, he even knew about his move to the United States. And as he learned of Aron's family relationship with London, he professed he even had a vague memory of a son-in-law. "I remember, there was a rumor about marriage. What was the daughter called, Rosa?"

"Linda."

"Right, Linda London."

Now Tennenbaum was apparently in the position of

placing Aron in the picture. He became friendlier; he opened a hidden closet in the bookshelf and took out a cherry liqueur. "I must confess, I've been waiting for you for a long time," he said.

"For me?"

"Not for you personally, but for a man with your qualifications. Of course, selling isn't a job for you."

The rest lasted barely half an hour. Tennenbaum outlined his future field of work. He was looking for someone who would keep his books, who would record all the incoming and outgoing movements — "Which is more than you think" — allowing a precise overview of the traffic. Until then, this had been done halfheartedly. He had taken care of this job himself, Tennenbaum said, as a bloody layman with a huge amount of effort and scarce success. "Do you trust you can do the job?"

"Who would I be keeping the books for?"

"For me, naturally. For who else?"

"You don't understand," Aron said. "I mean, for the internal revenue, for the tax office, for whom?"

"For me," Tennenbaum said. "We have nothing to do with the authorities. For me and my overview."

That simplified the matter enormously, Aron explains to me; there was no difference between gross and net amounts, a Sunday job for trained bookkeepers. Only the question of payment remained open. Aron had almost forgotten it, for him it had been secondary.

I feel that's exaggerated or understated, it could hardly correspond to the truth. I can't believe that money was such a side issue. "Excuse me, you're going to have to explain that," I say.

"What is there to explain?" he asks, irritated as usual because of the interruption. "That's the way it was."

"The pay couldn't have been secondary to you. On the contrary. I would understand if you had tried to get as much out of it as you possibly could. I keep hearing how anxious you were to catch up. How does that fit?"

"Who did you hear that from? From me?"

"If you like, not from you, but wasn't that so? Didn't you have an overwhelming desire to catch up?"

I mustn't always get in his way with my assumptions, Aron says. And I should not bother him with what I pick up from others. "If you really want to know, it was the other way around. I didn't want more and more; on the contrary, I was satisfied with so little that I thought I was touched in the head. In fact, I wasn't right in the head; the last few years had muddled my sense of priorities. I felt as if I was in paradise. A good-looking woman, an apartment, a rediscovered child, enough to eat — had I dared to imagine such luck in the camp?" he asks. "And with all this, I would stand there and haggle over money?"

In the end, Tennenbaum got around to discussing the salary only just before they parted. That late, because he evidently expected Aron to bring up the subject, but he had no other choice. He made him two offers — his decision — one was two thousand marks a month, the other was a one percent share in the total profit. By his calculation, he said, they both amounted more or less to the same thing. "I want to earn a decent wage but not to your disadvantage, as you can see. Not on my people," he said.

"I agree," Aron said.

"With which option?"

"You choose."

Tennenbaum smiled about his new bookkeeper, behind whose seeming lack of resolve refinement probably lurked. He opted for the percentage of profits. He gave Aron the existing documents — two books and many papers — pointed out the inadequacy of the previous bookkeeping, and asked if Aron needed some money up front, to get writing materials or for personal purposes.

"No," Aron said. "But where should I work?"

"Can't you work at home?"

"Not really."

"Then I'll try to find a room for you. It occurs to me that in the back of the bar there is a small room. Take a look at it, see if it's suitable."

"Actually, I can work at home," Aron said after brief consideration.

The work was easy; it didn't require particularly difficult bookkeeping tricks. After all, it was only for Tennenbaum's overview. Child's play, Aron says, that cost him hardly two hours a day; it would have been accomplished more quickly if it weren't for incredibly small entries that would pop up time and again. Eighteen pins or twelve shaving mirrors; nothing was too great a loss for Tennenbaum, and success proved him right.

The one percent profit share never, except in the

extremely slack months, fell below the two thousand mark barrier; on average it rose well above it. Tennenbaum had decided luckily or generously. A further advantage for Aron was that Tennenbaum gave him the possibility of getting part of his salary in goods from the current stock of the firm and at the buying rate, which no one besides the two of them knew. In this way, Aron's money was worth incomparably more than in the hands of *the Germans*.

He never tried to involve Paula in conversations about his new job; nothing ever happened that was important enough to mention to her. Paula took his occupation and his sudden wealth with composure; she showed no apparent interest, she asked no questions. Yet sometimes he had the feeling that he was participating in a small hidden war, as if it were a test of strength between them from which side the first word on the matter would come. Only at the very beginning, when he had explained the sense and purpose of his activity, which he never kept secret, did she hint at disapproval. "If you think this is right for you," she had said.

After that, nothing more. The issue of making Aron's days less empty appeared to be dealt with for her, since he looked more satisfied. She had other issues, other worries. For example, she hadn't as yet succeeded in finding a home for Mark in the neighborhood.

"Please don't drink so much," she said.

Aron was taken aback. Though Paula's words didn't sound presumptuous — rather they were expressed casu-

ally — they felt like an outrageous attack. Also the fact
that she immediately left the room, almost coyly, didn't
mitigate their effect. He was a drunkard, and that was not
acceptable to her. She had never made any demands, neither direct nor indirect; *that was exactly what was so outrageous*, suddenly he guzzled too much for her. He took the
bottle and got *intentionally* drunk, way beyond norm, as a
punishment to Paula. A punishment so severe that he
woke up the next morning only long after Paula had left
for work. He soon noticed something shocking: Paula
hadn't spent the night in the apartment; the bed was untouched and there were no leftovers from breakfast in the
kitchen. She must have already left the apartment in the
evening while he was asleep in front of the empty bottles.
Aron checked to see if her clothes were missing, cosmet-
ics, her nightgown, yet everything was in place. So he
could still hope that this wasn't a permanent departure,
simply an irate reaction to his behavior, their first serious
tiff. She'd be back in the evening, he reassured himself.
If not, if such a trifle sufficed as a pretext for separation,
that proved he was nothing more than a whim for her. But
considering everything that had happened between
them, that was out of the question.

He took an aspirin, made coffee, and considered
with what right Paula asked him not to drink so much.
That he drank too much lately, an average of a bottle a
day, was beyond dispute. He could not compare himself
with other drunkards, he didn't know any, but a bottle a
day, was undoubtedly a lot. And yet liquor had meant
nothing to him before the war; he hadn't been a drunkard
back then. For the first time he noticed and confronted
the mystery of how, in such a short time, such a large vice

could have taken hold of him. A not too illuminating reason may be that it was easy for him to get cognac. That
explained nothing; at most it facilitated the quenching of
a sudden thirst, the origin of which was still unexplained.
One could rather quote loneliness as a reason. The passive waiting for Mark, Paula's absence until evening, the
mindless calculating and occasional meetings with Tennenbaum or a dealer, with whom he didn't find, or look
for, closer contact. All this put together spelled boredom,
which was easier to bear under the effects of alcohol. Yet
boredom didn't explain everything either, *a third of the
bottle at most;* the remaining two-thirds, according to Aron's
own words, remained unexplained.

Since I'm already talking about those times, this also belongs to the story. But I don't like talking about it."

Aron drinks in little sips, his fourth or fifth glass today; he's not drunk, just a little tipsy. He doesn't drink
very often during our conversations, for my purposes, not
often enough. When he's drunk my questions seem to
bother him less than usual. He doesn't react so sensitively
and, what is more, he almost anticipates my questions.
He takes a break on his own initiative and answers them,
even if, as is the case today, they haven't yet been posed.

"You mustn't think that a camp like that ends from
one day to the next. That would be nice. You're freed, get
out, and everything's over. Unfortunately it's not like
that; you imagine it's far too easy — the camp runs after
you. The barrack pursues you, the smell pursues you, the
hunger pursues you, the beatings pursue you, the fear

pursues you. The lack of dignity pursues you, and the insults. Years later you still wake up and need several minutes before you get used to the fact that you woke up not in the barrack but in your own room. But it's not just like that at night with your damned dreams. Also in the middle of the day you suddenly see someone who isn't even there, and you hear someone talking to you who has long been buried, and it hurts you in a place where no one has hit you since then. From outside it looks like a normal life; in reality you're still sitting in the camp, which continues to exist in your head. You fear that this is how insanity starts. And you suddenly notice that liquor helps. Sure, it doesn't erase anything from existence and it doesn't change the past, but it blurs, eases, helps you get over the dreck. How could I simply tell Paula, Fine, starting tomorrow I'll stop drinking?"

The closer the clock hand advanced to half past six, the more restless Aron became. In the early afternoon he had a little drink, just a glass; he didn't want to let it come to an open battle should Paula — as he firmly believed she would — appear punctually. Actually, he knew perfectly well that the abstinence to which he'd committed himself would be only temporary, yet that wasn't what it was about. Paula mustn't find him in the same condition in which she had left him yesterday. He was prepared, but only over a certain period of time, to return gradually to his quota of one bottle a day; perhaps he could even drink less than that. After all, Paula had said, "Don't drink so much" — he remembered that clearly — and not "Stop drinking." He was prepared to explain in all candor that he was trying to do what he could, that he was doing his very best.

Paula arrived at the usual time. She didn't give him a kiss and acted like nothing had happened between them. She went into the kitchen to prepare dinner as usual. Aron remained seated at the table, relieved, until he heard her call, "It's ready."

As they sat across from each other, he got the feeling that she was different, unwilling to speak, and more serious. He didn't exclude the possibility that she was waiting for an apology. Yet it still wasn't clear to him who owed an apology to whom — he to Paula for nothing other than his usual behavior the previous night, or Paula to him for her absolutely unusual one. He thought, he says, it best if neither one apologized.

"Did you listen to the radio?" she asked.

"Today? No."

"Did you read the papers?"

"No. What happened?"

Paula went out, took a newspaper out of her bag, laid it on the table, and went on eating. Aron leafed through it quickly; nothing particular caught his attention until Paula said irritably, "Can't you read? Right on the first page."

The news was that the Americans had dropped a new type of bomb on a Japanese city. Ghastly devastation, the paper said, an unbelievable number of victims. Aron asked, "Is this what you're talking about?"

Paula found this question cynical. She had firmly believed in his indignation, and here he was asking whether

she meant this or something else. Aron felt no indignation. Not because, he says, he was looking for an argument; on this of all days, with the smoke of yesterday's
fight still burning in his nostrils, he was in the mood for reconciliation. But concerning this bomb affair he thought
radically differently from Paula, and he didn't want to tell
her what she wanted to hear. He told himself, and then
her too, that far away a damned pack of fascists still hadn't
given up, and with all the goodwill in the world he couldn't
see why he should get upset if someone gave these criminals a colossal slap in the face.

"You call this a slap in the face?" Paula cried out. She
was, in a way that he hadn't observed before, angry. First
of all with the bomb droppers and now with him. Her
voice cracked so that to Aron, so he says, it sounded almost childish. The war was decided long ago there in
Japan, she said, everybody knew that. "Only to spare a
couple of their own men, they kill hundreds of thousands" — what was this if not outright murder, hysterical
murder? she cried. They demonstrate their pointless
power and turn themselves into criminals. This Truman,
she said, wiped out an entire city with just one bomb,
"and you dare to call it a slap in the face?"

"Don't stick to that one expression," Aron said.

Paula stood up and slammed the door. Aron sat,
frightened, and wondered from how many directions
fights brewed; he was positively surrounded. When he
walked into the living room he didn't find Paula at the
table; she was lying in bed and had taken the radio with
her. He could hear the voice of a speaker indistinctly
through the door. He had waited the whole day and

hadn't got around to working. He took the books and co-gnac from the cupboard and sat down. At least this time she had stayed home.

Hours later he also went to the bedroom. Paula was asleep, the radio was still playing music. Aron made an ef-fort to be quiet so as not to wake her up. Though he didn't feel drunk, he was afraid she would smell a relapse, even after a particularly thorough brushing of his teeth. When he turned off the radio she woke up and lit a ciga-rette, ready for a new exchange of opinions.

"Please don't start where we left off," Aron said.

She didn't react curtly; she pushed an amicable hand under his head — *that's how she was*. "Ah, Arno, you don't understand anything," she said.

"What don't I understand?"

"Because you're full of hate," she said.

"I'm full of hate?"

"Maybe it's understandable, maybe it's quite nor-mal, but it's not right. In any case, it's not right like this. I'm sure I'm making it simpler than it really is, but still, you have to stop seeing only enemies everywhere. One has to try to overcome the desire for revenge. If the old laws are still valid, then the same things will keep hap-pening over and over again."

"When did I speak of revenge?"

"Then you just think of revenge."

"You seem to have good sources."

"Do you seriously want to assert that when an evil government makes war, it's all right to drop a bomb and kill a whole city in one blast?"

So she had reverted to her earlier argument; Paula was stubborn. "First of all," Aron said, "there is no government that can make war by themselves and, second, of course it would be good if one could abolish the old laws. Peace, happiness, quiet, do you think I have something against that? But everyone must abolish them, everyone without exception. Just one exception is the crack through which new evil can crawl. Only an idiot would stand up and call out, From today you can do to me what you will, I'm keeping the peace. If you try that today, tomorrow you'll be in the gas chamber."

"Yes, you would react like that." Paula sighed and pulled her hand back.

Aron was still far from asleep, perhaps not drunk enough; he wanted to change the mood. After an *appropriate pause* he asked, "Is there any news about Mark?"

His trick worked; Paula straightened up. Yes, she said, there was news. She lit a second cigarette. That is, there was basically nothing new, the novelty lay in the fact that she now saw the pointlessness, having considered her resources, of making further efforts to settle Mark in a different home. She had been able to trace only two homes altogether in Berlin and the surrounding area; she had gone to one of them, Brüningslinden, herself; it was cheap and pretty but overcrowded, with no respite in sight. She had to convince herself with her own eyes. And in the second home, after a phone call with the director, things didn't look all that different.

"So what do we do now?"

"There's only one thing I can think of," she said. "You must ask the Russians. There might be a place."

"The Russians?"

Though not at all absurd, since he lived in the part of the city that was called the Soviet sector, this possibility had never occurred to Aron. Until then, everything had been run by Paula.

One moment. You just spoke of her indignation about the bombs in Japan. So, in other words, indignation against America. And it was American aid that was available to her. Did she perhaps feel that it wasn't right to accept help from this source any longer? Is this why she thought that Mark would be better off with the Russians?"

A rare event: Aron praises me, in that he says I asked a good question. He had thought about that himself, yet he had come to no conclusion. "It may have been a coincidence. It was peculiar, however, that of all days she chose this one to make her suggestion. I never asked her, as you can imagine, but I don't think your suspicion is nonsensical, hypersensitive as she was."

Mark's accommodation through the Russians went so smoothly that Aron was annoyed that he hadn't considered the possibility earlier. He went to the Soviet headquarters at the address Paula had found, which was the last service Rescue provided him (aside from the monthly food packages, which he saw no reason to cancel). After a brief search he sat in front of the officer in charge, who welcomed him politely, but on hearing Aron's request, in his mother tongue too, soon behaved as if his very own brother was sitting in front of him. Waves of warmth, Aron says, bounded toward him; even a bottle of vodka appeared in a heartbeat, taken from the desk in a wink of an eye. The officer promised his full support. He said he wasn't a specialist in such operations, yet there was no doubt that in three days at most Aron could pick up the necessary authorization. "We already saved your son from the fascists, it would be really unfortunate if we couldn't tear him away from the Americans, too." They sat there for an hour and emptied the bottle, the first glass to success, the others, for several reasons, to Odessa, because they spoke the same language, or simply because they liked each other.

A week later Aron held a paper in his hands in which Mark was assigned a place in the children's recovery home. In a green suburb, toward the north of the city. Aron inspected the former inn that very same day. Above all, determined to visit often, he wanted to verify the transportation connections; a city railroad stopped nearby. From the station to the home there was almost an hour walk, so he decided to get a bicycle and deposit it somewhere in the vicinity of the station.

He's coming in two days, in the morning," Paula said. "Where do you want to keep him? Here in the apartment?"

"Yes, here."

Aron went to Tennenbaum — it turned out that he was always available to talk to him — and said he needed

a car two days later. Tennenbaum made a face and asked
if Aron had mistaken him for a magician.

"I need a car," Aron said.

"What for?"

Aron explained, at which point Tennenbaum wasted
no more words about difficulties. "Of course you'll get a
car. I still don't know how, but the day after tomorrow
morning it will be at your door. Why didn't you mention
before that you have a son?" he said.

"There's more," Aron said. "I can't drive."

The following afternoon he put all his money — a considerable sum — in his pocket and went to the Hessischen Weinstuben. As he had expected, he met Kenik and
asked him, "When do you actually work?"

"When I'm not here."

"But you're always here."

"Not always," Kenik said. "It only looks like that to
you because you come so rarely. What are we drinking?"

"Not now. Do you have a little time for me?"

"As much as you like."

"I have to buy a couple of things," Aron said, "and I
don't know where to get them. You know your stuff."

"Are you crazy?" Kenik said, shocked. "You want to
buy in the black market? You should know best what
prices those scoundrels make. One doesn't go to the
black market to buy, one goes there to sell. Is that clear?"

"Is it your money?"

Kenik tried to convince Aron that even if he absolutely wanted to shop in such an irresponsible way, at least he shouldn't pay cash, rather he should get barter goods from Tennenbaum or from his apartment. Only in this way would he get a reasonable rate of exchange. "Otherwise they'll rip you off, you'll see."

Aron declined; he didn't want to barter, he wanted to buy in the traditional way. Kenik reluctantly agreed. "But don't blame me afterward."

They set out in a direction known only to Kenik. After a while he stood still and asked, "We walk and walk, and you still haven't even told me what you need."

"Isn't it irrelevant?"

"There's a specific place for everything."

"Okay then," Aron said, "first I need some chocolate."

Kenik looked at him, Aron says, as if Aron had informed him that he wanted to buy a green airplane with yellow polka dots. He put his hands in his hair and whispered, "Chocolate."

At this stage, Aron's patience was exhausted. The help he had secured himself proved to be more of a hindrance than anything else. "Listen, Kenik," he said. "Either you want to help me or you don't. I barely utter a word and you already faint from astonishment or try to convince me of the opposite. Please stop it. What's so unusual about chocolate? Show me where I can buy some, or I'll look on my own."

"Fine," Kenik said, "I'll be quiet. But I swear it's just out of gratitude — I won't react to your craziness only out of gratitude."

"Don't forget it. Where can I buy chocolate?"

"May lightning strike me," Kenik said, "I don't know. I must think."

Then it occurred to him; it was in the exact opposite direction. He guided Aron down a little road that didn't look special at first, it gave the impression of being almost uninhabited, but this changed as soon as one looked at the entrances. The black marketers and the buyers stood in the doorways and entrances of houses; they spoke quietly and perused the passersby with alert, wary looks; hardly a house was unoccupied. Kenik grabbed Aron's arm, stood still, and said, "Wait for me here, I'll be right back."

He behaved as if Aron was a child who might be traumatized by the tension typical of these places and as if his duty was to protect him. Aron just stood there for a couple of minutes and waited, too long for the people who were in the entrance nearby; they left their post and strolled a couple of houses farther away; some left. Every idler meant potential danger; he could be an informer or a harbinger of an incumbent raid. Aron allowed himself a spiteful joke. He assumed an emphatically harmless attitude — a manner that was particularly conspicuous here — in front of the closest doorway in order to see if the buyers and dealers there behaved in the same way. The experiment succeeded; with his method he could have emptied the whole street. Yet he preferred to stop before it became self-defeating or someone beat him up. He had been the target of sufficient evil looks, he says.

Kenik came back with a young man dressed in shabby clothes; he wore a countryman's hat and had a shopping bag in his hand. Aron had a feeling that the young man, like himself, was not at ease in the surroundings. His face was bright red; he lowered his eyes in embarrassment when he was spoken to. "He has what you're looking for," Kenik said.

"How many bars of chocolate can I buy from you?" Aron asked.

"I have eight altogether," the young man said so quietly one could hardly hear him.

"Shouldn't we get out of the street first?" Kenik said.

In fact, they were the only ones there who formed a visible group; they went into an empty, recently cleared, doorway. Aron said, "Eight, you say. How much does one cost?"

"It's Dutch," said the young man, again almost inaudibly. Aron felt sorry for him already, but this didn't alter the fact that he wanted chocolate.

"Dutch is very good. How much is it?"

"Dutch isn't good at all," Kenik intervened. The young man cleared his throat and said, "I thought around a hundred fifty marks per bar."

The price sounded high to Aron, but he had no benchmark other than the old one. He looked quizzically at Kenik. He had already rolled his eyes, nodded, and said, "Come on, let's go, he's crazy. We'll find others soon enough."

Aron didn't know if this was honest indignation or routine business practice, *Kenik was that good*, and he also saw no way of finding this out without an embarrassing aside. So he said, "Leave us alone."

Since Aron had so obviously made it clear that he was the one in charge and not Kenik, the young man produced a bar of chocolate from his shopping bag and held it out to Aron, as if to let him check its value. "Maybe I can go down a couple of marks," he said.

"I'll make you an offer," Aron said decidedly. "I'll take all eight bars and pay eight hundred marks altogether. Deal?"

"Fine," the young man said immediately.

While Aron was counting the bills Kenik said, "Good God." The young man handed over his wares and hurriedly distanced himself. Kenik had hardly left the entrance when, beaming, he patted Aron on the shoulder and said, "Congratulations."

"For what?"

"You dealt like a professional. Until the end I was afraid he would change his mind. I don't have great experience with chocolate, none at all to be precise, but I bet we made a bargain. It probably costs twice as much today; he's still wet behind the ears."

"Twice as much?"

Aron stepped onto the street and spotted the young man, who was already some distance away. He called out, waved, and ran after him. The young man, evidently afraid that his trading partner had discovered an impropriety or felt cheated and wanted to undo the deal, or at least to lower the price, began to move faster. Aron called out several times "Please wait!" and had trouble catching up with him. When he stood before him at last, he fumbled in his bag and said, "I've changed my mind. Here."

He gave the young man three hundred marks. The young man couldn't bring himself to thank him; he just stared at the additional money in his hand as if it contained some hidden danger. Aron went back to Kenik without turning around.

"What did you want from him?"

"Nothing."

Next, Aron wanted to buy a toy. Mark, he explains, had been born so *inconveniently* he had never owned a toy, except for a wooden car Aron had built for him in the ghetto, which hadn't lasted two days. Aron had no idea what kind of toy it should be; one would have to wait for an offer. He knew only it should be suitable to play with in bed. When Kenik heard what Aron had in mind, he kept his promise not to comment. Aron looked at him and saw that it was all he could do to hold his tongue. So, a toy.

Kenik thought for a long time before he said, "There are no toys anywhere; we might as well stay here. Wait, I'll be right back."

The dealer he came back with was an old lady; Aron estimated she was over sixty. She didn't have anything with her, not even a bag, so Aron couldn't imagine where she kept the toy hidden.

"You have toys to sell?"

"Not really," she said. "I just happened to be here. But when I heard this gentleman asking about toys, I had an idea. Naturally I don't have anything here, it's at home."

"And what, may I ask?"

"All sorts of things," she said, "things that children need. But they're used."

"Do you live far away?" Kenik asked.

"No, right around the corner."

They accompanied the woman. She stopped in front of her door and looked around on all sides as if she were looking for someone; she even looked into the courtyard without offering any explanation. He immediately had a hunch, Aron says. He asked Kenik to wait in front of the house. He didn't think that a man like Kenik would make a suitable trading partner for a woman like this.

"Feel free to come upstairs with us," the woman said to Kenik.

"He doesn't want me to," Kenik said, upset. "He's afraid I'll rip you off."

The woman smiled at Kenik's words; apparently this was a joke, she didn't know how to react to it. Once in her apartment, she led Aron into a room that immediately struck him as a children's room. She explained, embarrassed, "I have two grandchildren, you know. Thank God they aren't here. There would have been some loud yelling when their evil grandmother sold their toys."

She took two stuffed toys from a shelf and said the animals were not for sale, they were needed to fall asleep. Otherwise the gentleman had free choice among the playthings in the room. It was fortunate for Mark, Aron claims, that the children weren't present; otherwise he probably wouldn't have bought anything. He decided in favor of the wooden construction set, several figurines of American Indians, a farm of considerable size, and finally a couple of picture books. When the toys were lying on the table, Aron asked the woman if in addition she could spare a bag; he didn't have anything to carry them in and still had a long way to go. She didn't have a spare bag, but she had a suitcase that was far too large. Unless he wanted to come back another time, Aron had to take it. "It's useless; at this point we must talk about the price," he said.

The woman became even more embarrassed. She said she had no idea how much these things were worth.

"You'd better name a price, you surely know better than I do."

Aron gave her five hundred marks and a bar of chocolate, whereby he was firmly convinced that she would have taken three hundred, *perhaps even two hundred.* The woman helped him pack the toys in the suitcase.

"You are definitely a good person."

"Then again, not so good," Aron said and thought her judgment was influenced by the price he paid; at a higher one she would have been even more effusive. Seconds later he was obliged to check himself; the woman's train of thought had veered in a different direction. "Whoever buys toys at a time like this must be a good person," she said.

Aron took his suitcase and said good-bye. To Kenik he said, "And now I need a bicycle."

"A bicycle?"

"A bicycle."

"He wants to finish me off," Kenik whispered.

First of all, before even considering a bicycle, he pointed out to Aron that it could be attributed only to astonishing gullibility, if not to stupidity verging on naïveté, if someone seriously believed he could get through the black market unscathed with a suitcase that size. And, second, it had occurred to him in the meantime that their shopping would be much more efficient if Aron made a list of all the things he was looking for, then went home and left it up to him, Kenik. "It has to be more convenient for you," he said. "Besides, we'd save time and nerves."

Aron declined, particularly since he wasn't looking for anything else except the bicycle, but the argument

about the suitcase made perfect sense. He was prepared
to give up on further support from Kenik; somewhere, he
hoped, he would find the bicycle, for a lot of money, *sin-fully* earned and easily given out.

"Fine," he said. "First I'll bring the suitcase home.
You don't have to go with me any farther, you've helped
me enough."

"Why are you angry all of a sudden?"

"I'm angry?"

All at once it occurred to Kenik that he had something urgent to do. He said, "Let me suggest something
else. I'll run my errand while you go home and wait for
me. In an hour I'll be there and we'll go buy a bicycle together."

Aron agreed and carried the suitcase containing the
toys and chocolate home. He made himself a snack and
looked at the picture books. Less than an hour later
Kenik came with the bicycle; *that was to be expected.*

3

Mark's move went according to plan. Rescue delivered him punctually on Aron's doorstep, where Tennenbaum's car and chauffeur were waiting. They drove out to the home together. Mark had memorized his lessons: the name Arno, the familiar form of address, and the relationship between father and son. He didn't confuse things anymore. Aron found that, though he was far from recovered, his condition had notably improved and he looked less apathetic than he had a few weeks before, more alert, more like a normal child.

"How long will he have to stay in bed?"

The doctor declared that he couldn't say for sure, all he knew was that proper nutrition was more important than medicine. Mark would survive in any case, though whether or not he would be released without irreversible damage depended primarily on his nutrition.

"Anything specific?"

"Nothing specific. Everything that is good and expensive."

Calories, said the doctor, vitamins until they come out his ears. Mark would probably have some stomach problems, but that was nothing to worry about. "Fatten him up. If another doctor tells you something different, don't believe him. Believe me," he said.

Till then, Aron's job at Tennenbaum's was nothing more than a stopgap measure, killing time; now it gained sense and purpose: the lavish salary that in the past month had procured *unimportant comforts*, or had served as a tranquilizing hoard, could now be used to heal Mark. Aron invested some of his money in groceries, vegetables, cheese, candies, juices, sausage, cookies; however, it wasn't a big part, he earned much more, he says, than what Mark could eat. Kenik helped him with the shopping. Aron wrote his shopping list on a piece of paper and sent Kenik out. At first Kenik refused. "If you absolutely have to eat tomatoes in the middle of winter, then go look for them yourself," he said. But when he learned whose health was at stake, his resistance crumbled and he was of great help; he knew the sources like no one else. He made his own suggestions about how to enrich Mark's meal plan and occasionally would come back from his raids with delicacies that weren't on the shopping list. "What do you think? He'll definitely like this," he would say.

For a pack of cigarettes per week, Aron could leave his bicycle with the stationmaster. He rode out with his packages almost every day, at least at the beginning, he says. At the home they must have thought he was a millionaire.

*   *   *

And Paula?"

Paula's time was much more restricted; during the week she was tied up at Rescue. Aron was certain she would go with him to see Mark the first Sunday. "I still haven't said a word to him about you. It'll be an exciting moment," he said.

Much to his disappointment, she didn't seem at all excited at the idea of her first meeting with Mark. On the contrary, he found that she looked rather glum. To be on the safe side he asked her, "You are coming with me?"

"I don't know."

"You're not coming with me?"

"I don't know."

Aron was puzzled; it made him angry that she should pretend not to know whether she wanted to keep such an important appointment, her head full of mystifying scruples. Her reasons, he says, were bound to be petty and, in his opinion, without substance. Perhaps that was precisely why he loved her, he suspected a particular kind of sensitivity behind all this insecurity. Yet her behavior this time really got on his nerves. Only later did he realize that his reasoning was based on the wrong assumption. His thinking had been more or less along these lines: if a father is happy to have found his long-lost son, how can the mother not be happy? It wasn't her fault if he thought that way.

But at the time he had lost patience with her and saw no reason to conceal his anger. "Have it your way," he said, "go ahead and stay home. There's just one thing I don't understand. Even if you don't care about him, why can't you do me at least this one small favor? Is it because it's a long walk from the station to the home?"

He posed this hurtful question on a Saturday; they didn't talk to each other until Monday. Then he asked, "Can you at least give me an explanation?"

"I'm a little scared."

"Of what? That he won't like you?"

"Nonsense."

"Of what then?"

Paula didn't explain; she just put her hand on Aron's arm, smiled, and said, "Of nothing. I'm a silly goose, of course I'll come with you. I'm sorry."

The following Sunday they took the train out to the home. Aron had promised her a nice hour-long walk from the station to the home. It suddenly occurred to him that they had never gone anywhere together, not even out of the house. He had the feeling that he had *come a long way* with Paula at his side, but strangely it became clear to him only now that all his movements involving her ended within the walls of his apartment. Paula said that so many trees made her dizzy.

"You should see them when they're green."

She acted as if the road were going through a museum, as if she were parading past an endless row of extraordinary treasures, which is apparently how she categorized every second bush and every third tree, and the blackbirds, too. She was extremely reserved, held Aron's hand, only now and again would cry out, "Look over there!"

Aron's pleasure in the surroundings was *worn-out* because he had seen them so often, but he was delighted by

Paula's joy and spent his time thinking. It's always been that way with him, he says, his mind works best while walking. *But now don't immediately say you want to go for a walk with me.*

He started to brood over what Paula could have meant when she said she was scared to meet Mark. Her only hint, that it wasn't for fear of being disliked by Mark, seemed credible to Aron; otherwise, he was sure, she would have easily admitted it. She probably had the opposite fear, he thought, the fear of being horrified by the way Mark looked and of not being able to cover it up sufficiently, so that Mark, seeing the expression on her face, would be frightened and Aron, hurt. Yet he dismissed this thought too; she was unlikely to have such a fear, he told himself, which was *inhuman somehow*, she was too clever and sensitive. Besides, during her work with Rescue she had certainly been confronted by similar experiences. But what kind of fear was it then? The only explanation Aron could think of was not only uncomfortable but, the more he thought about it, even alarming: Paula was afraid of getting too involved in his affairs. Her behavior, he thought, was noncommittal — in spite of all apparent trust, she always kept her options open. The most obvious of these was that Paula still kept her own apartment, didn't in fact use it, just owned it, why? Surely not to waste extra money in the form of rent, surely not to challenge Aron, or to threaten him. She didn't give up the apartment, Aron told himself, because the apartment was an escape route from which she found it rash to part. Till then, Paula's affection had been limited to one man. Yet a man and a child were *incomparably* more people than just the one man. If a woman came into the picture, the scene would look distinctly like a family, overpoweringly so in Paula's eyes, hence the fear.

I point out to Aron that Mark wasn't just born that day; not only had Paula known for some time that he existed, but she had met Aron because of Mark in the first place.

"That's true," Aron says, "but you can't compare the time before to the time at this point. Before, Mark wasn't a real child; he was nothing more than a problem to solve. A reason to write letters and make phone calls. Our personal relationship aside, it was her job to take care of him. Mark became a real person for her only now, with our first visit to him. There lies the boy, and she walks in with his father. Isn't that different?"

They arrived at a most unfortunate moment. The previous night, Mark had come down with a fever. No cause for concern, a doctor reassured them, but he advised against a visit; the excitement, which is often caused by visitors, should be avoided at all cost. They stood in the corridor. Aron wanted to see him at least for fifteen minutes. Then a nurse passed by, hurriedly pushing a bed on wheels ahead of her. A child was lying on the bed, motionless; the doctor ran after them. This, Aron says, was like an alarm signal, like a thick red line under an imminent danger. He gave up the idea of introducing Paula to his son that day after all; he gave the nurse a little package and asked her to say hello to Mark from the two of them.

"May I take a quick look in the room?" Paula asked the nurse. "I won't say a word and I'll leave right away."

The nurse gave her permission without Aron having to intervene; he didn't go with Paula into the room. The doctor's warning still ringing in his ears, he thought that the sight of Paula could hardly excite Mark, for him she was just another woman. He waited by the door and was happy that Paula had expressed *that wish*. A little while later she came back out and said, "He didn't even see me, they're all fast asleep."

And when they were outside, on the way back to the station, she said, "He's a handsome boy after all."

Aron says it sounded as if he had previously claimed the opposite. In any case, she had seen Mark even though she could easily have *avoided* it. The motives that Aron had attributed to her before, and that had appeared to be so plausible on the way there, no longer seemed valid.

Toward the end of our afternoon I ask Aron if he remembers the address of the Hessischen Weinstuben.

"Of course," he answers.

I then ask if the building is in West Berlin, and he replies, "No, it's on our side."

After that I ask if he would agree to drive there with me once — right now if he'd like.

"What for?"

"I don't know," I say. "Out of pure curiosity. After all these years, wouldn't you like to have a drink there again?"

"No."

"You're a spoilsport."

A couple of days later he says that as far as he's concerned we can visit the Weinstuben, if I haven't changed my mind in the meantime. I call a taxi, Aron gives the driver the address.

The bar is now called Balkan. When we're inside, Aron's eyes dart restlessly from one side of the room to the other — a lot must have changed. He looks at me only when the waiter puts on the table the two glasses of cognac I had ordered.

"Do you know how many years it's been?" he says. "Twenty-eight."

I ask myself if emotion will take over now, because often when I see old people remembering things long past I find that they are moved, no matter whether their memories are pleasant or unpleasant. Perhaps they belong to each other, perhaps remembering is a form of emotion — not for Aron apparently. He takes in the room with one last glance, then he's finished, as if a curtain has been drawn over his thoughts, or as if he has decided to consider any further memories superfluous. He drinks his cognac and orders another. "And now what?" he asks.

"Have things changed much?"

"Everything's changed," he says. "You can't recognize anything. Did you bring me here to find out how much it has changed?"

"Of course not."

"Why did you then?"

I don't know what he's getting at; the waiter comes

to my aid by bringing more cognac. Aron drinks and then says, smiling, "If you thought that something extraordinary would happen to me while I'm here, you were dead wrong."

"That's not what I thought."

"Then it's okay."

"Where was the room where you'd always meet?"

"Over there," Aron says. "Pay now, I don't like it here."

We walk leisurely to the next taxi stand; Aron makes fun of me. He says that if someone hears the story of Spartacus, or the story of gladiator fights, he can understand that this person would like to visit the Coliseum; the grandeur of the story justifies such a wish. However, what brought me to the Hessischen Weinstuben wasn't clear even to me.

I talk my way out of it; I never claimed to know why I wanted to go there.

Mark made his first attempts to walk, initially in the corridor, then in the snow in front of the home. The muscles in his legs, which had become as thin as birch twigs because of his constant lying in bed, needed to be strengthened. Aron attentively registered Mark's progress.

He felt that his frequent presence was necessary especially now, not so much to oversee Mark's training — for that he trusted the personnel — but he thought Mark required treatment of a different kind.

*   *   *

Of what kind?"

"I was convinced that the years in the camp had
damaged his mind too. That is, I was convinced, it was totally clear — everyone could see. He was seven, and you
had to talk to him as if he were four. Not to mention that
he couldn't read or write. His vocabulary was ridiculously
small and his knowledge was small and his interests were
small. Who should have taken care of that if not me?"

"Did you give him lessons?"

"Lessons?" Aron said. "I sat down and talked to him."

First he spoke to the doctor, not to strengthen his deter-
mination but because he wanted to make sure Mark's
physical condition would allow for daily conversations
without causing him too much strain. The doctor had no
doubt. He said, "I'm an internist, not a pedagogue, but
what you're planning to do sounds sensible."

Aron decided to look for a room in the neighborhood. He found that the three hours it took him each
time to get back and forth were better spent by Mark's
bedside. He asked the stationmaster if he knew someone
with a small room to spare, without any particular ameni-
ties and for a good price. The stationmaster asked Aron to
wait for a moment, he wanted to talk to his wife; then he
came back and said he knew someone, in fact, himself.
"We came to an agreement about your bicycle, why not
on this, too?" Aron could have a room right there in the
train station, a pretty one, if he would consider a pound of
real coffee appropriate monthly rent.

Aron was pleased by the quick resolution of his search and accepted. But he used the room only at the very beginning. On the one hand, his work suffered while he was away. His duties had increased in scope; Tennenbaum's business affairs were improving steadily. Still, he would immediately have given up the job if doing so had been useful for Mark. On the other hand, and above all, the few nights he spent in the attic room depressed him terribly; he suffered from an insomnia that fatigue couldn't overcome. He would lie awake and hear the trains pass below him and yearn for Paula. He saw pictures and heard noises that he had forgotten in bed next to her; now they returned in full clarity and volume. That was too high a price to save three hours a day.

One of the conversations with Mark *as an example.*

"Are you cold?"

"No."

"Still, pull the blanket higher, we don't need you to get the flu now. What did you eat for breakfast?"

"Bread and jam and butter and an egg."

"Very good, and what did you drink?"

"Milk and cod-liver oil. But they forced me."

"They have to, you won't get healthy without cod-liver oil. Do you want to know what cod-liver oil is good for?"

"No. It tastes bad and the others don't have to drink any."

"Because they don't have it. Do you know how hard it is to get cod-liver oil these days?"

"The others will also get healthy again."

"But not as fast as you."

"That's not true. Just yesterday they released Her-mann. He didn't drink any cod-liver oil."

"Then he wasn't that sick. Should I tell you where cod-liver oil comes from? It's a really crazy story, you'll be surprised."

"All right."

"But let's take a little walk. Lean on me and I'll tell you. Up to the tree over there and back."

They set off, and Aron began the story. "The biggest fish on earth are called whales. They are so big that all the rivers are too small for them. They would constantly hit against the shore. That is why the whales live in the sea."

"How big are they?"

"At least a hundred feet long. That is from here to the wall and as tall as a house."

"And where do they live?"

"In the ocean. Have you already heard that word?"

"No. But my legs hurt."

"That's all right, we're almost halfway there. And now listen to what an ocean is."

Quite by chance, in one of the children's books Aron had given him there was a picture of a whale.

However, Aron told himself that the explanation of wonders, like whales and oceans, would not suffice in the long run; they were just a small part of the big picture. More urgently, Mark needed a goal and a role model, be-cause he must become healthy *from the inside out*, he must want to be healthy, and Aron decided that he must find a way to stimulate this wish.

The issue of the goal was hardly a problem; he is still convinced today that no goal is *more senseless* than that which lies in a nebulous distance. To give Mark courage, he says, the only goal that could work was: get healthy so that you can come home. Aron portrayed the near future as colorful, told him of visits to the zoo, of ice-cream parlors and cinemas, intentionally inflating the time dedicated to pleasures. But he also spoke of school, which awaited him; he described it as a fun kind of institution, the only one that could open the door to the greatest happiness, namely the joy of knowing.

On the other hand, the role model was more of a problem for Aron. For a long time he wavered. Which circle of people should he choose from? It must be a man. An imposing figure, but one that didn't exceed Mark's imagination — there was no one like that in Mark's entourage. Two candidates, from which Aron had to choose, elbowed themselves clearly into the foreground. One was a made-up person called Anatol. Aron could easily credit him with all sorts of characteristics and merits that he felt were desirable, according to his educational purpose. Courageous like Anatol, he could say, friendly like Anatol, clever like Anatol. Anatol had been an old acquaintance he lost track of during the war. The second candidate was Aron himself, and in the end the choice fell on him, though he realized that it was more convenient for role models to dwell in remote places, where their true nature could not easily be verified. Mark, however, would be able to keep an eye on him constantly, especially when he would come home from the sanatorium. This was clear to

Aron — he knew what he was letting himself in for. Yet the risk was smaller than I may think at first, because it wasn't actually he who was the candidate, but the man that he could have been once upon a time. And this man was naturally far beyond Mark's reach.

In short, Aron decided that all the talent, all the skills he would otherwise have bestowed on an Anatol looked just as good on him. Furthermore, he was convinced that the constant presence of a role model could only be an advantage and would have a positive effect on Mark. (He expressly emphasizes that it wasn't vanity that made him come to this decision, though he concedes that, in a way unknown to him at the time, vanity may have played a small part. First and foremost, however, his starting point had been cool calculation.)

The first story he told, in his new job as role model, concerned how he had overcome a terrible illness when he was a boy of barely thirteen, with tenacity and great energy. How he had followed to the letter both the doctor's and his parents' instructions, understanding the urgency and not in fear of punishment. How he had told himself that this was only about him, about nobody else, because it wasn't other people's health that was at stake. It was his own time that he frittered away in bed, denied of all pleasure — visits to the zoo, ice-cream parlors, and cinemas. Aron didn't expect to change Mark with a flick of the wrist, he rather hoped for gradual changes. So his joy was all the greater when during his following visit the nurses told him that lately his son swallowed his cod-liver oil without grumbling. He doubted that his old acquaintance Anatol would have been capable of producing such surprisingly speedy results.

*   *   *

One afternoon in February, Aron remembers exactly, he was working on the books when Paula came home. This was surprising — she usually appeared two hours later; Aron immediately knew that something was wrong. She sat down at the table with her coat on and didn't kiss him as she usually did in greeting. He waited patiently for a word of explanation, yet Paula was silent, *like someone who doesn't know where to start.* "What happened?" he asked.

Paula remained silent; he thought that the premature return home had something to do with her health. The mysterious pills came to mind; he stood up to get a glass of water. At that she finally said, "Stay here, I've resigned."

Not an alarming novelty, Aron found, rather pleasant in fact, even though Paula, according to her face and posture, seemed to think differently. "No harm done," he would have liked to have said and taken her chin in his hand, yet she was silent again in such a peculiarly embarrassed way that he preferred to sigh as a sign of solidarity. Financial problems absolutely did not arise, he told himself, the only problem they could face now was: what would Paula do with all her free time? She would have more time for him, time, too, for Mark, whose arrival was imminent; she would follow her passions or discover new ones; in the worst case she would be a little bored. Perhaps she would finally warm up to the idea of a family, of being a housewife and a stepmother; her momentary mood would soon vanish into a bright picture of the future. A daring thought shot through Aron's head: *to have a child with Paula.* "At least take your coat off," he said.

Paula went out and didn't come back; he found her in the kitchen, where she was making coffee. He sat next to her and asked, "Why did you resign? What kind of trouble was there? Come on, tell me."

"There was no trouble," she said, "only joy."

"Then why do you look so upset?"

"Rescue found Walter."

I hardly know anything about this Walter. I asked her ten, twenty times, but she acted as if she couldn't hear me. She was in a state similar to that of a woman I had seen before the war in a vaudeville show — a magician had hypnotized her. She began to pack, her packing went on till evening, she forgot half her things and took half of mine, all I could understand was what she let slip."

Aron, downing another cognac, wanders from the subject; he talks about the vaudeville show and the hypnotized woman. I see that the memory of Paula's last day affects him. Perhaps he regrets having mentioned this part of the story; he could have said, One day Paula didn't come home for reasons unknown to me.

"So what did you find out?" I ask.

"Yes, what did I find out?" Aron says and works his face into a funny grimace, as if this question forces him into extreme concentration. "This Walter was a man she had known for a long time, that's for sure. Her boyfriend or fiancé, certainly not her husband. They had lost track of each other during the war, just like Anatol and me. After the war she had started looking for him. That's why she went to Rescue in the first place; she wanted to be right there at the source. With time she had given up hope but kept her job anyway. Then I came along and she must have decided to start a new life, that's all. And then this damned Rescue has to find her Walter."

The first days after Paula left were *unbearable*. All duties became tedious — at first just the books, then the messenger who delivered the bundled accounts, and then Tennenbaum himself, with his cold gaze. Aron's mood led to an unjustified abuse of Kenik. Even the trips to Mark's home were suddenly more problematic; he went less than before, and when he went he stayed only briefly. The bed was his preferred haunt — open the door to no one, do nothing, think of nothing, but how does one do that, think of nothing? Again, out of bed, Aron clung to the conviction that no person is irreplaceable, so Paula couldn't be either. Hundreds of Paulas, he told himself, were running around. Thousands, in a city like this. Aron moved through the city and looked for them, in an angry action of self-defense. Until the evening when he found a *poor* woman whose willingness, he says, and poverty, must have been one and the same. He took her home with him. But it took only a couple of minutes before he noticed the differences between this woman and Paula; Aron paid the full price and sent her away. He paid the full price out of a sense of justice, he says, because she was not to blame for his change of heart.

He went to the Hessischen Weinstuben, to get drunk. He could have done it at home too, but he felt that in his state it would be better if he stayed among people.

People greeted him and treated him with respect; his role in Tennenbaum's business was well known. Someone told him that his friend Kenik was sick and bedridden for a while, kidney problems.

Aron sat in the backroom, which was reserved for Tennenbaum's men, but he soon felt irritated by the curious looks and pointless questions. In fact, the *whole backroom* looked silly to him; this sitting around was nothing more than the ostentation of belonging to a clan. He went back to the front room, the common bar, where people played billiards and where the ordinary customers would stay. The people from the backroom thought he was an eccentric and shrugged.

Aron had to come to an agreement with the barman; drinks were far cheaper in the back, and the barman was scared stiff of jealous customers: why him and not me? But Aron didn't want to give up on cognac; they agreed on camouflaged glasses.

Paula looked at him from the cognac glasses; only rarely did he recognize Lydia, *actually as good as ever.* Most of the time Paula was laughing; although at their actual parting she had looked quite serious, she laughed because she was looking forward to seeing her Walter. Or she turned her back on Aron and repeatedly went away. Once a glass full of cognac broke in the process. The barman appeared, cleaned up, and said, "What a shame."

Another time the barman, in a whisper, brought Aron's attention to the fact that he was talking to himself, clearly audible monologues, and that he was mentioning details that surely were not meant for the ears of others. Aron quickly paid and went home for the day — he heard giggling behind him all the way to the revolving door.

Later on, he worked on his books or went to visit Mark.
Yet he came again, the following day; consistently, for
months, he was one of the first guests in the afternoon
and one of the last in the evening; *they* noticed that. A paper was handed to him; he should, as soon as he could, go
to see Tennenbaum.

"I was told," Tennenbaum said, "that you spend entire days in the Weinstuben."

"Is that forbidden?"

Tennenbaum's reproach seemed impudent to Aron,
just like the *summons*. He had timed it well so that he
would be sober when he got to Tennenbaum's and now
he was regretting it.

"It's not forbidden," Tennenbaum said. "But you
must allow me to be worried."

"About me or the accounting?"

"About both, Mr. Blank, about both."

Aron asked Tennenbaum to spare him his worries;
he was mature and old enough to organize his private life
his own way. Business was another issue entirely; he
would be happy to talk about it any time. "Did you notice
any inaccuracies?"

"Not yet, Mr. Blank, not yet. But I fear that I soon
will, if you keep behaving this way."

"I'll make a suggestion," Aron said. "When it comes
to that point, have me sent for again. Okay?"

Then he thought about whether or not he should
look for another bar, but in the meantime he kept going
to the Weinstuben. Cognac was a scarce commodity everywhere. Besides, a change implied that he recognized
Tennenbaum's authority and was hiding from him. So
he sat again in the front bar, with the firm intention of

avoiding monologues in the future. Paula laughed anew
or went away. Aron found a further explanation for her
strange reticence: she had never talked about her job at
Rescue, though he was sure that this job hadn't been indifferent to her. Had that been the case, he would have
noticed it at their very first meeting, when he stood in
front of Paula like any other person in need. Furthermore, it was as if Paula were *made for* sympathy; in the
blink of an eye she made every client's concern her own,
that was her nature. Nevertheless, not a word.

Then, Aron says, Ostwald had come to his table.
Aron looked up when a stranger spoke to him. "What
you're drinking looks good."

"It tastes good, too."

"I believe you."

The man sat down; in disgust he drained the glass he
had brought with him, all in one shot. Aron knew that the
fluid was called Alkolat. Up front everyone drank Alkolat;
he had never tasted it before. The man called to the barman, "Bring me more of this swill."

At first sight Aron didn't like him, he was too
loud — someone who talks loud even without the help of
Alkolat no doubt, someone who wants to be noticed. And
to notice him, Aron claims, was anything but a pleasure.
Ostwald was *the opposite of beauty*, sixty years old or just
under, tall and scrawny; his hair grew in a small crown
around his head. In the middle of his bald spot, Aron describes, bulged a big red scar that looked like a cockscomb.
His gray skin hung from him everywhere in folds, like
that of a person who lost half his weight over a very short
period of time. Better still was his suit, the only one Aron
ever saw him wear. Aron was certain that this man would

soon ask him to get him a drink that looked as good as his, it was only a question of time; he kept an appropriate answer ready.

"Why are you looking at me in such an unfriendly way?" Ostwald asked. "A moment ago you were smiling at me."

"I was smiling at you?"

"Of course. Otherwise I wouldn't have dared to sit at your table. Besides, you look like a person with whom one can have a sensible conversation."

Aron was confused by this compliment; he couldn't remember having ever received a compliment that was based on his looks. His eyes looked friendlier; the man's last words had sounded unassuming, almost in need, and the way he had explained why he preferred Aron's company to that of the other customers sounded credible. Besides, the question of cognac was still unasked; perhaps Aron had been wrong all along.

"You're mistaken," Aron said. "Why should I have anything against you?"

Ostwald smiled, as if he didn't know either; then he went to the counter and got his drink himself because the barman was taking too long. When he came back, Aron offered him a cigarette. Ostwald took it with no surprise, though cigarettes were still worth *their weight in gold*. He introduced himself with his first name. "I've seen you often here in the last couple of days," he said.

"How do you do it?" Ostwald asked. "How do you get him to sell you cognac? That is cognac, isn't it? I've been coming here longer than you have, but that dog never gave me a drop. Are you one of the local dealers?"

"Are you from the police?"

"No," Ostwald said, "I'm not from the police."

He emphasized the word police in a peculiar way, Aron says, almost as if in reality he was a murderer and a thief, who was wanted by the police for a long time — and here comes someone who asks him if he's a policeman. He shook his head several times and looked at Aron with amusement, as if Aron couldn't guess even in his wildest dreams what a great joke he had just made. His amusement had such a provocative effect that Aron, disregarding possible consequences, said, "Yes, I'm one of the dealers. And that's why I drink cognac. And you're not a dealer, and that's why you drink swill."

In that moment, I hear, Ostwald's face turned sour; he furrowed his brow, surprised at this sudden change of tone. "You know what — screw you."

He stood up. Aron heard him mumble on his way out, "I've had enough anyway . . ."

Ostwald paid at the counter, came back to Aron's table, and snuffed out the only half-smoked cigarette in the ashtray; then he left. Aron called the barman and asked, "Who's that man?"

"His name is Ostwald," the barman said. "He always comes and goes alone."

The next day Ostwald didn't come, but he did on the following day. Aron saw him through the window as he approached the Hessischen Weinstuben. Without a coat, he wore only a hat and scarf against the cold; he stopped directly in front of the window and counted his money. Aron put on the most good-natured face possible and made a welcoming gesture as soon as Ostwald walked through the revolving door. Ostwald stopped in his tracks right there at the entrance. He looked around extensively, then went to Aron's table and sat down without further ado. Without a greeting, he remained silent and looked at Aron curiously, as if he expected an explanation, perhaps an apology. Aron snapped his fingers at the barman, at which he immediately brought two disguised glasses of cognac, as agreed. When the glasses were on the table, Ostwald accepted this conciliatory gesture; his eyes moved from Aron to the glass. They toasted and drank, Ostwald in an exalted manner, reveling in the sensation as if he had just drunk the first cognac of his life. Then the last touch — a cigarette. Aron said, "But don't throw it away again only half-smoked. They're very expensive."

"I wish I hadn't," Ostwald said.

"Why did you leave like that?" Aron asked. "So angrily?"

"And you ask? It's none of my business if you're a dealer, that's your choice. If you have a bad conscience it's your choice. As far as I'm concerned, you can even be cynical, if you can't think of anything better, because most people can't think of anything better. But if you want to say something at my expense, then it is very much my business."

"Not at your expense."

"How can you think of mocking me, of dumping all your complexes on my back? Did you get the impression that I deserve this, because I'm not a dealer and must drink swill instead of cognac? Do you think I'm too stupid to become a dealer? I'm not a dealer because I don't want to be."

"All right," Aron said.

(He had noticed what was actually remarkable about Ostwald's words, he tells me, weeks later, only when they knew each other better. It was the fact that Ostwald accused him of cynicism although he himself, Ostwald, was the greatest cynic he had ever met. As far as I can see, there's no evidence in Aron's story to back this assertion.)

Aron told himself that his first impression of Ostwald as a primitive drunkard had been rash. The direction their conversation could take was still a mystery; *schnapps aside*, neither knew the interests of the other. In the meantime, Aron was looking forward to developing a conversation. He decided however to wait and see; he sat, as it were, with his arms crossed. After all, he hadn't been the one to sit at Ostwald's table, it was Ostwald who had come of his own free will. Aron didn't want to relieve him of the burden of beginning.

"Are you a Jew?"

This was, Aron found, not a very happy choice. He said yes with appropriate reserve. "So?"

"Were you here during the war?"

"Where here?"

"In a camp?"

"Yes."

"How did you survive?"

Aron didn't understand how his life in the camp could be of interest to someone who was, at least for now, nothing more than a casual acquaintance. He said, "Tell me about you. You already know practically everything about me. That I'm a Jew, that I'm a dealer, that I have complexes. I only know that your name is Ostwald and that you like to drink cognac. And that you probably don't have a coat."

Now Ostwald asked for a cognac after all, and Aron didn't have the impression that he found it embarrassing. Ostwald expressed this wish as if it were a demand; the barman will sell it to you and not to me, so why wait? Aron came to an understanding with the barman. Ostwald was silent until the glasses were on the table.

"To your health."

Ostwald still said nothing about himself; Aron thought he looked pensive. Finally, he asked, "Why do you sit here in this gloomy bar every day and get drunk?"

"Is that any of your business?"

"Why don't you sit in the backroom at least, with your people? Why do you get drunk here, up front?"

Aron was taken aback by his lack of diplomacy, but at the same time he had to admit that Ostwald was an uncommonly sharp observer. The directness of his question was almost annoying, but it sprang not necessarily from bad manners, rather from simple thinking, and this is why Aron didn't react curtly. "You won't hear another word from me until I know who I'm sitting with at this table," he said.

"With a fifty-three-year-old idiot."

"You'll have to elaborate on that."

Ostwald drank the last drop of cognac, *demanded* a cigarette, and began, Aron reports, the story of his life with these strange words: "My father had a whitewashed house in Stuttgart by the Neckarstrand."

Aron tells me the Ostwald story for an entire afternoon; it's clear that the main character is a man he loved, I had

suspected this from the first. Just the way Aron had announced that one day Ostwald, whom he hadn't mentioned till then, came up to his table was evidence
enough that a very important person had entered the
scene. Aron languishes in details; he elaborates on anec-
dotes from Ostwald's life, which, as far as I can tell, have
nothing to do with Aron himself. Should Aron go on with
such detail, I fear that Ostwald will hold us up for days.
"Excuse me, but you're wandering a bit far now. This is
no longer our subject."

"Is that so?" Aron says. "What is our subject?"

"Not this Ostwald in any case."

He says he can't recall an agreement between us that
tied him to a specific topic. In the worst case, he says sar-
castically, I must summon up a little forbearance for his
garrulousness. When I risk further objections, he declares
today's meeting is over.

The next day he says, "Listen to me, young man. If
you'd like us to remain in business, there's one thing you
must understand. You can do as you please with the
things I tell you, you can even forget them. I have just
one request: you must let me finish speaking."

So in the name of God, in the year 1912, Ostwald started
studying law. Shortly before his final exams, his presence
was requested on the stage of war. Several experiences as
a soldier confused him; his knowledge of life was turned
upside down. After the war Ostwald, who had been non-
political up to his conscription, made contact with a group
of anarchists in Munich. Before that he had looked around

briefly, to see where a person with his opinions and incli-
nations belonged. The Communists were too unworldly,
planning too much for the long term and not concerned
enough with the present. Apparently he said, "If I had
the certainty that I'd grow to be two hundred years old, I
would have become a Communist." He didn't like the
Social Democrats either; they were far too conservative
and fearful of the law. Because they didn't challenge the
rules of the game; first they tied their hands behind their
backs and then they went into battle, which consequently they lost. Only the anarchists remained. He finished his studies, no longer only for his own sake but also
under the instructions of his new friends. They thought
of the future too and wanted to position their people
everywhere, even in the legal system. Ostwald was to do
everything that was expected of a jurist; he led a double
life. During the day he wore the mask of an industrious
young man, but after closing time he was an anarchist. He
visited the secret meetings regularly, participated in the
preparation — never in the execution — of assaults that
failed without exception. Often he was implicated in
skirmishes with the Nazis.

When he took stock years later, he was disappointed.
They had achieved nothing, and the group had gradually
become smaller. Ostwald realized that his activities had
had no significant consequences whatsoever, that they
had only served the purpose of self-gratification. He left
the underground movement, dedicated himself completely to his job, and came to the conclusion that his anarchist activities were nothing more than a tardy youthful
folly. He advanced steadily but not sensationally; by the
age of thirty-three, he had made it to the post of judge in

the regional court of appeal. He never strayed into serious conflicts with his superiors. At times he regretted the fact that he wasn't any different from the other jurists. For his liberal views, which he openly expressed with his colleagues, never found expression in his judgments. He had to, Aron says in his defense, judge according to the laws after all.

When the administration of justice fell into the hands of the National Socialists, Ostwald was fired. He did not accept the dismissal, the reasons for which he didn't know. He issued a complaint, once and then again, not so much because he was worried about making a living, Aron says, but rather because he believed that, in times like those, men like him must counteract evil. His resistance had fatal consequences. It led to the Nazis' thorough examination of Ostwald's tiresome person, and this uncovered information that had serious repercussions. Colleagues accused him of subversive activities and proved their suspicions with quotations. One day the main inspector told Ostwald to his face that he had been a member of an anarchist group. Instead of denying it, Ostwald said, "So what?" That was a decisive mistake, he was arrested on the spot. After he'd spent two months in custody, a trial took place. The prosecuting attorney demanded the death penalty; in his opinion substantial evidence indicated that Ostwald had participated in the attempt to assassinate the Führer in Munich. The judge was lenient and sentenced his former colleague to life imprisonment. Ostwald spent four years in prison, the following seven in a concentration camp.

After his release he put himself at the disposal of the Allies, coincidentally the English — they were the ones who had taken his camp. Men like him were badly needed, at the time; jurists with a clean past were a rarity. Ostwald was allowed to practice the law again. Since there were no German courts, he was assigned to an English authority as an expert for the prosecution of National Socialist crimes. This was the very job he had yearned for during those eleven years; Ostwald *grabbed whomever he could grab.* He used every millimeter of leeway the Allied law offered; Aron names examples.

Then one day, just before the beginning of an important trial, Ostwald was called to a commanding officer he had never seen before. The officer accused him of bloodthirsty behavior; he said he had watched long enough while Ostwald misused his position as a means for personal revenge. Despite fully understanding Ostwald's tragic past, he said, this proved once again that the victim does not belong in the judge's seat. Ostwald was fired *again;* since then he had taken to drinking heavily but not outrageously.

Aron wanted to order more cognac, but the barman objected. He said the other guests had noticed the preferential treatment and, since he didn't have enough cognac for everybody, either Mr. Blank could drink the same thing as everyone else or he should go and sit in the backroom. Aron decided to leave.

"Where to?" Ostwald asked.

They went to Aron's apartment, where they drank cognac without remorse. "I immediately knew you'd be a great catch," Ostwald said.

In the following weeks they met almost daily. Ostwald didn't have a family. Once he accompanied Aron to
visit Mark in the home. Yet most of the time they sat in
Aron's apartment in front of glasses full of cognac. This can
only be the beginning of a great friendship, Aron thought;
he felt attached to Ostwald, having suffered similar sor-
rows and bitterness. The only difference was that Ostwald
had suffered yet another injustice to be added to the already long list.

"Why don't you join the Russians?" Aron asked.

Ostwald laughed bitterly, waved this suggestion
away, and said, "They're all in cahoots."

Aron was decidedly of a different opinion. It was at
least worth a try, he maintains; one couldn't be so blind as
not to see that the Russians had made a clean break with
the past, unlike the other Allies. He named examples of
this, even though he had to admit that he didn't follow
politics much. Ostwald waved this away too and said
Aron's so-called proof was tomfoolery.

"Then tell me why you think they're all in cahoots."

Ostwald wouldn't say. He said all further discussion
on that subject was unnecessary, the sentence he had just
uttered was a *fundamental* fact. "I wouldn't argue with you
whether this table is made of wood or iron."

"Unfortunately, that's exactly what you're doing,"
Aron said.

At first I thought he didn't want to get involved in that
conversation because he realized that what he had just
said was absolute nonsense. But I soon realized that I was

mistaken, that it wasn't nonsense. You must understand, every claim is made from a certain standpoint, and only those who know that standpoint can judge it correctly. What had he meant when he said that the English, Americans, and Russians were all in cahoots?"

"I presume that in Germany at the time there was a widespread misapprehension. What he meant was that the Allies discussed their policies with one another."

"Wrong. Hardly anyone thought that. Not Ostwald in any case, he was an educated man."

"What then?"

"You forgot his point of view," Aron says. "Think of what he wanted."

This is followed by an encouraging nod that helps me guess what he might mean. Ostwald wanted to see heads roll, that's what Aron's hints indicate — he wanted maximum penalties. He had set himself the task of cleansing the land of all the people he held guilty and, considering his extreme experiences, they must have been many. Therefore his lack of faith in the Russians had its foundation in his certainty that they wouldn't give him a free hand in his cleanup operation either, and that was undoubtedly right. From this perspective, they were all in cahoots.

"Bravo," says Aron.

A few days before Mark's release, the following occurred: Aron was on the way to the sanatorium; he had picked up his bicycle from the stationmaster when suddenly he thought that he didn't need the room, which

had cost him a great deal of coffee, anymore. He wanted
to resolve the matter right then, before the next rent was
due. So he leaned his bicycle against the wall and went
back into the house. The stationmaster wasn't enthusiastic but had to accept his notice. When Aron stepped out
to the street for the second time, his bicycle had vanished.

I still can't understand why he was so indifferent toward
his possessions, toward objects that at the time must have
represented great wealth. I am up to my ears in examples.
He paid a pound of coffee a month for a shabby little
room when, I hear from others, for such a price one could
have rented the Sanssouci castle, with all the servants to
boot. He burned linens, threw away cuckoo clocks and
paintings, gave away chocolate, and now, in the spring of
1946, he let someone steal his bicycle. "You must have
been out of your mind to leave your bicycle by the wall
unsupervised. Didn't you know how much it was worth?"

"How could I not have known?" Aron says. "After
all, I'm the one who paid for it."

"Stop trying to be funny," I say. "Isn't it true that in
the camps everything was worth a thousand times more
than in normal times? And a hundred times more than
that after the war?"

"That's true."

"And before the war you weren't exactly a millionaire?"

"That's also true."

"So there. How do you explain your sudden care-lessness?"

"I explain nothing," Aron says. "I'm simply telling a story."

He often retreats to a place where I can't follow. I don't exclude the possibility that now and then he tells me of an Aron he would have liked to have been, but I can't prove this assumption, because, like him, I'm just telling a story.

The theft of his bicycle infuriated Aron beyond all measure. The material loss itself carried less weight than the arrogance of the thief, whose deed Aron took as a personal offense. A thief would not have robbed an anonymous bicycle owner thus; he had a chosen victim: Aron. A woman stood nearby and looked on, interested. Aron asked her, "Did you see anything?"

"Was that your bicycle?"

"Yes."

"He's over there," the woman said and pointed down the road. At a hopeless distance, Aron saw a man riding away on his possession and immediately turning a corner.

"Do you know that man?" Aron asked.

The woman came *uncomfortably* close and whispered that it was a Russian, she had seen him perfectly well. Then she moved away quickly, as if she didn't want to get involved any further in this explosive case. Aron caught up with her and stood in her way; the woman tried to get past him. "Leave me alone," she said. "I didn't see anything."

"Where are the Russian headquarters?" Aron asked.

"You actually want to go there?"

"Why not?"

The woman wasn't prepared to answer this question either; she finally left. She almost ran and looked back only once at the dangerously naive man, fear of Siberia, Aron presumes, in her eyes. He had had to ask other passersby for directions to the headquarters. The whole way, I hear, anger seethed in his head. He thought, If you want compensation, please go ahead, help yourselves, you have a right to it. *But not from me.*

The guard at the door looked at his papers. Irritably, Aron demanded, in Russian, to speak to the officer in charge. The guard went to ask a second soldier for help. He took Aron to a bare room and told him to wait. Aron waited for over a half hour. He cooled off and started wondering what he would say to the officer in charge, should he ever get to see him. From a legal point of view, his position wasn't favorable. He would be asked what led him to believe that the wrongdoer was a soldier of the Red Army, and the only proof he had was the pitiful claim of a woman who in the meantime had disappeared, no further witnesses. He soon realized that his plan was unlikely to succeed, that it would be more sensible to write off the bicycle and disappear before any words were exchanged. The soldier who had taken him to the room came in and waved Aron toward the stairs. Aron asked, "Where are you taking me? To the officer in charge?"

"Deputy," the soldier said grumpily and in German,

even though Aron's question had been asked in Russian. It was as if he refused to let himself indulge in familiarities with someone he didn't know.

The deputy was a bearded man of uncertain age. Aron wasn't acquainted with military ranks, but could see that this man was certainly an officer. He pointed at the empty chair in front of his desk. When Aron sat down, before a word was spoken, he asked, "Where did you learn our language?"

Aron's response could not be brief and, in explaining, he had to reveal a couple of details of his biography. He thought that it would only be to his advantage in the resolution of his case if the deputy knew *who he was dealing with*. When at last the question was satisfactorily answered, Aron wanted to speak of his case, but he was interrupted. The officer asked, "Why aren't you working for us?"

This unexpected turn disconcerted Aron; he imagined it was an offer to join the secret service. "I can't think of anything I could do for you," he said.

"You could be an interpreter, of course," the officer said. "Interpreters are important people in our endeavors to get along with the local population. We have problems enough, but not enough interpreters."

"First listen to why I'm here."

"Everything in due course," the officer said. "Where are you currently employed?"

"I work in the market."

"The black market?"

"Yes," Aron said.

The officer grinned, the first expression on his face

so far — perhaps he was impressed by Aron's openness. He tore a strip of paper from a newspaper, rolled himself a cigarette, and gestured to Aron to help himself. Aron smoked one of his own cigarettes, American.

"We probably can't offer a salary as good as the one you earn now," the officer said, amused, "but what we offer is certainly a more durable post. I can vouch for that."

Aron liked the joke. "It won't work for one simple reason," he said. "I live in the middle of Berlin, and I'd never travel twenty miles here and back every day."

"You live in our sector?"

"Yes."

"I'm not speaking only on my behalf. Interpreters are needed in Berlin just as much as they are needed here. I'll give you a letter that you can take to any one of our departments."

Aron shrugged and made an effort to appear undecided. He was afraid that a determined refusal would be an obstacle in the path of his actual concern. He said, "I'll think about it."

"Good. And now to you."

Aron explained what was to be explained. He named the few facts, which were rather pathetic in his own opinion. The officer took a paper and pencil and asked for the name and address of the woman. He did this even though Aron had just described the manner in which she had disappeared. At this, Aron stood up and said, "Please excuse me for disturbing you, the problem is solved."

"Sit down."

Aron stayed standing, awaiting a lecture. The officer said, "Do you realize what you're asking of me?"

"Yes," Aron said, "my bicycle."

"And how am I supposed to find it?"

"That's not my problem."

The officer blew out his cheeks pensively and played with his beard; he had barely finished smoking the first when he rolled himself a second cigarette. Aron sat down again *because he was so bewildered.*

"Is it really such a great loss?"

"Should thieves be punished only if their victims' loss is great?"

Renewed bewilderment. With a heavy heart, the officer said, "If you really insist, I can give you a second letter. Perhaps our supply center in Berlin can get you another bicycle. Okay?"

Apparently he thought that letters were magic potions, trump cards in all situations. Aron says he felt sorry for the bearded officer, who suddenly seemed vulnerable. Nevertheless, he had to tell him that apparently there had been a misunderstanding; Aron didn't want any old bicycle, he wanted his own, and the rightful punishment of the delinquent. Yet, as things stood, he realized that it was obviously quite impossible. He says the Russians could have made a reason of state out of such a trifle, searched all the barracks and examined every bicycle. Then doubts arose in his own mind: How could he be certain that the woman wasn't a liar? Or perhaps she had made a mistake; there are all sorts of strange stories about the mistakes of so-called eyewitnesses. "Never mind," he said, "the case is closed."

The officer looked relieved and on parting reminded him of his offer and of his willingness to write the letter. "Don't think about it for too long. An interpreter is more than just an interpreter for us."

*   *   *

When Aron arrived on foot at the children's home, several surprises awaited him. Mark wasn't in his room but in the park — for the first time in the park on his own. Aron recognized him through the doorway in his green coat; he secretly observed him for a couple of minutes. Mark didn't play with the other children, who threw a ball at each other between the trees. He walked on wobbly legs all the way from the house to the wall, time and again, silently, over and over again. At first sight Aron was puzzled by his peculiar behavior, wanted to go up to him and ask him what was wrong. Yet it soon became clear that Mark had a plan, that he was training himself hard. A couple of times, while he took a little break, he looked at the children, not with envy, Aron says, rather with anger. They were the looks of a person who has serious work to do and becomes understandably upset when other people fool around under his nose. Only when Mark, suddenly tired, sat down on a bench did Aron go up to him and kiss him. "Did you see how well I can walk?" Mark said.

"Yes."

"There's a letter for you in my room."

"What does it say?"

Mark smiled secretively; he seemed to know its contents, which must have been good news. "Go in and read it," he said.

"Go on, tell me."

"You're to take me with you," Mark said.

Aron ran into the house. A letter from the doctor lay on the pillow. The doctor wrote that from a medical point of view he could see no reason to keep Mark in the home

any longer. On the contrary, what was still to be done for
the child could only be achieved outside, in normal surroundings. And if Aron would allow a recommendation —
he felt so close to Aron — he should immediately treat
Mark like a normal child and never give him the feeling
that he was different from the others. Because, aside from
the peculiar occurrences of his past, he wasn't different.

Aron wiped the tears from his face and went back to
Mark, who was still resting on the bench. "You're right,"
Aron said. "I'm taking you home with me today."

"Are you happy?" Mark asked.

This question really touched him, Aron tells me.
Until then, Aron had been certain that the prospect of
going home mattered to Mark only for his personal
joy. But now he had the impression that Mark was, above
all, happy for Aron's sake, as if he had been training only
for him.

"And how I'm happy!" Aron said. "How did you
know what the letter said?"

"Irma told me."

"Irma? Who's Irma?"

"You don't know Irma?"

Mark's amazement wasn't feigned; apparently Irma
was a very familiar name for him, and his own father, the
all-knowing, didn't know Irma. "Irma is the nurse."

He dragged Aron into the house, went into his room,
then to another one, and knocked on the door. In the
process Aron caught himself thinking of other things: *He
walks like a real person, he knocks on the door like a real person.* Mark asked an elderly nurse if Nurse Irma was there.

"She's out."

"When will she be back?"

"She didn't say. Probably this evening."

"I'm taking him home today," Aron said.

"Well then, our young man will be happy," the nurse said indifferently.

"Is the doctor available?"

"He's not here either."

"Please tell him that I'll be back."

In Mark's sleeping hall Aron said, "You must say good-bye to your friends."

"I don't have any friends."

Aron opened Mark's bedside table, took everything out, and Mark started to cry. He turned his head to the wall and brought his hands to his eyes more and more frequently; soon he gave up trying to hide his tears. Some other children had come closer and stared *as if they were at a circus,* but they left solemnly when Aron chased them off shouting. Aron unfolded his handkerchief and *gave it a shot.* "Tell me about Irma."

With this he had found the exact source of Mark's tears. Mark described, at first interrupted by sobs, an unearthly being. Beautiful, clever, friendly, selfless, so it seems. Aron couldn't understand why his son had hidden such a treasure from him. If Mark was telling the truth, then Irma had taken care of him ten or a hundred times more lovingly than was to be expected of a nurse. She had read to him both books Aron had brought and others too, she had an answer to every question, she had gone walking with Mark so that he could see what was beyond the walls and the parks of the home. Once she had built an entire person out of snow for him, *a snowman* — that's how Irma was.

"Did she spend as much time with the other children?" Aron asked.

"No, only with me," Mark said. It sounded as if he had meant "That's the whole point!" And he sounded proud.

"Did she give you your food?"

Mark said that sometimes he had offered her his chocolate but she never took even one piece, as if this was the ultimate proof of how special she was. He said, "Sometimes we also talked about you."

"About me?"

"She asked me and I told her."

"What did you tell her?"

"About how you got healthy that time."

"And what else?"

"I can't remember."

Only when Mark asserted that they had also spoken about him, Aron says, did he suspect that Irma's attentions were directed not only to his son but to himself, and that Mark had played the role of a go-between. "I told you how I brought lots of packages. Wasn't it understandable, then, that she should be interested in such a father? And that he didn't have a mother, he would have said that, too. Don't get me wrong, I'm not saying that it must have been that way, but wasn't my suspicion logical?"

"No, it's illogical."

"Why is it illogical?"

"How do you explain the fact that up to the last day

she didn't try to meet you? Surely there had been plenty of occasions."

"Perhaps she had tried but I simply didn't notice."

"That's splitting hairs. In the end you'll claim that her reserve was purely a sign of refinement."

Aron smiles at me — that's exactly what he thinks — however, he prefers not to answer my loaded question immediately but to let the facts speak for themselves.

Mark's move brought considerable changes that were greater than Aron had predicted. The biggest and most notable change was that Mark was *present twenty-four hours* a day.

Like Aron before him, Mark had to get used to the apartment gradually, with the additional awkwardness that most of the objects in his new surroundings were not only unfamiliar; they were completely unknown to him. For example, he had never seen a closet, never heard a radio; the first rocking chair of his life was the subject of day-long experiments.

What had hitherto been the living room was converted into a bedroom for Mark, and Aron slept in the master bedroom. Conveniently, both rooms had doors leading to the corridor. Aron didn't let Mark sleep with him in the double bed, not even for one night. He would have liked to, but *just in time* he remembered when as a child he was allowed to sleep with his mother for one week in his father's bed while his father was away on business, and the tragedy that followed when his father came back.

Mark's presence did not affect his work — Aron could take care of it in the evening or when Mark took his afternoon nap — but it did affect his relationship with Ostwald. Ostwald came as usual, at any time of the day, and sat down, to talk and drink. He hardly noticed Mark. He didn't actually ignore him, he just reduced their relationship to what was unavoidable — as if he didn't want to appear impolite. Ostwald wasn't crazy about children, Aron says, and had made it clear that the reasons for his visits had nothing to do with Mark. On the other hand, Mark wasn't an obtrusive child but was self-contained and shy. Aron presumes he must have sensed Ostwald's reserve. In any case, as soon as Ostwald would turn up, Mark would retreat to his room, where he would play or look out the window. Then Ostwald tried to behave like he always did, but Aron sat there with a bad conscience, and in his thoughts he was in the neighboring room. He looked past Ostwald and restrained the drinking; he didn't want Mark to see his father drunk. Ostwald said, "The only way out is to get some help. You can definitely afford it."

Though Aron promised to find a housekeeper, for several weeks he did nothing. Ostwald didn't pressure him, *he never said things twice*, but his behavior changed noticeably. Until then their meetings had been entertaining mainly because of his liveliness, now he hardly spoke. Aron had the impression that he came only for the liquor, and Ostwald didn't try to challenge this impression. He drank hastily to reach the desired state as fast as possible and not have to extend his visit longer than necessary. Soon he came rarely and finally not at all.

For a couple of days Aron didn't miss him; he was almost relieved by Ostwald's absence. The cognac was locked up, Aron busied himself with Mark and was a *good father*, until this new situation felt like a sacrifice to his son. He started longing for Ostwald; he thought that with his absence Ostwald wanted to punish him.

Punish you? What for?"

"His staying away could have been a sign of a jealousy."

"He was jealous of Mark?"

"Yes, that's what I thought."

"Why did you care so much? Was it fun to watch him drink?"

"It was only like that in the last few days, it wasn't like that at the beginning."

"What first attracted you to him?"

Although he has already lifted his hand from the table to brush off my question, Aron declares himself prepared to name a couple of reasons after all: Ostwald was an intelligent person. He was original, meaning entertaining and amusing. With time he, Aron, had the feeling that Ostwald needed him for more than just the cognac — that behind Ostwald's self-conscious words was a person in need. Ostwald was like him; the past had damaged them in similar ways. And, not least, Aron says, Ostwald had been above every suspicion.

Aron did his best not to let Mark feel his vexation, but it became increasingly difficult. One morning he took him by the hand and went to see Ostwald. Normally Aron took advantage of walks to explain the world to Mark, often until they were both exhausted; *it had to be that way.* For example, shop signs were particularly suitable material for Mark's first reading lessons. This time, however, Aron was silent, and in his thoughts he prepared for the meeting with Ostwald. He planned a sort of reconciliation, which was problematic since no argument had taken place. There had been only a growing estrangement, which was the result of a new situation that could not be changed by any number of well-meant words. Thus Aron's visit was hardly more than a gesture; nothing could be clarified through an exchange of opinions.

In Ostwald's street he was suddenly afraid that his visit itself could lead to a fight. Aron was aware that he had a tendency to choleric outbursts, and experience had taught him that good intentions offered scant protection from them. A choleric, he says, does not choose when he shouts and when not. It could easily happen, if Ostwald stuck to his guns for too long, that Aron would shout at him. He would accuse Ostwald of coming to his apartment only to drink good liquor, everything else was just an excuse. And he pictured his reaction when Ostwald would answer, "That's exactly why I came."

Ostwald wasn't home. Aron didn't have a piece of paper on which to write a message, that he could then drop into the mail slot. He would have liked to leave some sign of life, he had nothing on him that could have reminded Ostwald of him. Only a banknote, he says but, as things stood, that was not a serious possibility. He even knocked in vain on the door to the neighboring apartment.

On the way home he was plagued by the suspicion that Ostwald had spotted him through the window and that was why he hadn't opened the door. He was thinking of going back when Mark announced that his feet hurt. Aron carried him part of the way home. People turned around to stare; the children grinned because nobody had to carry them when they were Mark's age. Aron started the lessons again. But Mark didn't want to listen; he brought up the topic of Nurse Irma. It wasn't the first time he had begged Aron to let him visit her in the home; he said that at least he would like to write her a letter, Nurse Irma would definitely answer.

"It's your birthday soon," Aron said, "then we'll go there. Definitely."

Mark asked what that was, a birthday. Time and again Aron was struck by *such* questions. He explained the reason and sense of birthdays and didn't forget to mention the important role of presents. He said, "For your birthday you can wish for something beautiful and, if you're lucky, you actually get it."

"Does everybody have a birthday?"

"Everybody."

"You too?"

"Naturally."

"Can you also wish for something?"

"Yes."

"From whom?"

"From you," Aron said. "From who else?"

He observed that this information, in addition to all anticipated joy, apparently brought a new preoccupation into Mark's life.

*   *   *

Now and again Kenik would come by and offer his services, more and more often since Mark's arrival. Aron gratefully accepted; Kenik soon became indispensable to him. It would never have occurred to Aron to leave Mark alone in the apartment for over a quarter of an hour, the time it took for a quick purchase. Whenever he had a longer errand to run he took Mark along, or Kenik had to come. He himself found such attention exaggerated; nevertheless, he took Mark along or called Kenik.

To Aron's question how he could show his gratitude for putting him through so much trouble, Kenik replied, "Don't talk like that, you've already done so much for me."

With time I liked him better. But I never knew what to say to him. He felt most at ease when the table was well set and he could talk about the past. Not necessarily about the camp, simply about the past. Probably he felt that the past was the most important part of his life. But he talked about it in a way that in my opinion led to nothing. The old times were one thing and the new ones something else and in between there were no bridges. Don't get me wrong, I'm not saying that I am better than he is. It's just that I didn't know what to do with him. I was bored. I once thought that Kenik was perfect for people who collect prejudices against Jews. He got along splendidly with Mark."

*　*　*

When the monthly statements were due, Aron went to Tennenbaum and found him waiting with tea and cookies. Tennenbaum's intention to solve the dissension between them could not be overlooked; right at the door he laid his hand in a friendly manner on Aron's back and led him into the room in which the table was set. He hardly looked at the columns of numbers Aron had handed him; he laid the paper to one side as if it would only disturb their cozy afternoon. He remarked that everything was bound to be correct, as always. Yet Aron saw no reason to share Tennenbaum's conciliatory mood — this unfounded heartiness — *without a fight*. He said, "You didn't think so for a long time."

"I don't understand."

"You'd better check. Just a couple of weeks ago you were worried about the balances. What has changed in the meantime?"

Tennenbaum looked at him like a wounded deer, Aron relates. With a little reproach and much patience in his eyes, Tennenbaum said, "Why do you have to remind me of that?"

"Because I remember. Either you are worried, in which case you should check, or you're not worried, in which case why did you say you are?"

"All right," Tennenbaum said, smiling. "Will you nevertheless drink a cup of tea with me, a sinner?"

While Tennenbaum poured tea into the cups, Aron wondered why his boss had become so friendly. Perhaps Tennenbaum had recently looked around in vain for a new bookkeeper, hence the about-face.

While they sipped their tea, Tennenbaum was preparing an explanation, Aron could tell. He discarded unexpressed formulas and searched for better ones. Finally he said, "In all honesty, Mr. Blank, something has indeed changed. If you remember correctly, recently we spoke about the books, with which I was always satisfied. The topic of our brief conversation was, if you'll allow me the pompous word, your lifestyle."

"And it has changed?"

"As far as I hear, yes."

"That's interesting," Aron said.

"I know you think that this doesn't concern me, you made that clear. But you are partially right and partially wrong. I must be allowed to worry about how my employees live."

The word employees, Aron says, was the most uncomfortable that he ever heard from Tennenbaum's mouth. In that moment, he says, he felt that he wouldn't be able to bear working for Tennenbaum much longer. "So, what do you have to reproach me for?" he asked.

"Nothing," Tennenbaum said. "On the contrary, I am very satisfied. I was told that you haven't been seen at the Weinstuben since our talk. I am even more pleased about this because, perhaps, I have a small part in it."

"That's right," Aron said, "I don't go to the Weinstuben anymore. I'll tell you why: I came to the conclusion that it's more fun to drink at home."

Tennenbaum didn't let this spoil his mood; he seemed to have an inexhaustible supply of good spirits that day. "No matter how hard you try, Mr. Blank," he said, "I will not argue with you. You'd better give up."

He held out a plate of cookies and posed the piquant

question, would Aron like something alcoholic to drink?
Aron *naturally* declined. Suddenly Tennenbaum's tone
became businesslike; he said that the preliminaries were
now over, he had plans to discuss with Aron. He poured
more tea and *made a speech.*

"The purpose of every business is, as you well know,
growth. As you also know, in our case there are limits
because our business is, from a certain point of view, illegal. We cannot expand unrestrictedly. I have thought
of where our future lies, and I came to the conclusion:
certainly not at the same level we're at now. The black
market — let's call the child freely by its name — has to
remain restricted. Aside from the possibility of reprisals,
it is such that we can't make plans for the long term; our
sources change constantly, and we are always dependent
on a thousand coincidences, in both supply and demand.
I concede that to date we have not been doing too badly,
but it won't always be this way. Because to the same extent that the economy gradually becomes stable, the
bread will be taken from our mouths. Besides, I don't particularly care for this kind of business; I'm telling you
honestly, it is too small-minded for my taste. I've decided
to shut down our enterprise — sooner or later. I'm sure I
told you once that I have good connections with the Allies. To be more precise, I know four, five people to
whom I could be useful and who would help me because
of that, if it can be done. In short, I have submitted an application for a trade license. I want to start a company that
deals with exports and above all imports. For the moment
it looks like we'll be getting the authorization in a few
weeks. But I don't want to stand there with a piece of pa-

per in my hand and nothing else, so certain preparations
have already been made. For example, I've looked around
for office space, for storage room, for example; already
there are some business connections, not bad ones by the
way. What I'm concerned about now, and this is why I'm
telling you the whole story, are good people. How would
you like to be head bookkeeper?"

Aron had listened attentively, even with a certain suspense; in spite of his dislike for the man, he still thought
that Tennenbaum had a *fine nose* for business. (He looks
for a newspaper article in his closet in which, years later,
Tennenbaum's company is mentioned. He can't find it.)
Tennenbaum sat there, his eyes full of expectation, Aron
remembers, like someone who anticipates gratitude, or at
least an enthusiastic consent. Since Aron's answer failed
to materialize for an inexplicably long time, he asked,
"Did that leave you speechless?"

Aron sighed and turned his cup; caution kept him
from immediately declaring that he could not picture
himself as a collaborator of that kind. Aron found this caution *cowardly* and was embarrassed, yet he couldn't shake
it. He simply hadn't found the courage, he says, to give an
answer off the cuff that to a significant degree would influence his and Mark's life for the following years. It was
certainly reprehensible to have nothing but one's salary
in mind, he easily admits; on the other hand, it was impossible not to worry about it at all, especially in such
complicated times.

"I see," Tennenbaum said, "you need a little time.
Sleep on it, but also know that I firmly count on you. Do
you have any questions about the details?"

"Yes," Aron said. "What will happen to the others after the closure?"

Aron listed the names he was familiar with, *all of them employees;* for example, he named Kenik. Tennenbaum smiled again; apparently he found these questions understandable and unnecessary at the same time. "Dear Mr. Blank, I want to make you aware of the fundamental difference that exists between our old enterprise and the new one. Till now we got along using speed and improvisation; that will change. A solid trading company needs qualified employees. Sympathy cannot play a role, it's all about knowledge and ability. We will have to part with most of our people, but I don't consider it tragic. First of all, our men have done very well until now and had a chance to put some money aside. And, second, in an economy that gradually strengthens, there is a place for anyone who wants to work. Please don't mistake me for a welfare institution."

At home, Mark and Kenik were playing checkers. Kenik opened the door, and while they were still in the corridor, he said, "He plays exceptionally well for a seven-year-old. I'm telling you, he has talent!"

Only when he was in the room did Aron understand what Kenik was talking about. He waited for the game to end. Kenik lost for educational reasons, or he played really badly. Then Mark was sent to his room; after his victory he was quite happy to go. Aron needed some peace for Kenik and himself. "What's your profession?" he asked.

Apparently Kenik didn't understand his question; after all, Aron knew exactly what he did and what he lived on. Aron had to say, "I mean, what profession did you learn as a young man?"

"Shoemaker," Kenik said.

"Kenik," Aron said, "you have to look for a new occupation."

That was wholly astonishing. Kenik asked, "Why should I? Don't I live like a king?"

"Not for much longer."

Aron passed on the news — Tennenbaum's plans and the predictable consequences. It made sense; there was no place for a veteran shoemaker in a trading company. Kenik sat there *flabbergasted*, unexpectedly deprived of his secure existence. He mumbled words to himself that Aron did not understand — probably he cursed Tennenbaum.

Aron tried to console him by saying that *the likes of us* had already survived worse things; he noticed himself how stiff his words sounded and how they only darkened the mood further. He stopped consoling Kenik, and they cooked themselves a meal.

In the kitchen Aron asked, astonished, "Why are you smiling all of a sudden?"

"I'm smiling?"

"Come on, tell me."

"I've changed my plans."

"Changed your plans?"

Again Kenik smiled; he bustled around the stove and gave himself plenty of time before he started to talk, his face averted from Aron and in a voice that was broken with embarrassment. Since being released from the camp,

he'd had only one dream, he said, not extraordinary perhaps, but *what does extraordinary mean?* Even if Aron
laughed at him now, he had made this dream his top —
indeed his sole — priority. Even his work for Tennenbaum:
it was only a means to reach his goal.

"Say no more," Aron said. "You want to open your
own business? A shoe shop?"

"A shoe shop?" Kenik said pityingly. Again he fid-
geted at the stove for a couple of seconds; then he confessed that he dreamed one day, as a wealthy man, of
moving to Palestine. Now the situation had changed. He
stood before the choice, he said, either to give up his
dream till later — because how was he going to come into
big money quickly if not through Tennenbaum? — or
to delete part of the conditions, namely the little word
wealthy. Palestine remained, he just wouldn't be a wealthy
man but one with meager savings, which he could only
hope would be enough for the long trip. Then he was
silent, as if he had to give Aron time to grasp the *entire
scope* of his words. At dinner he asked, "How about you?"

"You mean, am I going to Palestine?"

That was what Kenik meant. He pushed his plate
away and wanted to convince Aron at all costs that a rosy
happiness awaited them in the promised land — for
Aron, for Mark, and for him. The two of them, he declared, side by side in the land of the fathers, in the land
where milk and honey flow. He revealed an attachment
to tradition, a Kenikian trait Aron had never suspected
before, and that surprised him because it had made no
past appearance in their acquaintance. He spoke of millions of like-minded people. They all look like us and

think like us and leave each other alone; they were not that old yet, he said, it was still worth making the long trip. And while he didn't tire of inventing new reasons for their departure, Aron thought, He wants to convince me so that he won't be lonely there. Kenik enthused until Aron said, "Please stop. I don't want to go."

Before you continue, tell me why you didn't want to go to Palestine."

"Are you serious?"

"Yes."

Aron shakes his head and exhales audibly through his nose, yet I am convinced that he can't explain what is so absurd about my question. He stands up and turns on the TV in the corner of the room, as if he were turning to a new occupation and had simply forgotten to send me away. He sits there in silence and waits for the appliance to warm up; his face looks thoughtful to me, he's smiling at something. Then he says quietly, without taking his gaze off the screen, which is still black, "I understand why you ask. You want to hear a confession. You want to hear from me: This is my home, I grew up here. Here and nowhere else do I feel good, that's why I want to die here and want my son to grow up here." He looks at me again and his eyes ask, "Isn't it so?" He says, "Let's leave open the question about how much this country means to me. Rather, let's consider how much it meant to me then, in the kitchen with Kenik, for that's what this is about. If I hated it, you would learn nothing, and if I loved it, you would learn even less. Whenever I heard people talking about it, they sounded ridiculous to me."

The television buzzes now; Aron zaps through all the channels, none of them is of interest. He turns it off again and comes back to the table. Again he muses a little before he says, "Naturally, you mustn't take into account what you have heard about Israel since then; don't forget I was talking to Kenik in 1946. He yearned for Palestine and I didn't yearn for it, that's all. I had never thought of Palestine for a second before then. For me it was the same as if someone had asked me if I wanted to go with him to Australia. Why on earth would I go to Australia?"

When does Tennenbaum want to shut down?" Kenik asked.

"It sounded as if it would take a couple of weeks," Aron said.

Apparently Kenik wasn't worried about his livelihood anymore; he made no further attempt to convince Aron and was preoccupied only with himself. He smiled into the future, laid his hand on Aron's arm, and said, "Aron, exciting times are coming."

Toward evening, when Kenik was about to leave, Aron asked him to postpone the beginning of the exciting times to the day after next because he absolutely needed him to stay with Mark the following day. He had, he said, urgent matters to settle. Kenik agreed.

The next morning, after Kenik had arrived punctually, Aron took the train out to the suburbs. His first destination was the Soviet headquarters. It took him forever to explain to the guard who he wanted to talk to — Aron didn't know the name of the bearded officer. Finally the man was found; he immediately remembered Aron, though a full three months had passed since their first and only encounter. Aron said he had thought at great length about the offer, and only unfortunate circumstances had prevented him from coming sooner. Yet he was ready now to accept the post as interpreter, if they were still interested in him. The officer remembered that, too; Aron only had to remind him that he had mentioned a post in Berlin. The officer ripped a sheet of paper from his notebook, wrote a couple of sentences, and put a stamp under it all. He called a soldier and ordered him to find an envelope somewhere in the building.

After that Aron went to the home. The weather was splendid, he says, light green spring; the road felt shorter than ever before without a bicycle. In the garden again there were many children. Aron waited until a ball rolled to his feet so that he could kick it back. He asked for the doctor's office.

The doctor opened the door in his pajamas and excused himself for being asleep so late, he had been on the night shift. He asked about Mark's health and wondered if there was an urgent reason for Aron's visit. Aron said Mark was doing fine, he had only come, though tardily, to thank him for everything that had been done to cure his son, by the doctor himself, and everybody else. As a present he had brought a bottle of French cognac — after having considered and dismissed the option of giving him money. He maintained that money could easily be taken

as a tip and annoy, whereas cognac was *neutral*. The doctor behaved as if the present had nothing to do with his
small achievement, which had only been his duty after
all. Should Aron need his help again, he said, concerning
Mark or anything else, he could count on him. Aron said,
"There is something else, Doctor. There's a nurse here
called Irma. I don't know who she is or what she looks
like, but Mark talks about her all day. I'd like to speak
to her."

"Certainly."

The doctor pulled on his pants, asked Aron to wait,
and went out. A little while later he came back, took Aron
to the window, and said that the blond woman sitting on
the bench below was Nurse Irma, she was waiting for
him. "Or would you prefer to meet her in this room?"

"No, no, that's fine."

When she saw Aron walking toward her Nurse Irma
stood up and smiled, embarrassed. Aron was also embarrassed; the arrangement through the doctor had lent the
rendezvous a certain weight. Aron describes Nurse Irma.
(He has many photographs of her. Irma was an average-
sized woman, blond as mentioned, thirty-one years old at
the time. A good figure, as one can well see from the photos; she smiles in all of them. Her face looks pleasant,
with really big eyes — whose color, as Aron tells me, was
a greenish gray — a small nose, a mole on the right side of
the chin. The plucked eyebrows bother me; on all pictures they look as if they weren't real but drawn in pencil.
A good-looking woman, unobtrusive.) Aron thought that
the best means against embarrassment was a *quick* beginning; he said, "My name is Arno Blank."

"I know."

They sat on the bench; there was a lengthy pause. Aron fished cigarettes out of his pocket; Nurse Irma was a nonsmoker.

"I came to see you," Aron said, "because to this day my son, Mark, hasn't stopped raving about you."

"We did get to like each other," Nurse Irma said. "I'm glad he still thinks about me."

She looked straight ahead toward the trees, Aron still recalls, her face attentive. Aron observed her closely, in profile; for a few seconds he compared her with Paula, then immediately dismissed this comparison as unreasonable. His first impression, *I honestly confess*, was very good. In spite of all Aron's reservations, Mark's reports had already won him over; he was also, he says, relieved to discover that she wasn't an ugly woman. And quite suddenly he had the idea of solving, with Irma's help, several personal problems *all in one go*. "Would you do me a favor?"

"Yes?"

Aron found that her "yes?" betrayed a little too much expectation, considering his unrevealing question. He told her about his promise to organize a meeting between her and his son on Mark's birthday. She said, "Why not? If I can work it out, I'll come."

This statement was an even clearer hint, because he had originally thought of bringing Mark to her. Now she wanted to take on the trip herself. It was her business, he told himself, what her expectations were, while his own wishes were his affair. Counting on their fingers, they figured that Mark's birthday fell on a Saturday, one of Irma's days off, or so she *claimed*. Aron described the way to his apartment and said that he and Mark were already looking forward to her visit. Coincidentally he looked at the home and noticed that a man who till then had been standing at an open window stepped back into the room as soon as Aron raised his head. It may have been the doctor. Aron wanted to leave. Nurse Irma asked if she could walk a little way with him, she had plenty of time.

"With pleasure."

Between the home and the station Aron learned that Irma had been a nurse only since the end of the war. Before that she had wanted to become a pianist, which never came to pass because her parents didn't have enough money. The lessons were too expensive and her talent was, she admitted with a smile, not great enough to justify going into debt.

"And what did you do before the war?"

"I gave piano lessons until I was married."

"You're married?"

"I was," she said. "My husband fell during the war."

A detail that had almost made all other words unnecessary, but *fallen means fallen*. Aron asked if she lived with her relatives. She said no, she was *independent* and lived with a colleague in a room in the sanatorium; her parents lived in Thuringia. "Listen," Aron said, "I want to make you an offer. You know that I have a son. He doesn't have a mother, she died during the war. Since he left this home, no one takes care of him except me, and that isn't enough. Every day I clearly feel that I need someone who has more time for him than I do, and more patience. Until now I have never hired any help because Mark won't be helped by a woman who just does her job. Now that I know you — and above all I know what Mark thinks of you — how would you feel about moving in with us?"

Aron wondered if he should immediately raise the financial question himself, yet he felt it was inappropriate, perhaps even offensive. Everything had happened so suddenly, he says, and was so unhoped for that there had been no time to contemplate the details. Instead he said, "Obviously I won't get angry if you decline."

Nurse Irma took a long time to answer; her eyes stayed fixed on the road. Aron says she hadn't wanted to *keep him in suspense*, and yet she had a look, she seemed rather confused. However, he had noticed that he had not pressured her into an embarrassing situation; he had almost *made her wish come true*. And the more firmly he reckoned that she would accept his offer, the more the pause she made seemed appropriate. It would have been highly awkward for him if she had immediately stretched out her hand and said, "Okay."

"By when do I have to decide?" she asked.

"Whenever you want," he said. "There are no other applicants."

"May I give you an answer when I come to Mark's birthday?"

"That's actually a very good idea. First you should see where I want to abduct you."

Then he sat in the train and was satisfied with the results of the trip. When he first met Nurse Irma, he says, it wasn't clear to him why he had looked her up. Everything had come to light only during the course of the conversation and actually without his assistance.

*　*　*

For a couple of minutes now I've been sitting at the living room table. Aron went to the kitchen to get some refreshments; it's a muggy day. I hear ice cubes clink. Aron brings two tall glasses of lemonade; he sits across from me and lets his hands fall on his knees as if now he's ready to start. He asks, "Where did we stop yesterday?"

I drink, then I say, "If you won't get too upset, I'd rather cancel today's session."

"Why, what's the matter?" Aron asks.

The real reason has nothing to do with him, personal troubles, I say. "There are days on which one simply doesn't want to do a thing."

"Yes, I understand," Aron says. Suddenly he looks amazed at me and says, "Do you know what I just realized? What a balanced fellow you are. Until now, if there was someone who didn't want to do anything it was me, never you. Why is that?"

I shrug and say, "No idea. I have plenty of other faults."

"Don't get me wrong," Aron says, "it isn't necessarily an advantage."

He lights a cigarette. After the first puff he starts coughing horribly and snuffs it out in the ashtray. I ask him if he would agree to go for a little ride. I came by car today, it's right in front of the house. Aron walks over to the window and leans out a little. "The yellow one?" he asks.

"Yes," I say.

"Okay then," he says. It sounds as if he wouldn't have accepted had it not been the yellow one.

The airstream makes the mugginess bearable; Aron holds his hand out the window to cool off. The driver in the car behind us honks vehemently, probably because he thinks that an idiot like himself could be irritated by this hand and think that we want to turn right. Aron withdraws his hand and I turn right. I don't have a destination, I want only to drive a little way out of the city, but at the sight of the first fields an idea forms in my mind. We could drive to Mark's home, I think, without expecting any revelations, there is nothing to reveal. I only think, instead of simply driving out into the blue, we could visit the children's home. At first I don't tell Aron; otherwise he might think I already had the home in mind when we were sitting in his room. I more or less know the direction. When we reach the train station I'll look surprised and ask him if it this isn't the station. And he will say yes and perhaps be a little surprised himself, and then I'll ask him, "Don't you think that while we're here . . ."

Aron seems to feel good. After a couple of miles he even starts whistling, quietly; I never heard him whistle before. He's not very musical; I don't know the melody, but in any case he is whistling it wrong. I ask if I should stop at the ice-cream parlor; he shakes his head, without interrupting his whistling. I'd like to know what's making him so jolly all of a sudden.

When the tune ends he asks, "Where are you taking me?"

"For a ride," I say. "What did you think?"

"That you have a precise destination."

"Then you know more than I do."

"All right then."

Aron turns on the radio, a Russian folk song. He says he had the feeling that I suddenly started driving more resolutely than before, determinedly, as if I had decided on a route. I tell him that he is wrong, that I definitely don't have a secret destination, and if he wants, from now on he can decide the route. Again he says, "All right, then."

We drive until the day comes to an end, no more thoughts of Mark's home. In the afternoon we eat at a village inn; Aron insists on paying for both of us. When I drop him off at home, it's already dark. He says, "For once that was a good idea."

4

*T*HERE IS NOTHING TO SAY ABOUT IRMA.

She appeared punctually, at the stipulated time. Mark was delighted and forgot about both the toys and the birthday cake. He made such a fuss about the hand-made rag giraffe she had brought that all the other presents faded into the background. Aron was very pleased with Mark's liveliness; never before had he been able to make Mark so euphorically happy. He repressed a momentary pang of jealousy by resorting to logic. Either he hired a woman who meant nothing to Mark, he told himself, and then such joyous outbursts would never materialize, or the woman would be lovable in Mark's eyes, like Irma. With his choice, he told himself, he had wanted to create the conditions for jealousy, and that was exactly why being jealous made no sense. And, furthermore, he says, the way children love is unpredictable.

Aron avoided the topic of Irma's decision, which was still pending. He would have preferred that she bring up the subject, but she did not. She had her hands full with

Mark. There was also the distinct possibility she might
have felt restricted by Mark's presence, but now and
then, by a couple of glances she cast in Aron's direction — which he calls meaningful — she showed that she
hadn't forgotten his offer. In any case, the shyness that
usually came over Mark as soon as guests arrived had vanished into thin air, so much so that the grown-ups could
hardly get a word in edgewise. At one point Aron asked
his son to go and play in the other room for a while, to no
avail. Evidently Irma guessed the reason for his request
and smiled.

Only when Mark was in bed that evening did they
have a chance to sit down alone at the table, across from
each other. Aron had bought a bottle of champagne; he
wondered if the right moment had finally come to fetch it
from the kitchen, or if it might lead to some kind of misunderstanding. Still, he thought, what kind of misunderstanding could it possibly cause? In the last few days he
had become conscious that the offer to run his household,
live in this apartment, and take care of Mark *in the end*
boiled down to a marriage proposal. And if Irma had her
wits about her — and nothing said she didn't — she must
have come to the same conclusion. And if she had, Aron
thought, then the very fact she had come that day was a
clear answer. Her friendliness, he says, her determined
dedication while playing with Mark, were only meant to
prove that he would never find anyone better. He didn't
get the bottle. Irma said, "You've fixed up the apartment
very nicely."

"Why are you beating around the bush?" Aron asked.

"Is that what I'm doing?"

"Yes."

"You've been watching me all day."

Aron admitted to himself that Irma's words, although he found them inappropriate, rang true; of course he had been watching her closely. More than ever, he believed that they would get along well; therefore her saying yes was important to him. Contrary to this was his brusque tone; after all, he had asked a favor of her, not she of him. He decided that from that moment on he would offer her the image of a man with whom she could picture a pleasant life.

"Whether I watched you or not," he said, "you owe me an answer."

"Yes," Irma said, but Aron didn't know if she was accepting his offer or only confirming that she still owed him an answer.

"If I understand you correctly," Irma asked, "you would like me to live here?"

"That's right."

"The apartment has only two bedrooms?"

For the life of him, Aron couldn't bring himself to say that he had the intention of sharing the bedroom with her. It would have been the most practical solution, he says, yet he simply couldn't say it. Instead he suggested that she should take the living room while he and Mark would share the bedroom.

"Wouldn't that be impractical?"

"Perhaps," Aron said. "Do you have a better suggestion?"

She shook her head as if to say she honestly didn't; she didn't give Aron the impression, it occurred to him later, that his question was *profoundly suggestive*, or she simply hadn't noticed. Aron said, "Don't forget, you're also bringing us many advantages. All in all, Mark and I are making the better deal.

"When can you start?" he asked.

"The first of next month."

This answer indicated that Irma's vision of her future with Aron was devoid of emotion — a contractual relationship between employer and employee. For reasons of salary, it is usually convenient to start on the first of the month. However, it could also be that she had to give notice at the sanatorium. Aron asked if he should pick her up. That wouldn't be necessary, she answered, her possessions fit into two small suitcases, which she could manage nicely herself. Detailed conditions, meaning pay, insurance, or annual vacation, weren't spoken of. Aron tells me I should picture the following scenario. What if Irma had asked one simple question? A question that in all cases is cleared, possibly early, between a housekeeper, particularly a relatively young one, and her employer — the question of male visitors. He would have had a stroke, he says, but she did not raise the matter.

Once the date was happily agreed upon, there were longer and longer pauses in the conversation; he had never been good at entertaining, Aron says. Finally, he went to fetch the champagne from its hiding place. Irma looked surprised. She read the label and said, Good God, she hadn't seen anything like that for ages. As she watched, he popped the cork. She put her finger to her lips and listened; Mark didn't wake up. Aron poured and said, "To a good beginning."

After the champagne he took her to the train station.

*   *   *

A few weeks later Irma moved in. The rooms were shared as discussed, but before that, significant events occurred. First of all, Aron took his letter of recommendation to the closest Soviet headquarters; when he left the building he was an interpreter. He would start the first day of the following month, just as Irma would.

He found some aspects of this new situation worrisome: the early start in the morning, every day at eight, and never leaving the office before five. The man he spoke to even hinted that he should count on some occasional overtime. Then the salary. Aron claims he does not remember the sum; all he recalls is that, when he heard what it was, he thought it was a bad joke. Nevertheless, there was a good food ration card, the man said, as well as the possibility of shopping in certain stores that had been set up only for members and employees of the Soviet army. Aron hadn't expected to get rich in his new job; he took it simply because he didn't like his old one. Fortunately he had saved up some money and could *afford* the post as interpreter.

The second important event was Kenik's departure. One day Kenik arrived and said, "I'm glad you're here. We're starting this afternoon."

"Starting what?" Aron asked.

"Did you forget what we talked about? The trip? My trip?"

Much to his surprise, the opportunity had arisen, Kenik said; the organization he had called responded very promptly. They told him that if he could make up his mind immediately, there was an opening. The next group would leave in three months at the earliest. "I grabbed it. Who knows what the situation will look like in three months?" People like Kenik, Aron says, spend half their lives getting transported somewhere.

Aron went with Kenik to the meeting place. Along the way, the thought occurred to him that with Kenik, the last *living* person to know that his name wasn't Aron would be leaving. Kenik carried a rucksack and a suitcase; there were still several things in his apartment that he would have loved to bring along, he said, but that was as much luggage as was allowed. The following day at this time he would be in Bremen, he continued, the day after that perhaps already on a big ship, and soon, if God didn't place any stones in his path, at his destination. "Of course it's too late," he said, "but doesn't the idea appeal to you at all?"

The meeting place was a courtyard. A man at the entrance with an armband let through only those people who could produce a certain piece of paper, like the one Kenik had.

"Well, this is it," Kenik said. Then he said, "Let me give you a hug," and he did. When they broke away from their embrace, Aron noticed that Kenik's eyes were filled with tears; he was crying, *don't ask me why*. He was sure he would never miss Kenik. Only taking leave of him would hurt a little. Farewells, Aron says, follow their own rules. He called out after Kenik, "I'll stay here until your bus comes."

"It might take a while," Kenik called back.

"I'll stay anyway."

In fact, Aron had to wait for almost an hour; then at last came a filthy truck chock-full of people. Aron

couldn't see Kenik. He probably was sitting at the far end
of the truck. Nonetheless, Aron waved; he was the only
one still standing in front of the gate. He thought there
might be a second truck, but when? And while he was
walking away he thought, What torture, going all the way
to Bremen on a truck like that.

Finally the third event, in Aron's eyes the most
pleasant, was tendering his resignation to Tennenbaum.
First, he took advantage of the privileges he had as Tennenbaum's employee — he went shopping in the storage
room. He stocked up on tea, liquor, clothes for Mark and
himself, as well as a wool sweater that he hoped would fit
Irma and that she would like.

As soon as he brought the things home, he collected
all the documents and went to see Tennenbaum, who
welcomed him warmly, though with a curious look on his
face. Aron still hadn't replied to his question, whether he
wanted to join Tennenbaum's commercial enterprise as
head bookkeeper. Aron spread out all the papers and
notes on the table.

"What does this mean?"

For a long time Aron had pondered how to let Tennenbaum know his decision *most effectively.* The point of
the visit, resigning, was clear from the start, but there
were various ways to proceed. He couldn't make up his
mind whether a blunt statement was better than recrimi-
nations, barging in noisily, for instance, combined with
making remarks about Tennenbaum's *inhuman behavior.*
Finally he decided to resolve the matter as gracefully as
possible. On the one hand, Aron says, he considered it a
given that Tennenbaum possessed a great many unpleasant

qualities and character traits; on the other hand, any hope of converting him by listing these qualities and traits was pointless. Besides, it would make him feel better for only a couple of minutes — the toll on his nervous system simply wasn't worth the effort. His *revenge* could consist of only the indisputable fact that by losing him, Aron, Tennenbaum was losing an irreplaceable employee. Yet pettiness and openly vengeful behavior could not arouse this sense of loss. For this reason, too, moderation.

"The month isn't over yet," Aron said, "but we have to close the books. I quit."

"What do you mean?"

"I'm resigning."

"Right now?"

"Yes."

"But why? Aren't you satisfied? Do you have any cause for complaint?"

"It's for personal reasons."

Tennenbaum looked truly unhappy, Aron says. He shrugged, as if he didn't understand, and grimaced thoughtfully. He asked, "Are you sure?"

"Absolutely."

"Does this mean you're turning down my offer?"

"It does."

Tennenbaum suddenly seemed to remember who he was. He straightened up in his chair and said, "Let's go through the numbers."

They checked each entry, meticulously, Aron remembers, as they never had before. When they were through, without finding a single error, Tennenbaum said, "So that's it. Thank you."

He stood up and walked Aron to the door; in the corridor he asked, "Oh, by the way, do you have any idea where your friend Kenik might be?"

"Why?"

"He asked me to pay him a month in advance. And now I'm told that no one has seen him for days. Please tell him I don't approve of such behavior, that he should come here to pay off his debts."

"If I see him I'll tell him," Aron said.

About four weeks after Irma's arrival, *the time finally came* — the rooms were rearranged. Mark moved into one, the other was shared by the two grown-ups. Irma suggested they call a contractor to build a children's room in the hallway, which was uncommonly long, but Aron felt it was *still too early* to let Mark live in a room without any windows, which would result from closing off the corridor.

There's not much I can do with this information, but he didn't want to keep it from me: The days until Irma and he agreed to *share one bed* were the most exciting in his entire life. Erotically speaking, at any rate — four long weeks. At the time, the problem was how to come to an understanding.

Irma was to be Mark's educator, the housekeeper, and Aron's lover all rolled into one, and yet they spoke openly about only the first two functions. The difficulty of talking about the third point increased hour by hour. It soon appeared to Aron that the first two aspects of Irma's duties were unimportant, that the still not discussed third point was the only one that mattered, but he was afraid of jumping the gun. Irma could easily have come to the conclusion that he had lured her into his house under false pretenses and only now revealed his true intentions. (These explanations are in clear opposition to Aron's previous claim, namely that when Irma was particularly friendly to Mark in the children's home, she'd actually had the father in mind. When I had subsequently asked for proof, Aron had silenced me with the promise of coming events. Well, here they are.)

For example, the feeling, he proceeds, when they sat across from each other at breakfast or dinner and talked about only the *other* things, those emanating from daily life. Or sitting side by side after dinner, he says. They sat next to each other for no good reason, or only because they were officially sharing the apartment — Irma's presence had been registered with the police the very first day. Sitting there in silence, once the empty topics of conversation had been exhausted, and searching for some reason to justify their presence in the room. *At least Irma had buttons to sew.* The many secret looks, always from an embarrassed face and always responded to with a friendly smile whenever they were observed. Or when Irma would play with Mark, when Mark forced her to play horse and rode her through the room until the people in the apartment below banged on the ceiling, *that was quite provocative.* Or the noises, Aron says, the noises late at night from the neighboring room. He lay beside Mark, who was sleeping, and couldn't fall asleep; next door Irma couldn't sleep either. She was always busy with something, night after night, no one knew with what; in any case she made noises, he says, like only a woman does. Now and then they would meet at the bathroom door, and inevitably Aron saw her in an outfit that made her even more desirable. He concedes that sometimes he would arrange accidental meetings in the corridor when she was on her way to the bathroom clad only in her nightgown or pajamas, since she didn't own a bathrobe.

Four weeks later there was clarification. Aron took the initiative, not because he had managed to summon up enough courage but because he felt the urge. *What urge?* The deadline of four weeks was not self-imposed; after a month Irma would, though they had still never discussed the matter, ask him for her first paycheck. He was afraid of that. He couldn't refuse her a stipend. At most he could pretend, if she reminded him, to have forgotten about it. It would have been more than embarrassing. Still, he thought that to pay her a salary would somehow create a distance between them, more than before. It meant an additional obstacle, which did not yet exist, and had to be avoided at all cost.

Four weeks later, late one evening, he knocked quietly on her door, in order not to wake Mark. He said he absolutely had to talk to her, and sat down at the bedroom table. Irma was lying in bed and had put down her book. She looked at him, attentive and serious, as if she knew *the importance of the moment;* how the situation evolved was his sole responsibility. He had to choose, at lightning speed, between two possibilities, between talking and acting. Then he noticed that he had already opted against action — he shouldn't have sat down. To sit first and then stand up again and kiss her — he didn't want to be responsible for such *clumsiness*, not to mention that he wasn't sure anymore if Irma would let herself be kissed.

She was of no help. She just lay there, serious and

attentive, so that he had to ask why they were making things so hard for themselves. To that she didn't respond either. Her entire answer consisted of a shrug, which could mean several things. Aron wanted to put *this affair* behind him at last; he said he had liked her from the first moment they had met. Actually, longer than that; he had been interested in her ever since he had heard Mark's stories about her. He was a man of flesh and blood, not of wood, they had been living under the same roof for weeks. In God's name, she mustn't misunderstand him, and if she felt differently, they could, even if he would find it rather sad, leave things as they were. But as for himself, he was ready, more than ready, he felt a strong desire — stronger than ever — to make their relationship warmer, more intimate. All this without looking at Irma, he says. The question lay on his lips, Did I make myself clear? Of course, he didn't say that. He envied Irma's *freedom of movement.*

She stood up and quietly locked both doors. First the one to the neighboring room, then the one opening onto the corridor; then she went back toward the bed, stopped halfway, and turned to face Aron. The inviting smile was still absent from her face. Yet her consent was as good as spoken; she stood there, her arms by her sides, the way women in the movies tend to stand, Aron says, ready to be possessed. And that was basically the end of any happiness with her worth mentioning. Later there was only satisfaction, *as when you've eaten your fill.* In sexual matters she was unimaginative, and this shouldn't be taken as a reproach, Aron says; he was even more unimaginative than she was, he mentions this only because his desires developed into disillusionment shockingly fast.

Rather, he found reason for reproach in the fact that there was almost nothing he could talk to Irma about. At most about Mark, with whom she was probably in love, he didn't exclude that possibility. He never managed to involve Irma in any deep conversation about anything. In the most extreme case she would listen to him patiently, *she was patient*. Her interests were limited to organizational issues; she had to organize the housekeeping, shopping, laundry, and so on — Irma was a fantastic housekeeper. Her fallen husband, a certain Herbert Wiesner, cabinetmaker, had probably trained her.

Aron never seriously tried to expand Irma's field of interest or change it in any way. He accepted the situation and never gave her any indication that she did not interest him. They never had a fight, a real fight, and *that's why* there's nothing more to say about Irma.

During one of the evenings they spent together, she asked Aron how much longer he thought he would wait before enrolling Mark.

"What do you mean?"

"Sooner or later he'll have to go to school."

Aron was struck by this. The problem itself did not worry him; what did was the fact that an *outsider* had to come and remind him of his most obvious duty. Of course, he had already thought of enrolling Mark, yet only briefly. It had been, as he says, a feeling rather than a thought. Now he could no longer maintain this fence-sitting; Irma's question implied that she would take the opportunity to ask him time and time again.

*   *   *

Where did you see a problem?" I ask. "To enroll a child in school is the easiest thing in the world. You go to the school, enroll him, and buy books; there's nothing to it."

"There's a little more," Aron says. He lays a hand on my arm and explains the situation without any irritability; his voice almost sounds understanding. It's as if it has finally become clear to him that an outsider like me can conjure up only an incomplete picture of the situation and therefore has to rely on questions. "If a dog is kept for a long time in a cage and is beaten and tormented," he says, "then the day they let him loose, humanity as a whole, for him, will consist of people who are cruel to animals. Even outside the cage." And he says, "Please excuse me if I talk to you as if you were a child, but if you ask me such questions, you leave me no choice."

"If I understand your example correctly," I say, "you hesitated in enrolling Mark because you didn't want him to go to a school where the teachers were not, in your eyes, free from the suspicion of being fascists, or even murderers?"

"That's right," Aron answers.

"And because you didn't want him to sit at the same desk with the children of these people?"

"That's right."

"Even taking your reservations into consideration," I say, "it could not have been your intention to raise an illiterate?"

"That first and foremost," Aron says. "And second, there are laws, school was compulsory. A few days later I enrolled him."

*   *   *

It would be exaggerated, Aron says, to call his job as an interpreter a source of happiness. He names disadvantages that can be attributed to any job — the pay was too low, it was enormously time-consuming, his lack of enthusiasm increased with every passing month. The greatest shortcoming, he says, is a circumstance characteristic of virtually every translation — the impossibility of bringing one's own opinions into play. One's opinions were not asked for. On the contrary, they stood in the way of exact translations, were spanners in the works. One had to concentrate solely on the task of repeating someone else's opinions, no matter how nonsensical they might be. During the breaks he could formulate his own opinions, but during the breaks an interpreter is an interpreter just as much as he is a doorman — the breaks didn't count. To be allowed to proffer one's own convictions only after working hours must, in the long run, be considered degrading.

If only, Aron says, the work had dealt with things that interested him. Usually a Soviet officer sat across from some frightened German mayor, or the representative of some authority, and they discussed problems that bored Aron to death. Since it was always the same officer, *even* entire idioms, whole sentences were repeated. Soon Aron had to start paying attention so that his lack of enthusiasm would not interrupt the flow of the conversation.

On several occasions, he says, he was sorely tempted to lighten his work by leading the interlocutors astray, by translating their words not exactly, not truthfully, but

slightly off to one side. In contemplating this, he had nothing special in mind — that is, nothing political — only his
desire to provide a little variation by creating confusion.
He never yielded to this temptation, never, of course; he
didn't want to pay for such inanities with reasonable
reprisals. Besides, conscientiousness is one of the tools of
the trade of a bookkeeper. The only freedom he allowed
himself now and then was, while truthfully repeating the
contents, of placing his own accents. For example when
the *German person* in question was dislikable, and this
happened more than once, Aron adapted his voice so that
the German's words sounded denigrating and the words
of the officer sharp and cool, like orders. This modus
operandi didn't change the outcome of the conversation,
he says; his unauthorized behavior only underlined the
positions more clearly and perhaps contributed to abbre-
viating the procedure.

Regardless, the breaks provided a certain rest. Aron
was at the disposal of the officer in charge, a forty-five-
year-old-man from Leningrad. His name was Leonid
Petrowitsch Wasin, and to Aron's frustration he was an
antialcoholic — just sweet tea morning, noon, and night.
After a couple of days they had exchanged their life stories, in installments. Once Wasin said his brother had *also*
married a Jew. He was a shy, reserved man; Aron felt that
every time he had to give an order, he had to overcome all
sorts of inner conflicts. Their relationship was good, civi-
lized up to the last day, Aron says. Neither of them was an
especially outgoing type.

Perhaps this too concerning us — after they had been
working together for several weeks, a company director
approached Wasin and complained that he was constantly

having problems procuring various materials; he thought the problem could be solved by the Red Army. He also requested a staff car, without which he had great trouble carrying out his duties. The German authority responsible had refused his request several times.

After he left, without getting what he wanted but with Wasin's promise to put in a good word for him, Aron regretted that Wasin hadn't reprimanded the presumptuous man. It's one thing to make promises, for what they are worth, he says, but not to react to such arrogance, or worse, even to respond sympathetically, that was an entirely different matter.

Since there was some time before the next appointment, Wasin made tea. "What are you upset about?" he asked.

"Does it show?"

"Well, what's the matter?"

"It's the way you treated that man."

"Was I impolite? That makes me uncomfortable. You should bring my attention to that in the future."

Wasin certainly knew what Aron had meant; he smiled because he found his observation *elegantly ironic.* And Aron felt the moment was opportune, or at least he thought he could make it so. "Why didn't you kick him out?" he asked. "Or, better still, why didn't you promise him a butler?"

Wasin was silent; he put tea leaves in two glasses and looked at the water for so long that it started to boil. Aron was convinced that Wasin refused to discuss such issues with his interpreter. Then he sipped his tea — *he could drink incredibly hot tea* — and he said, "You know, that's an issue about which neither of us is impartial. Perhaps it would be wisest if, after a war, decisions were made only by people who had nothing to do with the war. But that can't be done. When I started working here, I also asked myself what rights the Germans I was dealing with had and what rights they didn't have. Apparently you tend to think they have no rights; I've noticed this for a while now. I don't judge you, but I'm of a different opinion."

"Very magnanimous," Aron said.

Wasin scowled and asked Aron to save his mockery for some more appropriate occasion. He asked Aron angrily if he thought it would be a solution to kill all the Germans. If the result of the war for the defeated had to be exactly as it would have been for the victors if they had lost the war. Did the only difference in the chance of war consist of which side was struck by disaster, or wasn't it also a question of type of disaster?

"That's not what this is about," Aron said. "To kiss someone's ass or to kill him, those aren't the only two options."

"Did I kiss his ass?" Wasin asked.

"More or less," Aron said. "What do you think he would do to you if he could do as he pleased? I don't mean this man in particular, I don't even know him."

"Who do you mean then?" Wasin asked.

"The average German."

"You're starting from the beginning again," Wasin said. "Perhaps there are only two options, because there are only two sides. Our work cannot be determined by feelings. When a German stands in front of me, I can't keep reminding myself that my wife and my parents were killed. Of course, we're in a position of power here, the question is only what we should do with it. I'll tell you again, there are two sides. On one side we have you and me and most of our visitors, on the other side are those people against whom we fought."

Aron said he alone knew at least ten different sides; then the next visitor knocked on the door. He had the impression that Wasin treated the man particularly indulgently, as if to irritate him, Aron. Later they did not resume the conversation. Aron felt there really was no point; apparently Wasin came armed with convictions that precluded any discussion. And why Wasin never brought the subject up again, Aron says, he never knew, and never gave it a second thought.

In the first report card that Mark brought home, the teacher had noted under the section "General Assessment" that Mark possessed a remarkable intelligence for his age and was possibly in the position, with a greater eagerness to learn, to skip a grade. In particular she mentioned his gift for music and math. Aron rewarded him with a toy of his choice. On a walk he asked if Mark would like to learn how to play the piano.

"I don't know," Mark said.

"Other children would jump for joy and you don't know."

Aron explained to Mark the, in his opinion, unique enjoyment that came from being able to play the piano; he spoke of the pleasure one could provide others, visitors, for example, not to mention his own father. It soon turned out that Mark had already heard a piano but had never actually seen one.

When they got back to the apartment, Aron asked Irma to look around for a piano teacher for Mark, preferably someone in the neighborhood. Astonished, Irma said, "But, Arno, I could do it."

"Do what?"

"Do you have anything against my teaching him?"

"None," Aron said. *In the excitement* he had completely forgotten that Irma was a piano teacher. Why should he have something against it? So they didn't need a piano teacher but an instrument. Unfortunately Kenik, the expert on major purchases, was gone. Aron asked her to check around, here in the apartment house, in the streets, while shopping, to see if someone might have a spare piano, or knew of one that was not being used. "Only find out where it is," he told Irma; he wanted to discuss the price with the owner himself. "A brown one if possible."

Finally the piano appeared, thanks to Irma's diligent research and Aron's negotiating skills. Irma was happier than Mark, at least at first, until he mastered the finger exercises and was able to play short pieces. In the evenings she often gave concerts; Aron and Mark sat there and could request tunes. When she would bow deeply at the end, like pianists do, they would applaud loudly.

Once she interrupted her performance and listened; Aron thought something was wrong with the piano. But Irma said, "Somebody knocked."

Out of the three of us, she had the best ears. Mark ran out of the room; visitors were rare. He came back and whispered, "A man."

Aron immediately thought of Ostwald; a man at this time of night could be only Ostwald, he thought. Yet even before he was in the corridor he knew that Ostwald was out of the question because Mark knew Ostwald and, if it were he, Mark would have said, "Ostwald," not "A man."

Tennenbaum was waiting at the door. He wished Aron a good evening and asked if he was disturbing him, if so he could come back some other time. Aron led him into the kitchen. A little while later, when Irma, curious, stuck her head around the door, Aron told her, "I won't be long."

Tennenbaum wouldn't let himself be put off; he may even have feared they might not let him in. He had a request. First, he expressed his regret that they had completely lost sight of each other; after the long and, all in all, pleasant collaboration he found it a little surprising. As for himself, he could claim that the last few months had been successful; the trading company, whose existence Aron surely remembered, was thriving. He hoped things were also going well for Aron.

"I can't complain," Aron said.

Aron glanced at his watch. Tennenbaum finally came to the point. "I hear you are working for the Russian authorities?" he said.

"That's correct."

"May I know what you do there?"

"First please tell me your problem," Aron said.

Tennenbaum was expecting a shipment. From West Germany to West Berlin, he feared difficulties driving through the Russian Zone. He needed someone who could put in a good word for him; to be precise, he needed an authorization. Not for free, of course; that was

obvious, he said. He could think of several ways to show
Aron his gratitude — pettiness had never been his style.

Aron thought that only a small dealer, not one of the
important ones, would require such an embarrassing favor. He was silent for a long time, not because he was
thinking of how he could help Tennenbaum but only so
that Tennenbaum would think that that was what he was
doing. *I simply sat there and looked at the wall, and he sat very
still, not wanting to disturb me.* Aron said, "You know how
happy I'd be to do something for you. But you came at an
unfortunate time."

"What do you mean?"

"Between us, Mr. Tennenbaum, I have already
helped some people. Not exactly with shipments but
with other authorizations. As recently as last week. You
will understand that I can't bother the Russians every
day. Who am I anyway? They would throw me out."

"When is the earliest you can try again?"

Aron was happy that his little game was working so
well; he says it was *so* much more fun than simply kicking
Tennenbaum out. He said, "Not for another two months,
and that's pretty tight. Besides, the question remains
open if I can help you at all. I've never tried getting transport authorizations."

"I can't wait that long." Tennenbaum sighed. "Too
bad."

When he left, the piano started again. Aron couldn't
get Ostwald's name out of his head. Ah, he said, if only it
had been Ostwald knocking at my door. He pictured a reunion in full detail, a curtain drawn over all discord; the
lack of a friend made his longing for Ostwald strong and
tenacious. Even if liquor had become more expensive, he

told himself, *there was more than just liquor between us*. In
the evening they could sit and talk, complain and sound
out the situation. Mark could sleep or play or go out with
Irma. He even yearned for that being together without
saying a word; he claims Ostwald belonged to the category of people whose simple presence worked liked medicine for almost anything.

The following Sunday he went to Ostwald's house.
The worst thing that could happen was that Ostwald
would refuse to take his proffered hand, justifying himself with random excuses. Aron had decided to say, "If I
am to blame, I beg your pardon. If you're to blame, let's
forget about it. Or do you have a better idea?" Ostwald's
answer would settle everything. But a stranger opened
the door. Aron's first thought — *his new friend;* he said
he'd like to talk to Mr. Ostwald; the man led him to the
living room. No trace of Ostwald. Aron had never been in
that apartment. He looked around until the man asked,
"When was the last time you saw him?"

"Has he disappeared?"

"No."

Aron had the sensation, even before the man had answered, that something was wrong — he could feel it.
The man introduced himself as Ostwald's brother; his
name was Andreas Ostwald. He inquired about Aron's relationship with his brother; Aron explained reluctantly.
He wanted to see Ostwald, or at least hear a sentence that
would dissolve his fears, instead of the tedious questions.
The man said, "Forgive me for wanting to know who I
am talking to. My brother is dead."

He heard the whole unimportant rest, Aron says,
through a haze of tears; soon Andreas Ostwald was crying

too. He lived there now and as the only living relative had inherited everything. A couple of miserable letters were in his possession; most of the things he knew about his brother came from strangers like the neighbors. He explained that since childhood his brother had been hardly accessible to him — complicated, eccentric, and with a tendency to get involved in incomprehensible activities — but he didn't want to talk about old times now. The gentleman would surely find it hard to believe that he had last seen his brother in 1933, shortly before his arrest. After the war, only letters, and they were few and far between; he knew hardly anything about his brother's life after the war; the letters were circumspect, impersonal, nothing more than signs of life. And the information the neighbors gave was full of gaps; the image that he had tried to piece together was incomplete. He knew vaguely about a job his brother had had in the judiciary, under the supervision of the English; then he understood there'd been some kind of trouble, nothing precise, that had led to his dismissal. He said he could imagine that his brother never avoided a fight; he had never been a compromising type. Still, the rumor that his brother's only interest in life was alcohol was reliable. Several neighbors had independently confirmed that at a certain point he would come home dead drunk, unapproachable, night after night; nobody knew where he had been. It was his personal opinion, the brother said, that there, in that period of Ostwald's life, lay the evil influence that, months later, led to his brother's tragic death. In any case, one day, and again several neighbors commented on this, his brother had suddenly stopped drinking. People said that from one day to the next he started taking care of the way he looked —

clothes, shaving, posture. He looked like someone who was starting afresh, with good intentions. In fact, he accepted a post as one of four lawyers in a firm near the Kurfürstendamm. Good salary, and even better prospects, according to his lawyer colleagues, said Andreas Ostwald; his brother could have grown old and happy in that post. No one had the slightest inkling that things might take such a turn, this suicide from out of the blue. Gas.

"Do you have any idea why?" Andreas Ostwald asked. "Can you fill in any of the gaps?"

"I appear only in the booze phase," Aron said. "Not before and not after."

Andreas Ostwald, Aron says, did not make a good impression on him. Later he even goes so far as to say he had found him unpleasant, in spite of the tears; *for those people it is customary to shed tears when a close relative dies.* Andreas seemed to be irritated by Aron's words; perhaps he remembered the suspicion he had expressed in connection to his brother's alcoholism. "Perhaps you can tell me why my brother drank?" he said.

"What did you do during the war?" Aron asked.

"I was a soldier."

"He spent eleven years in the camps."

"I know," the brother said, surprised. "But what does that have to do with it?"

Aron stood up and went through all the rooms, looking for a picture of Ostwald, but found none. The brother asked him several times what he was looking for. Aron went home, the mourning lasted for weeks, Irma never knew.

All she saw was that he drank uncontrollably, day in and day out, that the stock of liquor was soon gone. Even

when he was drunk, Aron betrayed nothing, as if Ostwald
were a secret. From the very beginning, he says, his
mourning was infected with violent rage. Such a stubborn
idiot, he thought of Ostwald, such an irresponsible act.
He destroys something that doesn't belong to him, dis-
appears to a place where he can't be followed. Though
he could sympathize with Ostwald's foul moods, Aron
thought, this was too much: What right does he have to
put an end to the pleasure his presence gave others? How
arrogant! What right does he have to destroy the hopes
that he, Aron, held on to only for Ostwald's sake? What
right does he have to dissolve *so much* into nothing? (I
must confess that not even Ostwald's self-inflicted death
made me like him any more than before. Of course, I believe Aron, that he was attached to Ostwald. Why else
would he have told me about him? For me, this attachment is not all that interesting. Their relationship leaves
me cold. Aron's stories about Ostwald always contained
an element of unfettered admiration I simply can't relate
to, because one can truly admire only someone one
knows personally.)

A short time later — Aron was still in deep mourning — Irma looked so distraught when Aron came home
from work, it was obvious that something terrible had
happened. Her eyes looked unusually serious, and she
didn't greet him with her usual ceremony, a kiss and the
question whether everything was all right.

"What happened?"

"Go look at Mark."

Aron rushed into the room. Mark lay on his bed, a wet cloth on his forehead. Aron took it off and saw that Mark had obviously been beaten. Scratches, a swollen face, red and blue bruises, one eye was closed and the other open only a crack, and Irma had already *cleaned him up*. "His chest and arms are also black and blue. Should I have called a doctor?" she asked quietly.

"Get out," Aron said.

He sat on the bed, took Mark's hand, and hoped his voice wouldn't sound too shaky. "Who did this?" he asked.

Mark didn't answer. Aron repeated the question a couple of times and became impatient; then Mark started crying. Aron caressed him and in consolation told him a funny story about when he himself had been beaten like that as a young boy. He had come home in such a state that his own mother didn't recognize him; when she opened the door, she thought it was one of his friends, and she said her son was still outside playing. Yet Mark's condition was so pitiful that when he heard the punch line he didn't even change his expression; he looked as if he was ready to start crying at any moment. Aron said they wouldn't talk about that stupid story anymore. Tomorrow, "tomorrow will be a better day than today; now try to get some sleep."

Irma knew nothing more than he did. Aron sat there for hours; all he could conclude was that what had happened was an act of anti-Semitism, a *minipogrom*. In any case, it would not go unpunished. The only question was what kind of retaliation would be more expeditious. In that instant, at the moment when his anger was at its peak, he tended toward the idea of finding the name of the culprit, or culprits, and taking revenge in a way that was *appropriate*. However, one had to take into account that the culprits were children; that was clear even without Mark's confession. Children of Mark's age; therefore the real question was who had instigated them.

Aron went to the other room several times during the night; Mark was sleeping soundly as usual. Aron wanted to wake him up and get the name *out of him*, with or without tears. Only the thought that for Mark being awake meant being in pain restrained him.

W hy was he actually beaten?" I ask.

"Didn't I just tell you?"

"You didn't mention any proof. Did Mark confirm your suspicions later?"

"If you had seen the state he was in, you also would have realized immediately that it wasn't one of the usual fights between boys. I know how children fight. If one child has proven he's the strongest, he stops — that's how it goes with children. Mark looked as if he had been manhandled by someone who hated him. It wasn't a fight among children, it was an attack."

"And everything was so clear it didn't require any questioning? It never occurred to you that you were making something up that had nothing to do with Mark, only with yourself?"

"No," Aron says, "that never occurred to me."

He fills his glass and explains that he has been beaten often enough in his life. He has had so many

opportunities to look into the faces of thugs that in this
case he can permit himself to judge. He says, "Anything
else?"

The following day brought no greater clarification. Mark
didn't go to school and Aron stayed home from work; he
sent Irma to the nearest telephone with an excuse for the
Soviet headquarters — a sudden indisposition. Mark cat-
egorically refused to confess the names. Aron tried being
nice and then tough. Why do you want to protect your
tormentor, he asked, prevent him from being punished?
To no avail. Gradually the reasons for Mark's silence interested him more than the name itself; perhaps it was a
terrible threat. Some thugs, he says, prolong their victims' suffering by threatening them. In which case the
presumed threat didn't need to be terrible *in and of itself*,
it only needed to stay in Mark's frightened thoughts; not
everyone has the same concept of terror.

From then on, Aron tried to eliminate all traces of
impatience and anger from his questions and mix in sweet-
ness and a little coaxing. He says he already knew at the
time that trust wasn't something that falls straight from
heaven, that could be forced on request or even obtained
through extortion. It had to be built millimeter by millimeter, often with an arduous *attention for detail*.

Around noon he had reached his new goal. He did
not know who had hit his son, but he discovered why
Mark withheld the name so doggedly. He was afraid of
losing the only respect he still had after the thrashing — at least he wanted to be a *good loser*. He imagined

the catastrophic consequences if his father went into the schoolyard, grabbed the boy in question, and beat him in full view of the others.

"You needn't be afraid," Aron said. "I'll do it so thoroughly that he won't ever hurt you again."

Naturally, that wasn't a very good argument. Mark believed that, yes, an act of revenge would provide a certain protection from future attacks, but the price for that would be overall isolation, and that was a price he didn't want to pay. Aron asked him if he really wanted to take the risk of being confronted with such attacks from time to time, by the same person or someone else. Because if the others noticed that there was no reprisal, the attacks would just go on. "Revenge isn't useful only for others," Aron said. "Don't you want him to be beaten like you were?"

"Yes," Mark said, "I tried. But he's too strong."

"Now, tell me his name," Aron said.

Mark shook his head, amazed that the whole interrogation seemed to be starting all over again. *In the end*, Aron promised not to go to school, or to the boy's home; he didn't want to do anything at all, he said, only know the name, with the intention of forgetting it again, eventually. "If we both know it," he said, "you'll feel better."

Mark demanded that he swear on his honor. Aron had no choice, he wanted to know the name. The boy was called Winfried Schmidt.

When shortly thereafter Aron left the room, Mark, with more than a trace of suspicion, asked where he was going. For a little walk, Aron replied; he didn't know exactly where, but definitely not to the school. He never saw this boy, Aron tells me, this Winfried Schmidt, Mark and he never mentioned him again, yet to this day he can't forget that name, *ridiculous*. He then walked aimlessly; the nice weather and fresh air made his anger easier to bear, it never occurred to him to break his word to Mark. Then, *unintentionally*, he saw the school, an empty yard with trees. Aron didn't have the school schedule memorized and therefore didn't know whether or not classes were over. It didn't seem to make any sense just to stand there and wait in case he might decide to break his word after all. Still, he stood there for a good fifteen minutes, out of laziness, he says. A man, perhaps a teacher on his way home, came out of the school building and looked at him suspiciously. Aron moved on.

The more time passed, the hazier, he says, were his thoughts. He hardly knew what he was looking for anymore; *it's easy to say "a way out."* He knew only that Mark had been beaten up and that he had to make sure it would never happen again. The ideal, he says, would have been to convince them once and for all, convince them that it was inhuman to hit people, that they damaged not only the victims but their own souls as well. The convincing should go on until a new relationship had been established, however long it took. But what kind of a guarantee was that? The risk would be yours and yours alone; all you could do was act toward them the same way you expected them to act toward you. But who can guarantee that you will convince them before they beat you to death? And where do you find the patience? And who would protect you from relapses? And from misunderstanding?

He resolved not to go home before he found a

reliable solution to protect Mark. His first thought was to take him out of the school and send him to a different one, but all things considered that wasn't a solution. What had happened could reoccur anywhere. The idea of going with him everywhere he went was completely unrealistic. Mark had to learn to defend himself from this kind of attack; that was it, only effective self-defense would make him independent. *I had to arm him.*

Aron remembered the resolution he had made and eventually forgotten months before — of being a role model for Mark. A role model for all situations in life — but, aside from a couple of pathetic attempts, he hadn't done much. That would change now. Aron recognized the chance to turn his past good intentions into deeds and at the same time help Mark in a situation of need. How had he reacted to fights as a schoolboy? Specific images did not come to mind; there had certainly been fights now and then. Aron had forgotten them, but being able to remember them was irrelevant. What was clear was that, at the time, he definitely had not been the hero he wanted Mark to become thanks to tales from an invented past.

He sat by the bed and said, "Did I ever tell you that I was a boxer a long time ago? No? Strange," Aron said, "I was sure you knew. Well then, listen: it all began when I was as old as you are now, perhaps a couple of months older. I got along with everyone at school, but on our street lived this one guy who made our lives miserable. He was the one who always decided what game we would play, and he decided who could join in and who couldn't,

and if somebody didn't want to do as he said, then he
gave them a punch or two; he was the strongest kid in our
crowd. And one of us had to be his servant. He would
simply say: "Today, you!" and point at someone who
would be his servant all day. His name, by the way, was
Werner. You can imagine how much we wanted to get rid
of him, but no one could do anything, he was so incredibly strong. The only thing you could do, if you wanted to
go outside to play, would be first to look out the window
to see if he was on the street and, if he was, you would
stay in your room and get bored. That was almost just as
bad. He hit me more than once, and if my mother asked
me why I was crying I lied to her, because I was afraid
that if I told her who it was I'd get more of the same from
him the next day."

Mark winced with compassion; he was a *talented* listener. The fact that almost all the stories he had ever
heard tended to have a happy ending did not spoil the
suspense. He waited impatiently for the climax, the inevitable change in favor of the good guys; yet Aron felt he
hadn't done a thorough enough job on Werner, whose
meanness, he found, could easily bear a few more brush-
strokes.

"One day he threw a rock through a window, a huge
shop window, and ran away. Because I happened to be
standing nearby, I ran away too. Only I had been recognized, not him. When I got home the shop owner was already sitting with my father and telling him that I had
thrown the rock through his window. Just imagine: I was
so afraid of Werner that I simply couldn't tell on him and
took the blame myself. I got the punishment that he deserved, and when later on I told him the whole story, so

that he would praise me for my silence, do you know what he did? He laughed at me and said, 'Well, you were stupid enough to get caught.'"

"Did it go on like that forever?" Mark asked, at the end of his patience now.

"No, not forever," Aron said. "It lasted only as long as I kept waiting and hoping for a miracle, hoping that the torture would end of its own accord. Listen to what happened next. Once I read in the paper about a boxing match; rather, I read about how a famous boxer, whose name I can't remember any longer, was preparing for a world championship. How he practiced for weeks, how he ran alone through the woods, lifted weights, punched a bag full of sand for hours — all this only so that he could win this one match. It impressed me so much that I decided to become a boxer too and train for my match against Werner. I went to my father and asked him to enroll me in a boxing school. At first he refused, because it cost money; he said I should play soccer instead. But how could soccer help against Werner? I didn't give up and begged for so long that I finally was allowed to learn how to box."

A list of the difficulties of training followed, a description of what it took to learn a craft, because boxing, Aron claims, is nothing more than a craft and therefore, up to a certain level, talent has nothing to do with it. In fact, he says, he'd been interested in boxing as a young man, if only as a spectator — now and then he had watched boxing matches. The atmosphere in the hall where the matches were held had been a welcome change in his overly monotonous life.

It wasn't hard for Aron to spice up his career with

technical terms. Mark lay there amazed and heard upper-
cut, left hook clinch, straight right, sidestep. Aron didn't
forget to mention, among the many details, what *inspired*
him in his eagerness to train, what gave him new strength
when the next complicated trick was on the syllabus:
the thought of Werner, the hope of overpowering that
monster. But, he explained, Mark mustn't think that the
whole thing had been nothing but hardship. To learn how
to box, aside from the immense effort, was to learn a ver-
satile game, a game that is hard to explain, one should
simply try it out.

"Then the time finally came. I had never let anyone
in on what I was doing. I behaved the same way I always
had so that Werner wouldn't notice. I didn't want to start
a fight, I had simply decided that I wouldn't put up with
his shenanigans anymore. But in all honesty I was sort of
waiting for an opportunity. And it came soon enough.
Again he pointed at me and ordered — Today, you! You
remember, that's how he chose a slave. So I said, 'Get
yourself someone who's more stupid than I am. I don't
want to be your slave, not today or any other day.'"

"And what did he do?"

"He looked at me as if he hadn't heard me properly.
The others were also really shocked. One little guy whispered in my ear, 'Are you crazy? He'll make mincemeat
out of you.' Werner walked toward me slowly and rolled
up his sleeves. So I said to him, 'Why are you rolling up
your sleeves? It's not that warm today.' That's when he finally raised his arm. I was waiting for the right moment,
just as I had practiced a thousand times, and bang, I gave
him a good punch on the nose."

At this point Mark could no longer hide his feelings.

He clapped with delight and turned a somersault in bed; then he sat still again. The story had to go a little further; he really wanted to hear the happy ending. How Werner was flustered, how young Arno didn't even take advantage of his astonishment — didn't need to — when Werner attacked for the second time. A little step to one side and he hit the air — the famous sidestep. Blind with rage, Werner stormed after him and ran into a hail of punches. The horror of the others was soon transformed into cries of joy when they realized that rebellion led not to complete catastrophe, only to catastrophe for Werner. He didn't even see the hook and the straight punch coming, they flew at him that fast. When his nose was bleeding and his head buzzing because of all the uppercuts, he finally understood that his coarse hands were useless against a real boxer, only his legs could save him. So he started to run as if the very devil was after him, and from then on peace reigned in the street; the monster didn't show his face again.

Mark would have liked to have heard another couple of stories like that. He asked, "Did you box later?"

Once in a while, Aron said. His trainer had advised him to keep training, refine his skills, in time he too might become a champion, but he wasn't interested in championships. His purpose had been fulfilled, and no one could take from him what he had learned while he was training. He had felt prepared for any attack by loudmouths and tormentors, that was enough. A boxer, he said, isn't a man who boxes all the time, he's someone who knows how to box. Unfortunately, however, boxers often box just because they are boxers; *that's the whole problem.*

Aron succeeded far more easily than he had expected. It was one small step from Mark's enthusiasm to
his desire for heroic acts of his own. Children are predictable, Aron says, especially one's own. That evening
Mark asked if there were any boxing schools in the city.
Aron looked skeptical and said, maybe there were some,
but he wasn't sure, he would have to find out. He was
convinced that to keep Mark's desire alive an immediate
acceptance would be less effective than an indication that
it might not be all that easy; naturally there were difficulties he hoped to overcome, only not right away.

Every evening after that, as soon as Aron got home,
Mark asked him first thing: "Did you find one?" And
Aron said he had looked, but to no avail; he would keep
on looking. There was a dangerous moment, he says
thoughtfully, when expectation could turn into resignation; one had to be careful. "Guess what," he finally told
Mark a week later. "I found a place, we'll go tomorrow."

The next afternoon they went to a boxing union. Aron
had trouble getting permission to leave the headquarters
hours before closing time. Fascinated, Mark watched the
children train. A friendly man walked up to them, waved
at Aron, looked Mark up and down, and asked, "Do you
know how to box?"

Mark shook his head, so the man said, "Of course, I
can tell by your black eye. But we'll take care of that."

From that day on Mark went to the gym twice a
week — first with Aron, then by himself — and did his
best to learn the new craft. After each lesson he showed
off his progress at home. Aron stresses that it had nothing
to do with his own ambition; it didn't fill him with pride

in any way that his son could box better every day — it
only reassured him.

There's a letter from America," Irma said.

It was leaning against a vase on the table; the name
of the sender meant nothing to Aron, he recognized only
the word *Baltimore*. Mark waited for the stamps and Irma
for sensational news. They thought it was taking him too
long to open the envelope.

"Leave me alone."

The contents were in English; only a name caught
his eye in the incomprehensible text: Samuel London.
And, a few lines later, a sum: 50,000. Aron came to a conclusion that, should it prove to be accurate, would be ex-
cellent news. He dedicated almost an hour to London,
his first father-in-law. He had only a vague memory of
London's daughter Linda, Aron's first wife, but he saw
London distinctly, the textile factory behind him. To
Irma, Aron said, "If I'm not mistaken, we've inherited a
lot of money."

On the other hand, the same letter meant that old London must have died. Aron felt no pain, only a sense of
regret that didn't overwhelm him. So much pain lay between London and that day, he says, that he could easily
get over such a loss, especially if it was connected to a
handsome profit.

Aron took the letter to the headquarters. He wasn't
the only interpreter there; there was an English one too.
Aron took him aside and showed him the letter. Five
minutes later his suspicion was confirmed: London was

definitely dead and had left him fifty thousand dollars.
The legacy had not been challenged by the other heirs
and was therefore readily available. The notary who had
written the letter wanted to know where he should trans-
fer the money. The English interpreter said, "You're a
rich man now."

Not so rich after all, Aron opened a bank account.

Where?"

"In a bank in West Berlin. Where else?"

He sent the account number to Baltimore via telegram;
the money arrived one long month later. Except for a *few
thousand* right at the beginning, he says, he didn't touch it
for years, only much later, when Mark and Irma began to
have expensive tastes. And, he had to confess, he did too.
For example, Irma and Mark wanted to travel, but until
that moment the money had remained untouched; it paid
interest and had a reassuring effect. Aron didn't want
their lives to change because of a sudden external event,
and in a way that would make the neighbors jealous. He
had his way. Mark didn't know anything about the inher-
itance; only Irma was informed, and Aron soon regretted
this. She suddenly discovered shortcomings that could be
avoided, in her opinion, by using the money, but *that was
exactly* what Aron didn't want. They argued; Irma used
statements like "You only live once" or "You can't take it
with you" until Aron threatened he had better things to

do than argue endlessly with her. After that she no longer mentioned the money, maybe even found her peace, out of necessity or otherwise. Aron says, *So much about London.*

Then his first heart attack. He was diagnosed as having angina pectoris, severe chest pains. Aron describes having trouble breathing and the unpleasant feeling *when you think of nothing but what little life you have left.* He describes the fear, even if the doctor says that in theory one can live to be a hundred with that kind of damage — but without drinking.

What does survival mean? Till then, daily walks weren't undertaken for a reason, and therefore they used to be a pleasure. Now they simply had the effect of reminding him, with every step, of being deathly ill, a ridiculous attempt to *walk away from the end.*

No excitement. But how, Aron asks, does one not get excited? No excitement implies that in the past he had done his best to get excited as often as possible. Besides, the intention not to get excited is the most exciting of all; one swallows hard and keeps all one's anger pent up so that no one notices. There's an enormous difference between inner calm and forced self-control, and as far as he is concerned, he says, self-control is a thousand times more exciting than letting go.

Or the recommendation that he get more sleep than before. Until then he went to bed only when he was in a state of complete exhaustion, in a state that guaranteed falling asleep immediately or virtually. This meant an av-

erage of four to five hours sleep a night. The doctor demanded eight, which meant that Aron had to go to bed
hours earlier than usual, and those hours were unbearable, not to mention his having to forgo pleasure with
Irma. To help him sleep, he took sleeping pills or a slug of
cognac, which certainly wasn't part of the doctor's plan,
but the doctor's orders were right for the textbook model,
who only looked like Aron physically.

A cure, he says, that bored him to death: three
months in a home for the victims of fascism. Aron resigned from his post with the Russians, gave Mark and
Irma sufficient money and the most pressing instructions
for the time he was gone, and left. The prospect, he says,
of hanging around for months with *cases* like him, with
other *camp-ruins*, was more than he could bear. All they
did from noon till night was keep telling each other how
horrible everything was.

W ait a minute," I say. "Why did you resign from the
Russians?"

"Weren't you listening?" Aron asks.

I say, "You only said that you got sick and went to get
cured. You could have continued working as an interpreter after that."

"No, I couldn't," Aron says. "The strokes didn't stop
afterward; they haven't to this day. You know that."

"I do, but you couldn't have known it beforehand.
Why did you resign before you left for the health resort?"

In a flash Aron's face darkens, yet in a flash it's bright
again. He tilts his head to one side, he suddenly looks

cunning, he says, "For once, let me ask a question too. Why didn't you ask me the same thing when I resigned from Tennenbaum?"

"Because the reasons were clear, you spoke about it in detail."

"You're cheating, my friend, that's only a half-truth. You didn't ask about Tennenbaum because you agreed with my resigning. Now you're asking because you disagree with my resigning. For the sake of your story, you had hoped that something good would come out of my job with the Russians — Aron finally gets his act together — how should I know what goes on in your head? And now you're disappointed because my job with the Russians was nothing more than an episode."

"You may be right," I say, "at least partially."

"Partially is good," Aron says. "If you really want to hear my reasons again, I can easily repeat them. Listen carefully: first, it was a badly paid job. Second, I didn't find it interesting. Third, I got sick. Is that enough to justify my resignation?"

While he was recuperating, he read a lot, more than ever before. There was little else to do, aside from the daily examinations, the meals dispensed in accurate doses, and the controlled walks. Since he hadn't brought along any books, he was directed to the sanatorium's library. The librarian, who he realized was dissatisfied with the selection, gave him advice. With her help, Aron looked for what he thought would *most likely* correspond to his taste, primarily books by Russians of the previous century. He names Gogol, Turgenev, Saltykov-Shchedrin, and Goncharov. Since reading was an occupation born, as it were, out of necessity, he says, he started it with some reservations. Yet these reservations soon eased into real pleasure. A pleasure that wasn't in fact as breathtaking and unique as one hears now and then with connection to literature, but the books undoubtedly helped him make it through three months in which otherwise nothing happened. Reading, he proceeds, was but a brief experience for him anyway; in reading he was looking for distraction rather than stimulation. The lasting effect of impressions, which everybody talks about, was true only as they related to his own experiences and to people he had known, they never came from books. He did not think books were superfluous, dispensable accessories; on the contrary, he thought of himself as pro- rather than anti-book. But one should beware of overestimating their importance, expecting more from books than they are able to give, living more through books than through life. He wouldn't want to withhold this opinion, he says, especially from someone like me.

Bedtime was prescribed every night at eight; the lights were turned off at the central switch. Aron almost despaired trying to cope with the time between going to bed and falling asleep. To that, a further difficulty must be added: darkness. At home he always left the light on until morning. They wouldn't give him sleeping pills. Having decided that darkness was the biggest problem of all, he found some candles so he could read in bed until he fell asleep. Then a nurse discovered this major violation of the house rules. She confiscated the candle he had lit, found some others in the night table along with some matches, cigarettes, and a tin box filled with cigarette ashes. "Really! How irresponsible," she said, and reported him to the head of the sanatorium.

Aron was called before the director and confessed to everything. The director gave him a long lecture — what would have happened if an unexpected draft had blown the curtain into the flame? The whole sanatorium could have burned down, not to mention the damage to Aron's heart caused by his smoking and reading at night. "Really, Mr. Blank, if you can't be more disciplined, we have to expect the worst."

By "the worst" he meant the interruption of the cure. Aron promised improvement; he lay there in the dark and developed a new method. He thought intensively about the plot of the book he was reading. He made conjectures about how it would continue or tried to imagine how he himself would have handled the situation of the *written people,* and he did that until he ran out of thoughts. Learning this method, he says, was probably the greatest gain of the entire cure. He still uses it every evening; it doesn't necessarily have to be books he thinks about. He simply thinks about something complicated; with time he developed a knack for knowing which subjects were more likely to make him fall asleep and which were less prone to.

Aron didn't befriend any of the hundred or so patients; in any case he noticed that most of them, like him, were not interested in human contact. Contrary to his expectations, they were completely self-absorbed, intent on mitigating their own suffering, he says, and it was very quiet. Except for the few who already knew one another from the earlier days, no groups seemed to form; any type of approach was considered invasive. It was a small population of introverts.

One man interested Aron, but only briefly. They sat at the same table in the dining room a couple of times. It turned out coincidentally that the man had known Ostwald. He had spent two years with Ostwald in a concentration camp — no question about it, with the jurist Ostwald in the very same barrack. Aron hoped the man would tell him something about Ostwald, yet he was wrong. Having identified Ostwald, the man said no more. Even when Aron forced himself to ask the man for a little more information, he remained taciturn; he said he didn't like to talk about these things. Aron didn't pressure him any further; *perhaps it was better that way*, the man certainly had his own problems and his own methods. Aron didn't tell him that Ostwald had committed suicide. From then on they sat at different tables. The distance between them, Aron found, had only grown with the few words they had exchanged.

Twice a month was visitors' day. So Irma and Mark came six times altogether; Irma made herself pretty for every visit and never wore the same dress twice. Aron liked her more and more with each visit. He was often worried about whether Irma was as faithful as he was. External circumstances forced him to chastity — there were only old men and strict nurses in the sanatorium — whereas Irma lived in the city. He was not jealous of her, Aron says, on any other occasion during their time together, only for a couple of seconds in that sanatorium. He would have preferred to bite his tongue than to ask her a question involving trust; the question would have sounded like a sign of dependence, and that, he says, would definitely have been going too far.

The last visit brought Aron a new preoccupation. After greeting him, Irma sent Mark out of the room and said, "Please don't get upset, Arno. Yesterday a man came to me and complained about Mark. Apparently Mark hit his son."

"Have you already talked to Mark about this?"

"No, I wanted to tell you first."

Aron called Mark in and asked him why he thought he had been sent to boxing school — he should think carefully before answering. Mark said innocently, "To learn how to box."

"Why did you learn how to box?"

"So that I can box?"

Aron grabbed Mark's arm gruffly, he says, and pulled him close. "Listen carefully, young man. I didn't want to make a thug out of you, but someone who can defend himself from thugs. There's a tremendous difference. Do you understand?"

"Yes."

"I don't believe you do," Aron said. "You hit a boy?"

"Yes."

"What did he do to you?"

"He got on my nerves."

"Is that all?"

Mark was scared and close to tears, because of the unusual anger in Aron's voice or because of the tight grip on his arm. Mark said that the boy had drawn a naked man and a naked woman on the blackboard in their classroom and when the teacher asked who had been the dirty slob, the boy had blamed it on him. Mark said, "That was why after school I gave him a lick or two."

"Were you punished?"

"Yes."

"How?"

"I was reprimanded."

"Why didn't you tell the teacher it wasn't you?"

"I did tell him. But he didn't believe me."

"And the others?" Aron asked. "Didn't anyone see who had really drawn the pictures?"

"Yes," Mark said. "But they didn't speak up."

Aron let go of his arm, tormented by a new problem. Mark's answers only led to the conclusion that his fellow students didn't like him, perhaps were even hostile to him. Why else would they keep quiet when they knew better, when he was unjustly accused? Given all that, Aron told himself, it was only an advantage to have some boxing skills. Mark's revenge was obviously not to be forgiven, but he deserved a modicum of understanding for having *lost his head*. Aron said, "When I come home we'll discuss this further."

Weeks later, when Aron had been home for a while, Irma made a discovery while cleaning. She called Aron to Mark's desk and showed him drawings of naked men and women. Aron was about to say "So what?" and ask her if it wasn't normal, or at least not unusual, for children of Mark's age to make such drawings; then he grasped the connection. The other children had remained silent not because they couldn't stand Mark, he told himself, but because the other boy had told the teacher the truth. And

Mark had not hit the boy for having wrongfully accused
him but for having betrayed him. Mark had expected the
boy to show solidarity; he had not, thus the beating. At
this point, the only positive aspect was that there was no
real reason for worrying that Mark stood alone against the
other children in his class.

He knew, Aron says, that boxing was only an emergency solution, a precaution in case of need. Because experience shows that sympathy provides a more effective
protection than strength, he wanted to advise Mark once
again, and for the future, not to risk other people's sympathy through thoughtless outbursts of anger. On the
other hand, he remembered from his own childhood how
much easier it was for the strong ones to find friends; the
weak ones, he says, had much less choice. The best thing
was to be both *popular and strong*.

When Mark came home from the gym that evening,
Aron took him to task about the pictures. Mark confessed
everything; it was very embarrassing for him that his father had found the drawings. Aron said, "But that's not
what this is about, it's about boxing. If you hit other children again for such a small thing, not only will I take you
out of boxing school but you'll have to deal with me. I
want a popular son, not a feared one."

Aron had to set about reorganizing his life, his *future as a
retired person*. Till then, when important changes had
taken place — working for Tennenbaum or as an interpreter — he'd never felt they were definite. It was always
a temporary arrangement, recognized as such from the

start. By contrast, something definite was beginning now, a life without duties, a condition almost of unrestraint. He had known from the first, he says, that his main enemy would be boredom, and that's how it was. With the years this enemy proved to be overpowering.

Aron made an effort to discover his *true* interests. At first, he assumed that he'd simply be able to follow his passions, to say the least, but he couldn't find them.

Everybody has passions," I say. "Ask anyone, if you want, no one has enough time. Everyone would like to do something but doesn't get around to it. That's exactly why most people like the idea of retiring; it means they have more free time."

"Until the time came," Aron says, "I used to think just like you. But then I had to recognize that either the people you're talking about are mistaken or I'm not normal. I was scared to death because I couldn't find anything that I would have liked to spend my time doing. And I did try. For a couple of months I even started collecting coins.

"I sit there," Aron says, "and boredom gobbles me up. Otherwise we wouldn't be here now.

"No," he says, "everything was financially in order. The pension, while not impressive, was enough for our needs. People like me get paid more than most retired people do; my past is worth more. Besides, don't forget that I still had some money."

*　*　*

Mark often came home late in the evening; as well as his school and boxing lessons he got together with friends who were forever changing. He seldom brought these friends home, and when he did Aron always had the impression that the boy in question was not good company for his son. Yet he never mentioned this to Mark. On the one hand, he told himself, the fact that he changed friends constantly only proved that Mark was still testing them and hadn't yet found a friend that met his expectations. On the other hand, he says, he remained silent because he knew enough people who, by imposing unduly high expectations on their friends, painted themselves into a corner of solitude.

Irma only had to take care of the cleaning because Aron took up the cooking out of boredom; in the evening they often went to the movies. Irma spent half the day at the piano and practiced with an endurance that Aron felt was almost pathological. At first, he thought, Why not, if she likes it? But soon the incessant tinkling got on his nerves. Sometimes she would repeat single complicated parts for hours on end. He asked her, Why go through all the trouble, if she was not planning to give concerts?

"I'd like to start giving lessons again," Irma said.

"Where?"

"Here, of course. I don't have another apartment."

"Out of the question," Aron said. "I don't have another apartment either."

Because they were together all the time now, they began to fight. The problem was that Irma, who Aron admits was a quiet and by no means a know-it-all woman, was *only boring*. She never tried to back up her point of view with solid arguments. After a discussion she would retreat, hurt, to the kitchen or to the other room; in bed she turned to the other side. However, she bore the tension for no longer than three days; then Aron could be certain that her attempts at conciliation would begin, as was the case this time. When three days later she started to caress him, he admitted to being unjust. He said he could not expect her to lead the same inactive life he did and, if she still wanted to, she could bring her piano students to the house.

"Oh, Arno," she cried.

"But be merciful and don't take too many," he said. "There must be silence for at least a couple of hours a day."

She prattled away thankfully. She didn't know if she would find students in the first place; she wanted to ask around in the neighborhood and put an ad in the papers; it was definitely not for the money, even if a couple of extra marks couldn't hurt; he would not regret giving his consent.

In the end they found so many candidates that Irma had to turn some of them away. Aron had conceded her three hours a day, but demanded free weekends, so she could give fifteen lessons a week, earning five marks a lesson. Early on, Aron would sit quietly in the corner and listen, but I can certainly imagine, he says, how long he found this enjoyable. In the neighboring room he stuffed cotton into his ears and read a book or he went out for a walk.

He couldn't walk too far; the doctor had in fact recommended walks but at the same time had warned him against too much walking, *so the view always remained the same.* In the neighborhood there was a bar that Aron had never noticed before and that interested him more and more with every passing day; every time he walked by, an enticing noise was coming through the door. *Simple people.* He caught himself taking detours in order to avoid the place. If the desire became too strong, he would think of his last heart attack; that held him back for a couple of days. Then he told himself boredom could also lead to a heart attack and sat down at a table. He ordered cognac *again* and enjoyed the restlessness all around.

By the following visit he had already made acquaintances; at the tables most people played cards, skat or sixty-six. Aron still remembered the rules of sixty-six; he joined in, they played for drinks or small sums of money. More important than profit or loss was the distraction — *you look at the watch and are grateful at how much time has passed.* It often happened that he came home late at night and drunk, but Irma never reprimanded him. She only said he knew best about his health and should not exaggerate. Aron reacted curtly and would not be lectured. He reproached her that it wasn't the liquor that made him drunk but her; without her tedious lessons he wouldn't be obliged to drink a drop. She said no more.

In the middle of a card game he clutched his chest and fell from the chair. He was carried into a separate room; his fellow players didn't know what to do. They laid him down comfortably, opened his shirt, and waited for him to drink some water. An hour later he stood up; in the meantime an emergency doctor had arrived and given him an injection. Irma immediately understood what had happened to him. The next morning Aron told her, "You saw, I tried my best, but it doesn't work."

"What are you talking about?"

"The piano lessons."

"Yes."

She begged him to be patient, if only for one more full week, until each student had been to her once. Otherwise, she would have to go to the apartment of each child and resign, and she didn't know all their addresses. Aron agreed. During the last week of tinkling he no longer went to the bar. If I wanted to, he says, I could calculate exactly how many hours he was *forced to spend* in that bar. Irma had earned over *three thousand marks* with her lessons.

5

I CAN'T HELP THINKING THAT, FOR SOME TIME NOW, Aron's
stories have been becoming increasingly long-winded.
He often expands the most insignificant event into half a
novel or, worse, he tries to enhance the value of minor
matters by lacing them with generalized aphorisms. He
no longer simply informs me that after a bout of the flu
Mark got out of bed too soon and the next thing you
know he came down with pneumonia; now he also says,
"The greatest enemy of mankind is impatience."

To the question what is the explanation for this
transformation in his narrative style, I find only one reasonable answer: he wants to postpone the end of our in-
terview. He and he alone knows how extensive his supply
of stories is — quite small, I presume — and he's afraid of
having to inform me, sooner or later, that there is nothing
more to tell. He's afraid of being lonely again, the way
he was before we met. Which means he believes that,
as soon as he finishes his story, I'm quite capable of saying good-bye and never showing up again. This thought

concerns me. Of course I can't say, "Don't worry, Aron, go on with your story just as you have so far, but without these digressions that no one's interested in. I'll still come and visit you after our work is done, as often as you like." Instead, I just sit there trying to look interested, nodding at every third word, and feeling uneasy. For the first time I realize that I've taken a place in Aron's life from which there is no retreat, at least not an honorable one. And it is absolutely irrelevant whether or not that makes me comfortable.

I ask Aron if, like me, he thinks that he is largely to blame for his loneliness, and if he hasn't withdrawn from everything and everyone a bit too recklessly. Aron replies without hesitating, "I didn't choose what happened to me."

"That's exactly what I'm reproaching you for."

"One can only choose when there is an option," he says.

To tell him that such an option exists doesn't make much sense. He would ask for a list, then I would say first, second, third, and he would immediately start discarding each of these possibilities as silly and not worth talking about. "Such trivialities should be a alternative?" he would ask, without believing me when I say that only the sum of these little activities can lead to a sense of peace. Nevertheless, I tell him that, for example, he could have become caretaker for old people.

"With my impatience?" he asks. "With my heart? I need a caretaker myself."

Or he could have worked in some business, as a bookkeeper or company secretary, just part-time if he preferred. People like him are desperately needed nowadays.

"I have enough money to live off," he says.

"Who's talking about money, damn it!" I cry.

I force myself to calm down and explain that all my suggestions were simply hypothetical, what he might do on his own to extricate himself from his loneliness. Happiness, I say, comes only from interaction with other people, that's how I see it in any case, never in seclusion, and not through hobbies. Aside from a few technical acquisitions, I say, he still lives in the Stone Age. All around him the most important social changes are taking place, but he refuses to get involved. Not even his attitude toward these changes, be it pro or con, is clear.

I say, "You have papers that identify you as a victim of fascism and certify that you have a right to all kinds of special privileges. Nothing wrong with that, but does that suffice? Don't get me wrong, but in the long run is that a tolerable situation, to be nothing more than a victim of fascism?"

"Do you want me to return my papers?" Aron asks.

And I say, "Oh, my God."

And he says, "Don't get angry, I'm going to die soon anyway."

And I say, "I'm overwhelmed by compassion."

Go ahead and ask me," Aron says, "what I agree with and what I disapprove of. You can barely wait."

"I have no idea what you're talking about," I say.

"Of course you do," he says.

Another misunderstanding. Time and again, I think, he's tormented by the suspicion that our conversations are actually interrogations in disguise. But, it occurs to me, only people who are suspected of a crime are interrogated. What does he think I suspect him of? No, witnesses are also interrogated; I hope that in his conviction this fact doesn't escape him. I say, "I won't ask you something I already know."

Aron squints at me, because I think I'm so clever. "You know my political opinions?" he asks.

"More or less," I say.

"How?"

"We've known each other long enough."

"Really now," he says. He doesn't seem to be able to make up his mind whether to laugh or be angry. "Do me a favor and tell me what they are," he says.

"Your opinions?"

"Yes."

"I thought you knew them."

My weak joke doesn't faze Aron in the least; I can tell that he's determined not to say another word until I satisfy his wish. So that he won't consider me a charlatan, I start off by saying that, naturally, these are all suppositions, which nonetheless are founded on observations, or on sentences he has used in various circumstances. He nods impatiently, then I begin. For starters, I say that his attitude toward all social order — between the two of us or with anyone else — is primarily determined by self-interest. It all depends on how much he can gain from it personally.

"That's a cliché," Aron says. "What can be said about everybody can be said about me. Go on."

His relationship to East German Socialism I de-

scribe as well-wishing disinterest. Since he never took
the trouble to follow the laws that are at the basis of social
development, all his likes and dislikes must necessarily
be dictated by his moods, his whims. Given which, I say,
the situation of other people in the country does not concern him; that's what I had meant previously by self-
interest. He probably approves of the fact that prosperity
is more equally distributed now than before, but only
marginally. He probably finds that the greatest advantage
is that he is no longer persecuted.

"You mean as a Jew?"

"Yes."

"Am I a Jew?"

I laugh and don't know what to answer — a joke,
I think. Aron says, "All right, we'll talk about that later.
Go on."

Political objectives don't interest him, I continue.
Because he doesn't participate in life, the differences between socialism and capitalism are purely theoretical for
him and therefore relatively unimportant. The only thing
he's afraid of is fascism. An unsolvable contradiction: he's
glad that no one threatens his seclusion, which is his
greatest misery. A pinch of peripheral indignation, about
the war in Indochina, the persecution of blacks in South
Africa, the reign of terror in Chile — all this is both reprehensible and unreasonable, but the main point is that it
is taking place far away, outside his apartment. He has
enough money to afford the bare necessities; his pension
is generous because of the labor he was unjustly forced to
do in the past and therefore is not charity but salary. What
is most disturbing about this new state of things is that it

does not offer enough distractions. It's not colorful enough for him; as far as he's concerned, the entertainment industry is not doing very well. "You wanted to hear it," I say, curious.

Aron rubs his cold fingers, which suffer from poor circulation. He says, in a reproachful tone, I was better than he had suspected. I forgot only one thing, the most important, though, namely the justification for his apparently inexcusable behavior. Can I imagine, he asks, that there is a kind of weariness that makes all action impossible?

"Yes, I can."

And he who is overcome by that weariness barely has the strength, he says, even to take care of himself. The weariness he means should not be confused with resignation, although he understands that to an outsider they may appear one and the same, but he is referring to weariness. He didn't ask for it and he didn't want to give in to it so soon, on the contrary. The fight against fatigue was the last and perhaps the most difficult in his life, and he lost it. He is fully aware that it is more commendable to die with your boots on than to end your life in what one might call, to be harsh, inner infirmity. Like a wind, he says, that ceases so indiscernibly that no one is even aware of it. He had certainly never been a great fighter, yet he is totally convinced that this powerful fatigue has brought greater fighting natures than his to the ground.

"But I know that doesn't mean much to you," he says.

*　*　*

One day, a few weeks before Mark's summer holiday, Irma asked, "Why don't we ever go on a trip?"

And Mark immediately cried out, "Yes, let's take a trip."

Aron couldn't resist, simply because of Mark's enthusiasm. Traveling a little is a vital part of education, he says, and he wasn't uninterested either; a holiday meant distraction from the constant tedium that had come to plague him. He even thought it likely that, of the three, he needed a change of place more than anyone, the only question was where. He didn't know anyone in the country; he remembers the few trips he took before the war: To Carlsbad, Helgoland, Bad Schandau, an expensive holiday with Linda London in Davos; the sea had made the greatest impression on him, the sea was the most obvious difference compared with his daily life. "What do you think of going to the sea?" he said.

Irma smiled, satisfied, and Mark hugged *her* for joy. Aron saw that Mark whispered something in her ear, both looked relieved, as if they had expected him to resist rather than consent. This meant they must have already discussed their desire to travel, Aron thought, unless they have other secrets from me.

"But how and where?" Irma asked.

"First we'll take a map and look," Aron said. "Then we'll take money, then we'll get onto the right train, and once we've reached the sea they'll rent us a room."

Mark immediately fetched an atlas; they ran their fingers along the coast and called out names to each other, some places they'd vaguely heard of. Their only guide was how enticing the names sounded. Heringsdorf was briefly in the conversation, yet Mark resisted, Ahrenshoop provoked laughter, Zinnowitz, agreement reigned at Binz.

Halfway through the month something happened that jeopardized their travel plans. One morning Aron came across a crowd. He didn't understand why people were shouting, but he saw they were highly excited and, it appeared to him, close to getting violent. They were so agitated that he didn't dare ask them why they were so wrought up. He wanted to get away as quickly as possible. The people were chanting in chorus, he says, down with some law or other; he had no idea what their words meant and what was behind it. *Can you assure me that pogroms don't start like this?* Aron ran to the school as fast as his heart would allow; he wrenched open several classroom doors until he found Mark. Without asking the teacher, he took him by the hand and guided him through side streets to their apartment. To Irma he said, "You're staying home too."

The door was locked; through the window the city looked the same as always, the street was quiet. For three days no one left the apartment; they listened to the radio until they *had no other recourse* but to send Irma out to buy groceries. One news reporter spoke of unfortunate misdemeanors and called for people to remain calm and levelheaded; another man reported a revolt of the people and encouraged further resistance. When Irma came back from the store, she said she had seen some tanks.

Aron said, "That's very good, tanks are good news."

To Irma's surprised question about what he meant,

he replied that it was important to reestablish order and he could not imagine a more effective means to that end than tanks.

"You're against the demonstrators?" Irma asked.

"I'm against situations like this."

Aside from the defeat of the fascists, he says, he never witnessed a significant change that wasn't tied to a disadvantage for him. This is why, above all, he was concerned with maintaining the status quo. *If life is to be at least bearable, people like me have to fight against change.* (What he means by "fight," I think, is the locked door. And I notice that he often exchanges the unambiguous word "I" with "people like me" or similar expressions, as if he feels that his own will can be attributed to an entire group.)

Mark desperately wanted to go down into the streets; he was interested in the tanks Irma had talked about. Aron had to hide the key in his pocket. Disappointed, Mark stood at the window for hours on end, staring down at the empty street. He stopped pouting only when Aron promised to go to the sea as soon as order was restored. And then they just up and left, even before one of the two reporters announced on the radio that it was all over now, everything was under control. The next time she went out shopping, Irma, with Aron's consent, made a tentative trip to the train station and didn't notice anything suspicious. She had bought tickets for a train that left so early in the morning they met no one on their way to the station. Still, that mile and a half walk felt like a dangerous foray into enemy territory.

On the train the tension eased; as soon as they were out of the city they traveled *cheerfully*. They had the

entire compartment to themselves. Aron was proud of his
bold idea. They had escaped a dangerous situation unscathed, and from a distance, he says, every danger seems
to be only half the size it really is. "In these times, hardly
anyone comes up with such an idea," he said.

Irma praised his sangfroid but insisted that it was too
early to celebrate; unpleasant surprises could be awaiting
them at their destination. No one could say whether or
not an uprising was taking place there too. In the last few
days she had listened carefully to both the speakers, and
neither mentioned the name Binz. "And besides," she
said, "I'm curious to see where we'll end up staying."

When they reached Binz the following afternoon,
there was no sign of unrest. The small train station was so
sleepy that one might have thought, *We are in a place from
before the war.* Aron left Mark, Irma, and the luggage in the
restaurant at the station and went looking for a room. But
first he checked for any signs of unrest; nothing was settled yet, he could still go back and find another seaside
resort. However, either all traces had been removed or
there had never been *differences of opinion* in this happy
little town. No overturned cars, no broken windows, no
words on the walls, readable or covered up, and from the
station to the beach, Aron says, not a policeman in sight.

The search soon turned into a pleasant walk. The air
tasted of salt, the houses were white and pretty. In health
resorts, Aron declares, all the houses look the same. And
then the sea, the sight of the sea. Aron wondered why the
sight of a gray expanse of water — salt water, nothing
else — could move him so. Only an hour later Mark and
Irma would be expecting him back at the station —
he had to get cracking. The best houses are on the beach,

he told himself, the less good ones can wait. He went to the most beautiful — not the biggest, the most beautiful. There was the name of a woman in gold letters on the wall.

He tugged on the bell. On the lot next door he noticed there were five bedraggled wicker beach chairs. He had to ring several times before a suspicious old man opened the door. Aron said he was looking for a room to rent for a couple of weeks. He could tell immediately, he says, that the man was poor; only the poor display such a morose kind of mistrust. The old man, who smelled like cheap cigars, said he had no rooms to rent. He'd started to close the door when Aron said quickly, "I can pay more than you probably think."

"I already told you, we don't have any rooms," the old man said irritably. "Try somewhere else."

Then a middle-aged woman, *clearly* his daughter, appeared behind him. "Do come in a moment," she said to Aron, as if till then he had been reluctant. Suddenly the old man had nothing more to say. He shrugged and retreated to the depths of the house. The woman sat with Aron in the kitchen.

To Aron, the kitchen, tiled in blue and white, felt like the beginning of a holiday; there were some dried fish and a blazing hearth in spite of the heat. The woman said she actually did rent rooms, almost everyone here rents rooms, only this year she had already given her word to a family from Berlin. In ten days the ladies and gentlemen were due to arrive. On the other hand, she said, in recent times, as the gentleman would surely know, things have changed — she had no precise idea what the situation was like in Berlin. Only one thing tempted her to let him have the rooms, she said, namely that the family in question had not yet sent any confirmation about their agreement. Maybe they were just being careless, but then again, maybe not. Something might have happened to make the family change their plans, in which case she would be stuck with her vacant rooms. "At least they could have written," she said.

Aron asked her permission to see the rooms, and when the woman hesitated he added, "With no commitment."

She led him up a steep staircase to exactly the two rooms he was looking for. An open view of the sea, a small balcony, everything was clean and neat, above all, two rooms.

"I come from Berlin myself and I know what the situation is like there," Aron said. "You can't imagine. I think it's likely your guests won't be coming. Just in case, you should write a letter saying that you could no longer wait for news from them and that you have rented the rooms to someone else for four weeks. That's fair, no one can accuse you of anything. Otherwise you might get stuck with your rooms. Who travels in times like these? I'll pay you seven hundred marks for four weeks."

The woman didn't let him see how good she thought his offer was. She was silent and pushed chairs into place and tugged at the bed linen. Aron went out on the balcony and gazed at the sea for a while. Then he turned around and said, "Or shall we say eight hundred?"

The old man fetched a handcart from the shed. Aron went back to the train station with the cart. "I thought you had already forgotten us," Irma said.

"You'll be amazed," Aron said. He piled the luggage

onto the cart, with Mark on top. It was a pleasant holiday, without fights and without heart attacks. And, best of all, Aron says, when they went back to Berlin there was no trace of the ruckus. The streets looked just as they had before, no sign of violence, a miracle.

Encouraged by their experience, the following year they went on another holiday to the town of Ilsenburg, and the year after that a third trip to Sotschi on the Black Sea. Of the latter two trips, not much stuck in his memory, Aron says. As for comfort, neither one could compare with their trip to Binz. Perhaps just this much about Ilsenburg, that Mark, as far as he, Aron, could tell, had his first love affair. At this point he was fifteen years old, the girl was sixteen, the daughter of a baker who stuttered. Throughout the holiday *Mark hid with her;* Irma found it wrong. She said, "At his age already," until one day the baker came and asked Aron to please keep his son away from Veronika. "There you go," Irma whispered, but Aron didn't do anything about it; anyway their departure was imminent.

Later, Aron reports, Mark had so many girlfriends that he, Aron, eventually lost both track of them and his interest in the matter. He only followed this first one with a watchful eye because, beyond his general paternal feelings, he wanted to make sure that Mark, like himself, had survived ghetto, camp, and illness in all things, *including his manliness.* Apparently he had.

In the winter of 1955 Arno broke up with Irma. I shouldn't take this as a decisive event, Aron says, he mentions it only for the sake of completeness. It was simply one of the minor occurrences of which there were thousands in the course of his life. The first morning after the separation he did not feel the slightest regret — at most the apartment felt a little empty. Presumably Mark was the one who was most affected, because he was very attached to Irma, even loved her; after all, she had replaced his mother for years. Her way of fostering this affection had been patience, a patience that he, Aron, often found impressive, he was the first to admit. But patience is worthless if there's no purpose behind it, no purpose other than that of being patient. And buying a child's affection in this way is both easy and insignificant.

Irma was one of those people who always refused to see problems. If I'm not mistaken, she spent her whole life trying to find out what other people wanted. And when she found out what it was, she would immediately help, regardless of whether it was right or wrong. Don't picture that as being particularly pleasant."

"Like a handyman," I say.

"A born handyman. After a while the smallest objection on her part led to a fight; one simply wasn't used to her objecting."

"Did she leave on her own accord, or did you send her away?"

"I can't answer that in one sentence. One day it occurred to me that I couldn't care less whether she stayed or left. And then I said to myself, If I don't care anyway, then it's better if she leaves. Irma wasn't old, but she wasn't that young anymore either. I was afraid that one day we would have no alternative but to live together forever, purely out of habit. So I wanted her to leave."

"Couldn't you have left?"

"Are you crazy?"

"Okay, I'm sorry, that was nonsense. So did you send her away?"

"You can't say I sent her away."

After a night at the movies they had sat at the table and drunk a whole bottle of wine when Irma shifted close to Aron and asked him, shyly, if he had ever seriously thought about the future course of their life together. At first he felt hot, then cold, Aron says; he had never heard an important, or even notable, suggestion from her till then, and now suddenly this. He asked her why in the world they should marry.

"Then tell me why we shouldn't marry," Irma said.

Aron explained that nothing spoke for or against it, and if one lives in a situation that is just as good or as bad as the other, then one could logically avoid the effort implied by change.

In any other case, Irma would have been satisfied with his answers — not this time. She brought up the fact that other people got married too, that getting married wasn't a custom she had invented; even for Mark it would be an advantage to live in an official relationship. And not least, she said, as a wife she would have a sense of security that was missing in this precarious life.

"We are leading a precarious life?" Aron asked.

"Nothing is decided," she said. "We can break up whenever we like."

"Can't we break up even if we're married?" he asked.

"Not so easily."

"And you see that as an advantage?"

Irma smiled helplessly and said, "You always have to twist the words in my mouth."

Aron realized the significant difference between his and Irma's expectations: what he considered to be the end of all change, the irrevocably last station in his life, she thought was temporary. Apparently she was *full of desires*, which he had neither the will nor the strength to fulfill; she needed an energetic man, an agile one, he wasn't like that. He told her he was tired because of the movie and the wine, and they went to bed.

Soon after she was lying next to him and started to *busy herself*. He presumed that the kisses were supposed to put him in a compliant mood, and *in fact* a few minutes later she picked up her flag again. "If marrying is so irrelevant to you," she said, "and so important for me, why won't you do me the favor?"

"Please don't start that all over again," Aron said.

But Irma didn't stop. She pressured him with a stubbornness he had never noticed in her before; it was almost unbearable, he says. She hardly formulated any thoughts of her own, she only uttered words and expressions that he had heard or read dozens of times. She was forever playing a role, in his mind a miserable one. Would I perhaps be willing to marry a woman who reproached me for not having understood that the soul of a woman could blossom fully only in marriage? A tirade of sayings: "life as a couple," "sacrificing the best years of my life," "to be able to depend on one's partner for better or for worse," and more of the same. Several times he asked her to stop, but in vain; in the end all she knew how to do was to start crying. She shouted that he was too cowardly to get married, he was also too cowardly to tell her the real reason for his refusal, he didn't love her, she didn't deserve it. Then he said, "Finally we got to the point, I don't love you."

Irma immediately stopped crying, turned on the light, and posed the *insane* question: "How long have you known?"

"Since right now," he said, "let's go back to sleep."

The following afternoon, while Mark was at school, she behaved normally, but Aron found that her friendliness was affected. He figured that she regretted having opened yesterday's topic and having forced his confession. He felt relieved that Irma now knew where she stood; yesterday's conversation had clarified the situation. Now he hoped once and for all to be spared such sieges. She wouldn't provoke such a thrashing a second time, only a long silence would bring back the old ease.

But Irma was *too proud or too dumb* to be silent for long. After her housework was done, she started over from the beginning. She asked, "Were you being serious last night?"

"Yes," Aron said.

She nodded, as if that was the answer she were expecting. She then asked him to list all her flaws, openly and without mercy, she said; perhaps she could discard one or another. He found this funny and touching. He said, "Dear child, how can you say something like that? Do you think a man can tell a woman she should behave in this way or that, then love her?"

Irma raised her hand as if she had immediately recognized the simplemindedness of her request. She asked, to change the subject, if Aron thought that, in the future, marriage between them would be out of the question.

"I can't say that either," he said. "I'm only asking you for the last time to cut it out."

"Is that a threat?"

Her question, Aron says, sounded like the abrupt end of all modesty. He sat there in silence and thought, Irma would never become his wife, like Lydia had once been and Paula *playfully* could have become. He was angry that she should torment him with her foolish questions instead of demanding that he explain why he had lived with her for so long without loving her. *That would bother anybody.* But not Irma apparently; she was intent only on arranging a wedding, why, he still did not understand. Stubborn and nonsensical, she tried to change their current situation without realizing he would not be pushed in the direction she wanted. Aron went shopping.

When he came back, Irma asked him, as if no word had been spoken on the matter: "Please tell me, Arno, why are you so afraid of marriage? Did you have a bad experience?"

To this he said, "I won't be angry if you leave."

After a *frightful second*, she stood up and left the room. To cry undisturbed outside, Aron thought, but she came back with two empty suitcases and started packing. She was astonishingly composed, after all those years, he found. Her face betrayed nothing but concentration; she didn't want to forget anything. Aron watched her for a couple of minutes, then he asked if he could help her. She ignored the question, so he went out. He didn't want to give the impression that he was sitting there only to make sure she didn't take something that wasn't hers. When he went back to the room a while later, she had filled only one suitcase; all the cupboard doors and the drawers were open. He said, "Mark will be back in two hours. You'll say good-bye?"

Again she said nothing. Aron took a porcelain figurine from the closet, one he knew Irma liked particularly, and held it out to her. She ignored it. (The figurine still stands in his living room — two large black dogs fight while a very small brown one brightly holds a bone in his mouth. Aron says that if he hadn't offered the figurine to Irma, she would have taken it for sure.) Once she finished packing, she leafed through the common photo album and took out two photographs. In one of them Mark was wearing his boxing outfit; in the other he was with her on the beach by the Black Sea. She laid the pictures on top; then she closed the second suitcase and was finished. Aron knew that it made no sense to ask her, in her condition, if she wanted to drink a cup of tea with him. Suddenly he felt sorry for her.

"I only want to tell you one more thing," she said. "Think carefully about why I stayed by your side all these years."

"Well, why?" he asked.

"Think about it."

It was an outright demand to consider the worst reasons, the most disadvantageous for Aron, as the right ones. Nevertheless he was thankful that she spared him the list; even in anger she couldn't overcome *what re-mained of her modesty*. He said, "Fine, I'll think about it. Do you have enough money?"

"Thank you very much."

He took three thousand marks from his little box, he cannot explain why that precise sum. At the time, he says, he thought that three thousand marks were appropriate; there wasn't a fixed rate. He opened the second suitcase, put the money on top of the photographs, and closed it again; she wouldn't have taken it, he thought, in her hand. In the corridor he asked where she was thinking of going. "Don't worry," he said, "I don't want to pursue you. Just in case you forgot something."

"I didn't forget anything, Aron," she said. Those were her last words; she probably went to her parents'.

Aron stood baffled, staring at the slammed door. He couldn't for the life of him figure out how she knew the secret of his name; she had never used it before. Perhaps he had slipped up once without noticing — there were no documents in the apartment. In any case, he says, the last day with Irma had been the most eventful of their life together, and her very last word had been the most significant.

Since, with the passage of time, the house threatened to fall to pieces, Aron hired an elderly lady from the neighborhood to come three mornings a week to guarantee a minimum of order — an arrangement worked out with the help of the neighborhood grocer.

All of a sudden, the focus of the stories shifts to Mark; all the other people have disappeared. From this point on, Mark represents Aron's only connection to the outside world. Mark is described to me as a boy who didn't feel the need to communicate. Aron declares that while Mark's relationship with him was open it was not overly friendly. He often felt that Mark was struggling with problems he knew nothing about, and his occasional declarations that he was always available if his advice was needed never prompted Mark to discard his reserve.

Mark's career as a boxer was long over. Training took up so much time that two years later Mark lost all interest; his schoolmates didn't dare challenge him anymore. Instead he immersed himself in his studies; Aron wouldn't have been upset if Mark had studied less, because he considered him bright enough to get passing grades without working too hard. To rein in his eagerness to learn, Aron gave Mark theater tickets or money for other distractions, but he soon realized that for Mark the issue wasn't being the best; *the subjects* actually interested him. In which case, Aron says, any further attempt to hold him back would have been a sin, like an attempt to thwart his thirst for knowledge. He asked Mark how he could help him with his studies, Mark should call on him at any time. At first Mark didn't know how, then he gave him a piece of paper with titles of books and names of authors. Aron became the client of several bookstores and antiques shops in remote corners of the city; *it was a pleasure.*

*   *   *

What kinds of books did he read?"

"I can't remember, there were so many. The Bible was one."

"Where are they now?"

"Sold."

"Sold? After Mark read the books he sold them?"

"Not him, me. Just three years ago — they took up so much space. I put an ad in the paper and sold them all."

The closer graduation came, the more Aron was interested in which subject Mark wanted to study at the university. Aron would have liked him to become a *doctor or a jurist*, yet he knew he could not influence Mark's decisions. The possibility of influence, he says, had slipped from his fingers at one point; the need for advice had to be matured, but at this stage both of them decided their personal affairs on their own. To an outsider that may have looked like independence, Aron says, except that his own independence was purely theoretical: since he had virtually no personal affairs, there was nothing to decide.

"Maybe I won't study at all," Mark once said.

"Not at all?"

"We'll see."

He probably didn't realize how much he frightened his father with that statement. From then on, Aron refrained from any further prying; he wanted to avoid an escalation of Mark's aversion to the university out of defiance.

Thus he started his own investigation. Without telling Mark, he went to the university and asked how soon before one intended to enroll the application had to be submitted. He also wanted to know how good the chances were for applicants to be accepted in each of the various departments. He discovered that chances looked good for lawyers, less so for doctors. The employee at the admissions office smiled at the efforts of a solicitous father. He said, "If you want to be on the safe side, you should choose something like teaching."

One day, out of context, Mark said, "Mathematics."

"Mathematics?" Aron asked. "What about mathematics?"

"I will study mathematics," Mark said.

He was very confused, Aron says; until that moment he had never for an instant thought of mathematics — so, very confused, but no longer afraid. A few minutes later, after the word had been repeated several times, mathematics actually didn't sound bad. Mark declared he had decided for mathematics because he wanted to have a job in which the accuracy of the results could be determined by precise formulas and weren't dependent on other people's opinions.

Did you often talk about politics?" I ask.

"Almost never," Aron says. "What made you think of that?"

"Because the reason he gave you for wanting to study math is a political one," I say.

"How did you arrive at that idea?" Aron shakes his head. "What he said was that you can argue about taste but not about numbers. You think that's politics?"

Aron mentions something odd — on Mark's high school diploma there were an abundance of A's, except in the subject of mathematics, where the teachers had graded his performance with a B. Aron feared that this might make it difficult for Mark to be accepted as a math major. He took him to task for not having made an effort to shine in the very subject most important to him. Did he think this B was some sort of a joke?

"Stop grumbling," Mark said. "I did my best, it just wasn't good enough."

"I don't believe you," Aron said.

His worries proved unfounded; after a couple of nervous days the notice came to the house that nothing stood in the way of Mark's enrollment. At which point Aron, wanting to make a little speech, said, "Sit down and listen to me." He wanted to talk to Mark about how serious life was, as he would now find out for himself, about the end of his salad days, which he must not look back on with regret. Serious work, he wanted to say, above all when crowned with success, can bring great joy. And he didn't want to forget to mention that, as Mark must know by now, one was responsible for one's own progress. Yet after a few words Mark patted him on the back *paternally* and said, "It's okay, Papa, I already know that."

At first Aron was angry but, he says, he found Mark's interruption understandable — young people have their own idea of how to be polite — and soon after he even considered it a sign of character. With this remark, Mark had spared them a lecture that would have *naturally* sounded wooden and shallow. Mark wasn't the kind of person who pretended to be interested when he really wasn't.

Halfway through the holidays, Mark asked Aron for three hundred marks. He wanted to go camping with his friends. Where? That would be decided along the way. Aron gave him the money, and Mark disappeared for almost four weeks. The unfamiliar solitude made no difference to Aron; he was only worried about Mark. For the first time since the end of the war Mark was out of his sight; once he got a postcard from Mecklenburg: "Everything's fine, Mark."

During those four weeks Aron often had to dwell on something inevitable, the day when Mark would leave home. Mark had hinted at nothing of the kind, *but life hinted at it;* students everywhere lived away from their parents, and not just for lack of space. Aron dreaded that moment but resolved not to stand in the way if ever Mark should express such a wish. He decided, however, to refrain from doing anything that would encourage this desire. Therefore, no deciding for him; no prying as far as possible; no pestering over trivialities; tolerance.

When Mark returned from his trip unscathed, the days resumed their normal rhythm. Neither then, nor in the following period of time, did Mark indicate in any way that he wanted an apartment of his own. Now and then he would bring girls home; Aron didn't make any comments beyond the usual ones that men tend to exchange. As far as he could judge, the girls were decent in every respect. However, the nightly visits were clearly not to his liking; it was all he could do to keep his mouth shut. Otherwise Mark solemnly studied mathematics.

Our work is delayed by Aron's illness. He's sick for six months, so seriously in fact that I am afraid he won't make it.

We sit as usual at the living room table, and he tells me student stories that I would have gladly skipped; he interrupts himself in the middle of a sentence. He stands up and goes out without saying a word. I'm worried that my face didn't look attentive enough for his taste. I wait for a good ten minutes, until I have a feeling something's amiss. He's not in the kitchen; the bathroom door is locked from the inside. I knock and call out his name, but he doesn't reply, so for the first time in my life I break down a door. As I head toward it I can't help thinking how crazy this is, ridiculous. Aron is lying motionless on the tile floor, and I panic. I pull at him, try to lift him up — I can't — how will I get him to my car? I think, With help from the neighbors. The first neighbor I find is more level-headed than I am; he calls an emergency doctor. Together we carry Aron to the bed and moisten his forehead; he looks incredibly pale. The doctor answers me: "No, he's not dead."

For days I receive only general information from the hospital — his condition is stable — they won't let me see him. Finally I succeed in bribing a nurse with chocolate and pleas; she takes me secretly to Aron's room. She whispers that I must not get too close to him and must be

very quiet, he's still not responsive. He's in a transparent
oxygen tent, if that's the right term for it; dark blood drips
from a container into a tube fixed to his arm.

"Listen," I say excitedly to the doctor, "for days now
people here have been behaving as if his condition was a
state secret. He has no one to take care of him. Has anyone besides me asked about him?"

The doctor doesn't even look at me, he looks for
something on his untidy desk.

"Will you please tell me what's the matter with Aron
Blank?" I ask.

"Don't shout like that," the doctor says. He takes
out a file and leafs through it; he's making me wait longer
than necessary. Finally I learn why Aron was lying on the
tile floor so deathly pale. His stomach is consumed by ul-
cers; one had burst and this led to internal bleeding. He
would have been operated on a long time ago, if it weren't
for his heart condition. They couldn't wait much longer.
The doctor said he was constantly receiving blood trans-
fusions, but an open stomach is like a barrel full of holes.
For the moment the operation was delayed; they were
giving him medicines to strengthen the heart and increase
the circulation. He says, "If you insist, we'll proceed as if
he were twenty and operate right away."

"What are his chances?" I ask.

"Very poor," says the doctor.

At home, the question torments me — which worries me more, Aron's state or the danger that he will not
be able to finish his story? I listen to loud music, I leaf
through books; it's useless, the question won't leave me.
Of course I have to come to the conclusion that Aron
is important, far more important, incomparably more

important. I tell myself — what's in a couple of stupid notebooks. I toy with the idea of throwing all my notes into the fire; for a moment it appears to me that this would be convincing proof of my sincerity. I know that in complicated situations like this I have the tendency to go out of my mind. My final answer is: I care about both Aron and his story, I hope that's the truth, the end.

He is operated on and, against all odds, survives. When I am officially allowed into his room, he's pleased by my visit — for the first time since we met. He says, "There you are."

"I brought you something," I say and place a portable radio on his bedside table. He thanks me but hardly glances at it; he looks at me searchingly and asks me what he looks like.

"Very thin."

"Everyone is amazed I'm still alive."

"To tell you the truth, so am I."

We have only a couple of minutes. The sight of Aron — gray and scrawny and unshaven — is overwhelming; he asked the question for a good reason. This is more or less what he must have looked like, I suspect, when he came out of the camp. We talk about the most trivial things; that is, I do most of the talking, I can see with what difficulty he speaks. The nurse will knock soon, and I don't want to spend these few moments in silence.

From one visit to the next he seems livelier; the only problem is that he doesn't gain any weight. He stays away from the subject of his illness, I don't bring it up either, I wonder if we can't proceed with our interviews. We would have something to talk about and our work would progress; I wait for this suggestion from him daily. Once he smiles for no reason until I ask him why he's smiling. He replies, "You must have been really afraid."

"Of course I was afraid," I say. "You think that's funny?"

"Yes," he says. "You were afraid that the story would bite the dust right before the end."

I say, "Idiot." Luckily he doesn't insist.

Once he asks me, "How long have we known each other?"

"Let me calculate," I say. "It must be over a year and a half."

"It occurs to me that I know nothing about you," he says.

"Thank God," I say.

"Why do we always sit in my apartment?" he asks. "Am I a cripple? Why didn't you ever invite me to your place?"

Embarrassed, I say, "I would have done it long ago, if I had known you would have liked to come."

"Aha," he says.

Once we have a little argument because I refuse to smuggle cognac into the hospital. He calls me camp guard. In my presence he says angrily to the doctor, "He's such a responsible person. He won't even bring me a drop of liquor."

Six months later he weighs a hundred pounds.

Now and then Mark would not come home at night. Aron had to stop worrying about an accident every time; a twenty-year-old young man had every right to spend his nights as he saw fit. Most important, there was no indication that Mark's studies were affected — the results of his midterm exams were good. Mark showed them to Aron without being asked, perhaps with a little pride, but not primarily out of pride, Aron thinks, rather because he knew how much it pleased his father.

Although it didn't bother Aron anymore if Mark stayed out all night, it worried him that he wouldn't have been able to change things if it had disturbed him. He assumed that Mark would be surprised if Aron questioned him, as if his requests were breaking the rule of being mutually discreet. Luckily, Aron says, this never happened; he himself found it inappropriate to ask Mark to stay home at night.

Only lately, he says, and unfortunately not at the time, did he recognize a serious mistake he made with Mark, possibly a decisive one. At the time he thought only how Mark should be to fulfill his, Aron's, wishes, but he never posed the question the other way around. In other words, he had always taken for granted that Mark was happy rather than verifying what conditions his happiness was tied to. Meanwhile, he had come to understand how disastrous it was for parents to believe that they alone can determine what makes their children happy. Of course, it's a completely different matter when parents try to influence their children's idea of happiness; no one wants to deny them that right. But the certainty with which most parents think that their own desires are good enough for their children is arrogant and shortsighted.

Even today he doesn't know what Mark's needs were, but doubtless they were different from what he assumed. It now appears criminally thoughtless of him to have been

so dead sure Mark was happy as long as there was food on
the table and clothes in the closet and the place was warm.
He could hate himself a thousand times, but he couldn't
turn back time. In his naïveté, he had always cooked
Mark's favorite dishes and was happy when Mark said he
liked them. His conversations with Mark were incredibly
sparse, the kinds of exchanges one normally writes on
postcards to superficial acquaintances. For example, he
never succeeded in getting Mark to ask him for advice,
not once. Whenever they did talk he was simply happy
they were talking at all. He thought their conversations
were proof there was give-and-take between them. And
that thought calmed him down; courtesy has its limits after all, and children's courtesy toward their parents is especially limited. He couldn't expect Mark to sacrifice half
his day for sentimental reasons, no matter how gladly he
would have accepted such a sacrifice.

Once he decided to take Mark to task, when Mark
hadn't come home for three days and three nights in a
row. He couldn't stand it any longer, to be constantly tor-
tured by someone who, and this thought was the worst,
didn't have a clue he was the instigator of such suffering.
He intended to ask for a little more consideration, if not
for his age and health, at least for his feelings as a father.
He wanted to ask Mark if he thought that love between
parents and children went in only one direction.

So what did you tell him in the end?"

"Nothing."

"But why?"

"I'm tired," says Aron. He shuffles into the kitchen. I hear him putting water on to boil. He calls out across the corridor, "Do you want some tea?"

It's half past four; I know him well enough to know that he won't go on with his story today. I follow him into the kitchen. I say, "We still have half the day. If you've got nothing better to do, we could go to my place for a while."

"To your apartment?"

"Yes. I also have tea at home."

Aron smiles and shakes his head a couple of times, as if he were astonished at the transparency of my attempt to fool him. Then he dedicates himself to making tea; he warms the teapot, takes a sieve and tea — English — from the shelf. I ask, "So, what do you say?"

"You could have waited a bit longer to make the invitation," he said.

"Longer? Why?" I say. "We've known each other for two years now, surely I should be allowed to invite you to my apartment?"

"Stop pretending you're dumber than you really are," he says. "You know exactly what I mean."

He means the time since our conversation in the hospital, the time since his question, why hadn't I ever invited him to my place, the time since my flimsy answer — of course I know. Does he want me to hold off with my invitation until he forgets our conversation in the hospital? I can't change the order of our conversations in retrospect, I would have gladly invited him much earlier. I say, "I'll even bring you back home."

Aron is busy with the tea now, the water is boiling.

He looks at me briefly, irritated; his look says we would be well along on another subject if only I had a grain of tact. He says, "It's all right. You've invited me and I don't want to come. Do you want to drag me to your apartment by force perhaps? No one expects you to, don't worry."

Damned Mark didn't come home, not on the fourth day and not on the fifth. Aron's only consolation was the thought that the police would have informed him long before if anything had happened to him. He knew nothing about Mark's friends and acquaintances, he had no addresses, the only way to find out was to go to the university. He couldn't bring himself to go there — that, he says, could easily have ended in embarrassment, not so much for him as for Mark. Because if Mark had been missing only from home but was regularly attending his lectures, then a distraught old man in the middle of merry students would only have made his son look ridiculous — *who knows what their sense of honor is.* Or let's assume, says Aron, that Mark preferred a bench in the lecture hall to a girl's bed; days later she sees him and asks, Where have you been? And he lies out of necessity, he was at home in bed with a fever. *Then I come along and turn him into a liar.* And, in all fairness, there's a third point, he says; he felt like the man in the old joke. Do I know the joke about the man who lost his wallet? Well, a man loses his wallet with all his money and his papers. He turns the house upside down, he turns his clothes inside out and can't find it. His wife asks him why he looks everywhere except the right pocket of his brown coat. The man says, "It's very simple. If the wallet isn't there either, then I've definitely lost it."

On the sixth afternoon the doorbell rang. Mark had the key, of course; a young man stood at the door and asked for Mark.

"Are you a friend of his?" Aron asked.

To say friend is too much, said the young man; he had been instructed to come by his seminar group. Since Mark hadn't appeared at the lectures for a week, they assumed he must be sick; the young man wanted to pay a visit. Aron asked him in; the young man with his briefcase reminded him of the meter reader for the electricity company, *the right pocket of the brown coat was empty.* The young man asked, "You're his father?"

"Yes."

"He isn't home?"

"No."

The young man looked interested and asked when Mark was expected to return. Aron considered whether it still made sense *to stall for time;* then he shrugged and then he fainted. He remembers that the helpless young man stood over him and asked if he felt better.

"He hasn't been home either," said Aron.

The young man said several times that he hadn't thought it was possible until Aron inquired what he meant by that. The young man looked amazed and asked, "Well, do you know where else he could be?"

"No," said Aron.

"So there."

Aron asked the young man to keep his conjectures to himself a trifle longer, if he didn't mind; the young man replied that it didn't depend on him. Aron warned him against rash conclusions; he said, "And what if he suddenly reappears?"

"Then we'll all be delighted," said the young man.

For a couple of days Aron postponed certainty with excuses. He buried himself in the hope that Mark would suddenly show up at the door and explain his absence with an incredible story Aron couldn't possibly foresee. But his strength waned and also the idea, he says, of waiting like an idiot for a miracle to happen — *then he's simply gone*. Even the anger that follows initial mourning passed. At first, he was so angry with Mark he could have smashed furniture, he says; this was the most outrageous lack of consideration imaginable.

The first letter came five weeks later from Hamburg.

Dear Papa!

Please stop worrying, I'm fine. I have to beg your pardon for a number of things. For having left you without news for so long, for the fact that you are alone now, and above all because I acted behind your back. None of that can be changed now, but at least I'll try to explain it to you. The reason for my long silence is the initial excitement of being here. I had to find myself a room, some money. I am currently employed as a dockworker and will, if everything goes well, start studying again in a couple of months.

The reason for your loneliness, and I am firmly convinced of this, lies in you. I have never met a person who lives as separated from life as you, and I can't say that my presence changed things much.

But even if I'm wrong, in the long run I couldn't bring myself to be available as an excuse for you. Even if it bothers you, Papa, even if you find it self-ish, I don't want to keep this from you. You can blame me for not having talked to you about this while there was still a chance. Then I reproach you for having brought me up to be so reserved. I know you are a rather intelligent person, I probably am too, why didn't we ever talk about important things? It's not my fault if I could only guess what was going on in your head; I never heard it from you. And be-cause of this, it was the same thing the other way around.

This answers the third question too, why I acted behind your back. Since I'd been making all the im-portant decisions on my own for so long, I did it this time as well. If I had told you of my intention be-forehand, you would certainly have tried to stop me. It would only have been an issue of yes or no, but not about my reasons. And, in all honesty, I don't find these reasons tremendously convincing myself in the first place.

You should know that I don't particularly like the place I've landed in. So little, in fact, that I can't imagine staying here forever. To your question why did I leave, I can only answer because I didn't par-ticularly like the place I was in before, either. That's the difference between us, that you have long since given up searching while I see it as the only thing that I'd like to do. Searching means movement, and I want to move, that is what I wanted to explain to you. Dear Papa, I don't want to act as if I were happy now, but I'm not unhappy. Perhaps I'll come back one day, perhaps one day I'll be a "self-made man," perhaps one day you'll move to my place, we'll see. In any case you'll soon hear from me. Many greetings and kisses.

Yours, Mark

P.S. I haven't yet asked about your health. Write to me about it. Don't smoke too much and live to be a hundred.

I lay the letter on the table; curiously I think that I have never read a letter by an illegal immigrant from East Germany. Aron asks, "What do you think?"

"What should I think?" I say. "It's a letter."

He takes the letter and starts reading it, serious and concentrated, as if he were coming across each line for the first time. I don't disturb him, even if there is a long pause. Aron takes his time, he doesn't always read this slowly. Toward the end of the letter, his eyes fill with tears. "He wasn't even twenty-one at the time," he says quietly. He sounds full of admiration — writes such letters and isn't even twenty-one — he wipes his face. But it doesn't help, his face keeps crying. Mark releases emotions that aren't so easy to repress. Aron goes to the cupboard and puts the letter in a shoe box. I ask, "Did he write other letters?"

I see that he can't speak as he would like to; he goes up to the open window and leans out. Even his shoulders are crying on him, I know he doesn't want to irritate me with his silence, I understand him completely. I leave; when I glance up discreetly from the sidewalk, his window is closed.

The following day there's a little package on the table tied up with string, I estimate sixty to seventy letters. I undo the knot, pick up the one on top, and recognize it as yesterday's letter. As I'm about to remove the second one from its envelope, Aron says, "No, don't read it."

"Why not?"

"I don't want you to. They're nobody's business."

"Then why did you put them here?"

"Because you're skeptical," Aron says. "You asked me if he wrote other letters — here's the answer."

I'll only be able to read the letters with his permission, so for now, I have no choice but to comply. (Two days later we go for a little walk. When we get outside he notices that it's cooler than he thought, he asks me to get a jacket for him from the apartment. He gives me the keys. In the apartment I remember the shoe box. I think, the opportunity will certainly arise for me to put the letters back unnoticed, but the fear of being discovered keeps me from stealing them. I can't read them there, Aron is waiting outside the door; five minutes later he would know what I'm up to in his apartment. An hour later, when we're back in the room, I suddenly get the audacious suspicion that Aron may have marked the letters, he could have been testing me.) I say, "It's a shame. In this or another letter Mark must have answered your questions; correspondence is like a conversation. I could have a clearer idea of what you wrote to him."

"For the hundredth time," Aron says, smiling, "you are so skeptical. No matter what I tell you, you'll think I wrote something completely different."

"Nonsense. It's just that no event can be replaced by its description, not even the best one."

"You know what?" he says after a pause. "Let's per-
form an experiment." He talks loudly and has a merry
face; perhaps he wants to show me how thoroughly he has
overcome the mournfulness of the previous day. He says,
"I'll let you read all the letters, but first you must pay a
little price. First you must tell me what I might have written him."

"I can't," I say.

"Don't be such a coward," he says encouragingly,
"be a sport."

I'm not sure. I think of possible reproaches in the
letters to Mark, reprimands that may have lost their sharp-
ness with time, defiant and proud claims — one can get
along perfectly well on one's own, it was better than ever
before. I can imagine pleas, beseeching pleas for Mark to
return, promises even. But I won't play the game. I say,
"No, no, I can't guess."

Aron nods, as if my answer were the most self-
evident. In his eyes, I'm the kind of person who avoids
taking risks and always does what's most obvious — a
little boring. He says, "Relax, I didn't write to him."

"You never answered him?"

"Does that surprise you?"

"You never wrote him a letter?"

He waits for the effect of his punch line to end, then
he will let me know that he had no other choice. Mark's
departure had not only a physical meaning but primarily
a moral one. To him it felt like the evidence of the utmost
lack of interest in his father; he felt spat upon. Therefore,
he considered Mark's letters hypocritical, their intelligence couldn't change that. Perhaps they were also the
expression of a bad conscience, yet he couldn't do much

with a bad conscience if no attempt was made at reconciliation. And he, Aron, didn't want to be a party to this
hypocrisy. To enter a conversation, an increasingly cheer-
ful chat via mail, doubtlessly implied participation, he
says — Mark would have liked that. He asks me, "You
understand that these aren't my current thoughts? That
I'm only telling you what I thought at the time?"

I nod.

"If traveling means getting around," he says, "then
he got around the world a lot. Look at the stamps."

I leaf through the envelopes and see that they come
from a wide range of countries — France, Morocco, Yu-
goslavia, Sweden, Mexico — there isn't a single postcard.
Mark never stayed in the same place for very long; there
is only one letter from each country. In between there is
always a letter from Hamburg; yet even on the letters
from Hamburg I read different addresses below the
sender's name. If I'm not allowed to read the letters, at
least I want to register the information proffered by the
envelopes. Aron says, "Notice the last letters."

The last one comes from Israel, I see, the previous
one, the one before that, I count up to seven. With some
effort I manage to make out the date of the last stamp.
May 1967.

I want to be honest with you: to say that I didn't write to
him is only a half-truth. When I received his first letter, I
went to West Berlin — it wasn't a problem at the time. I
sat on an airplane and flew to Hamburg; within four hours
of the arrival of his letter I was in Hamburg. I showed the

envelope to a taxi driver, who found the road with no
trouble; it was a shabby house. I had no idea what I would
say to him; I thought that the moment I'd see him something would come to mind. But he wasn't home. A woman
opened the door; when I told her I was Mark's father she
let me in. The apartment was rather large, every room
was rented to a different person, doors were constantly
opening and closing. The woman said she had no idea
when Mark was coming back, I could wait if I wanted.
I sat down in his room and waited; the way he lived made
me sick at heart. A bed and a closet and a chair, not even
a desk but boxes. I sat there until nightfall; then the
woman came in, I was embarrassed. I said I would leave
and come back next morning, but she said it didn't matter to her if I slept there. I slept in his bed, but the following day he didn't come either. I looked around for a
hotel in the neighborhood, I bought a toothbrush and
underwear and went to his apartment twice a day to ask
for him. In the meantime I did some sightseeing. I even
went drinking once, on a road like that. On the fifth day
the woman asked me if it wouldn't be easier for me to
leave a note, so he could call me when he came back.
No one knew if he would come back the next day or in
a month or never. I went there for two more days. The
woman had to swear that she really had no idea where he
could be, then I wrote him a note. I wrote: 'Come back,
this business can't be so important for you to let your
father die.' Then I went home. In his following letter he
wrote that he had been to Dortmund for a couple of days
with an acquaintance and that he was upset he had missed
me. If I had the time and the desire, he wrote, I should go
visit him again, I should only warn him first. No word

about my note, not even in his following letter. And now you know why I didn't write to him."

Aron bought himself a television set. He finally retired. I don't understand what he means by that. He considered a number of ways to pass the time, he says: feeding swans by the river, attending events organized by the Jewish community, or events organized by the victims of fascism, buying himself a dog, taking a little trip now and then, studying the wedding announcements in the newspaper. He considered all these and more and gave up. He thought he realized that the loss of Mark hurt him particularly because he knew it was his last. From a certain perspective one might even consider it an advantage; he had nothing left to lose, at least nothing that might hurt him.

The housekeeper guaranteed a minimum of order; Aron hardly ever saw her. He usually slept so late that she would have finished her work by the time he got up. Once she asked if it would be all right if, from time to time, she and her husband came over in the evening to watch some TV. Aron was taken aback by her audacity but consented. But he already regretted his decision during their first visit; her husband was a primitive person who said hardly a word, he stared at the set, his face impassive, and only budged from the most comfortable chair in the room when the program was over. *Besides*, he never let his pipe, which stank hideously, go out. Aron had to ventilate the room for half the night. They came more and more often, in the end almost every day, until one day Aron set the alarm for the morning and told the housekeeper that in the future he didn't want any more visits. At that stage she resigned; she thought she didn't deserve such pettiness.

From then on the apartment went to seed. Aron had reached the point, he says, where one even stops trying. (At the beginning of our acquaintance I found his rooms were in a frightful mess, they looked like a rubbish heap. In the meantime things have come to look different. He has a housekeeper again; I had to coax him for a long time before I was allowed to find him one.) But he let himself go wherever he still could; for example, he no longer paid any attention to his health. He smoked and drank again as much as he pleased, he lost all notion of time. He slept when he was tired and got up when he couldn't sleep anymore, it had nothing to do with the fact that it was day or night. He didn't wear his watch anymore. When the TV program was over or too boring, he went to the bars; his heart caused him hardly any trouble, except for *understandable* little attacks.

No one knew him in the bars, there were different guests and owners. But that soon changed; the owners greeted him in a friendly way because he was a quiet customer and provided a good turnover; the guests liked him because he never hesitated to buy a drink for someone who was thirsty. Sure, he says, some of them thought he was a sucker and took advantage of his generosity; yet as long as this took place within limits he controlled, it didn't matter to him.

Once he had drinks with a man who had had some sort of argument with his wife. His wife was in love with another man, or he didn't love his wife anymore, *whatever;* after a couple of drinks the man said he didn't know where to spend the night. Aron offered him a bed, and the man gratefully accepted. A couple of days later another man said to Aron, You've already helped so-and-so, can I sleep at your place too? Aron granted him hospitality too, but soon he was sorry he had, because the man was very invasive. The next morning he disappeared with the second key, came back in the evening, slept there for several nights running, *completely at ease, as if he were at home,* one evening he brought a woman along. Aron threw him out and looked for another bar, in which nobody knew about his generosity.

Four times a year he received a postcard from the organization of those persecuted by the Nazi regime. Aron was required to go for medical checkups, or they offered him discussion groups if he wished to talk about his problems, or a member of the commission wrote announcing his visit. These last-named cards goaded Aron to a frenzy of activity. He was suddenly ashamed of the way he lived, of the apartment's state of neglect, the stifling atmosphere. Suddenly he would stop drinking, and for several days he cleaned the apartment until it looked liked a *human being lived there.* He put the card announcing the visit on the table as an admonition; he didn't want his visitor to think he was a case requiring special care — under no circumstances. The fear that they might force him to go to a home weighed heavily on him, and he succeeded in concealing his true condition, *sometimes just barely.* The member of the commission, usually a friendly woman Aron's age and with a similar past, would find Aron in a cozy room. Sometimes, he says, he waited impatiently for her knock; if she hadn't come with a purpose, perhaps he would have tried to make friends with her. They sat and drank tea and liquor, she was never in a rush. Topics of conversation were never lacking — they talked about new medicines or about the old times or about world politics or about children who outgrow us. When she left she was presumably convinced of leaving behind, as far as she could guess, a balanced person.

Mark's letters arrived approximately every four weeks. Unlike the cards from the organization, they weren't a reason to sober up; they always distressed him anew and hindered his attempt to forget.

After the first letters, in which Mark, as I learn summarily, primarily confined himself to describing his living conditions, he gradually turned to the question of why his father never replied. *He pretended* to be deeply concerned. He wrote that Aron had to understand how much his silence frightened him, even if he deserved punishment. He didn't even know whether Aron was silent because he was angry or because something had happened to him. Therefore he didn't even know if the silence was a punishment; apparently in one of the letters he wrote: "At least write to me saying that you will never write to me again."

One Sunday afternoon the doorbell rang. Aron opened the door, and a young woman he had never seen before was standing in front of him. She looked at him, smiled, and was silent until he asked her what she wanted. At this she mumbled an apology, saying she had gone to the wrong door. Aron says he didn't have sufficient presence of mind to interpret the situation correctly. Surprised, he simply watched as she went down the stairs. Her smile was suspicious. In the following letter from Mark he read: "Now at least I know that you're still alive."

After that, Mark didn't complain about Aron's silence anymore; his letters kept coming regularly, almost punctually once a month, as if at some point he had committed to it. They gradually lost all color, Aron says; with time they became inconsequential. To be fair, however, one must admit that in the long run it's almost impossible to write meaningful letters to someone who doesn't react. Yet, for whatever reason, in the following years he could only guess the important events in Mark's life. Since the possibility of asking was out of the question, often only vague hints were available to figure out *what actually happened*.

For example: Mark never pursued his studies. Aron can only assume why, he thinks lack of interest is out of the question. Even if one considers, he explains, that the *cities over there* hold many distractions, distractions capable of thwarting his son's thirst for knowledge had still to be invented. The only evident explanation: money problems. Mark worked all the time and earned a decent living but never enough to allow him to concentrate on his studies part-time. All those trips? I mustn't think Mark booked them through travel agents. During every trip he had a job — in France as a waiter, in Morocco as a tour leader; in Sweden he looked for snails in the woods with a friend and then sold them to restaurants in Stockholm. Not one of these trips had been what one usually considers a holiday, and yet Mark never complained about his financial situation. Aron only learned of it indirectly, in that Mark wrote constantly of new jobs he had. A person

changes jobs over a period of several years only if he has
money problems, of this he's quite sure. That Mark
didn't study, Aron also inferred, since the word "studying"
never appeared in his letters. Mark wrote that now he was
doing this, now he was doing that; unfortunately he never
wrote that he was studying.

Aron describes the contents of Mark's letters so thoroughly that I ask myself why he doesn't let me read
them. Mark delivers the plot from afar and Aron comments. Of his whole long story only Mark remains, and
since Aron seems determined to drag out the end as long
as possible, all he has left is thoroughness. I'm free to interrupt when I want, but I don't for several reasons. For
one, I think that digressions also contribute to complete
the image of a narrator. Second, an expanded story isn't
such a headache; no one is forcing me to take note of it,
and it isn't boring — there are worse ways of passing
time. Third, the longer I know Aron, the more I tend to
think that it doesn't make sense to be impatient with
people like him. I can't say what makes me so sure, perhaps I don't want to know, out of fear, or it could simply
be pity. I hear long commentaries about Mark's affairs; to
this day Aron can't stop wondering why his son went to
Israel.

He could understand that old fart Kenik, and in general those people who through experience and education,
identified themselves Jews, but how did Mark come up
with such an idea? In his estimation, Mark's experiences

during the war could not have been an influence; Mark had simply been too young, the experience factor was ruled out. Likewise the education factor — one could surely find fault in him, accuse him of having made many mistakes regarding Mark, but in no case that of having *made a Jew out of him.* What is that anyway, he asks me, a Jew, what is it if not a creed? Or aren't we finally living in times, he asks, in which everyone can decide for himself which party to join? Whether he is Turkish or German — of course he has no influence over that — but not even over the fact that he is a Christian or a Jew? The son of Catholic parents can, when he reaches maturity, freely choose whether or not he wants to become a Catholic like his parents. Why does one, he asks me, refuse the same right to the children of Jewish parents?

Since Aron cannot imagine that the decision to go to Israel had sprung from Mark's own head, *out of thin air,* the only possible explanation was other people's influence. They must have confused and convinced him, perhaps there was a girl behind it all; but in his letters there was no clue to support either hypothesis. Mark didn't even mention Israel until he was ready to go, and even when the *fateful* step was taken, he didn't give his reasons. He only communicated that he was there.

Apparently, Aron presumes, Mark liked life there, at least he didn't dislike it enough to leave. He didn't even leave when he couldn't find a *decent* job in Haifa, his first stop. He went to the countryside, a decision that, to hear Aron, nobody in his right mind would have even considered. He became a member of a kibbutz, *my son the farmer;* in one of the letters he wrote that he had decided for the time being to postpone his plans for the future, which Aron didn't know anyway; at the time he was occupied with the secrets of cultivating orange trees. And that's what he did till his death, says Aron.

No," he says, "I don't have an official notification. But I have common sense. How should the authorities have known about me in the first place?"

"That doesn't mean anything," I say.

"Think," he says. "For seven years he writes letters, regularly once a month, and suddenly he stops?"

"At most it's strange," I say, "but it isn't proof."

"Not proof? Didn't you see when he sent the last letter?"

"Yes, I did."

"Tell me."

"In May 'sixty-seven."

"So when should the following one have arrived?"

"In June 'sixty-seven."

"And what was going on then?"

"No idea."

"War. That's the proof."

I admit, Aron's conclusion is not completely unfounded, Mark probably did not survive the war. And yet a hint of uncertainty remains; surely there must be some way to make absolutely sure, a letter to the Red Cross ought to do it. But suddenly I ask myself, What's the point of making sure, how would that help Aron? With me he acts as if Mark's death were a foregone conclusion, but that doesn't mean much. Perhaps he doesn't want me to pressure him into an investigation, the consequences of which he fears. I remember his joke about the right pocket in the brown coat.

"You still have doubts?" he asks.

"Yes," I say.

"Then doubt."

We won't discuss anything that we can't prove here and now anyway; for the rest of the conversation Mark is dead. Probably fallen, Aron says; he died for a country, he says, in which he was lost. To my ears, it certainly sounds very self-possessed, callous perhaps, when he talks about the death of his son as if he were talking about a mathematics equation. Mark's death, he admits, was a conclusion that he *forced* himself to accept over the years. His pain had been really strange, at first a crawling one with a sliver of hope, a pain that grew from month to month but never as unbearable as it would have been if he had learned for sure in one blow. For instance, in the form of an official notification.

Once again, he started asking himself if Mark was really his son; for weeks he thought that doubt might alleviate his pain. There were just as many arguments for it as against it, except in the meantime Aron was a different man. He was no longer prepared to cheat and answer every undecided question to his advantage. For example, the question still open to this day — why it said Mark Berger on the papers. Mark may well be an uncommon name, but Aron increasingly tended to believe that Paula had *talked him into* a son. It must have been all the more easy for her, since he craved her truth, preferably this son than none at all, but in the meantime the situation had changed. Meanwhile, one had to ask oneself if one wasn't mourning the wrong person. An adventurous thought: Mark had found his parents, the Bergers, abroad.

Then Aron realized that Mark's family tree had no influence on his mourning, that he was mourning Mark independently of whose son he was. And if God, he says, would have appeared to him in person and proved to him that Mark was the son of a Greek goatherd, it wouldn't have changed an iota of his suffering. Once he was aware of this, he stopped the pointless questioning; Mark was without doubt his dead son.

In a certain way, Aron says, parents are always responsible for their children's actions. Above all when they are actions that emanate from free will and cannot be seen purely as reactions to someone else's actions, he must not ignore that. He meditated for a long time in order to fathom how important his role was in Mark's *escape*, in his move to Israel and, in the end, in his death. This had nothing to do with self-destructive brooding, rather I must understand that we are now dealing with the last important question that, to him, is still worth thinking about. And not for Mark's sake, *no one can help him anymore* — but exclusively for his own sake, for purely egoistic reasons. *What use is recognition to me?* I might ask, Aron says, since no one expects him to achieve great things, to rouse himself to notable actions anymore, yet that's not what it's about either. The degree of his guilt or innocence interests him because the *spirit* in which he will die isn't irrelevant to him. Parents easily tend, he says, to consider their children's intelligence, their intellectual activity, as a personal merit, while this rarely proves to be the case. No matter how uncomfortable it was to him, he had to admit that his influence on Mark's intellectual development was rather modest, it basically took place behind his back, and his *whole contribution* consisted of paying attention to Mark's physical well-being. Mark had been forced to draw from other sources, from sources that were beyond Aron's control and that might not always have been among the purest. A devilish mechanism was at the base of this course of events, a mechanism perhaps that someone else would have recognized at an earlier stage, but among all the things he was, Aron wasn't clairvoyant.

The worst thing was, he never succeeded in making Mark desire a specific lifestyle. Succeeded isn't even the right word, because it implies an attempt and Aron didn't even make a serious attempt. One is always wiser afterward, but assuming, he asks, that he had recognized the problem in time, how could he have made Mark desire a certain lifestyle? Such an intention can be fulfilled *credibly* only by those who desire a specific lifestyle themselves, and he didn't belong in that category. Wisely he says it's unfortunate, because he would be an idiot if he didn't recognize that the absence of this desire is a great disadvantage for him. Naturally every person yearns to give his life some deeper purpose than simply growing old. *But for the life of me,* he couldn't find that desire anywhere inside of him, he says; perhaps he hadn't looked hard enough.

*   *   *

Since I'm used to long silences from him, I wait awhile and think that this is just a silence like all the others — Aron is sorting out the sentences that will follow. But this time I'm mistaken; he says we should stop now, we've tormented ourselves long enough; he says, "This is getting boring."

He stands up and takes the teacups to the kitchen; the empty table should look like a conclusion, like the way chairs are turned upside down on the tables in a restaurant at closing time; the teapot is still half full. I understand. Everything that is to come, he wants me to feel, is a new story. Till now our relationship was nothing more than a mutual favor — that was our only connection. I think Aron is the proudest person I know.

When he comes back from the kitchen and finds me still in the chair, he asks me what I'm waiting for, he wants to know if I'm very disappointed. I laugh and reply, how could he think that, one can only be disappointed if one has expectations. Only expectations, I say, can be disappointed.

"Yes, you're right," he says. "So you came here without any expectations, and that's why you can't be disappointed now?"

"That's exactly right," I say.

Aron looks at me as if I were someone who's always making fun of him. He takes some cognac out of the cupboard, and as he pours he asks, "Tell me, how does someone normally react when he realizes that people think he's an idiot?"

"He gets angry," I say.

"Why do you think I'm any different?"